I wish I hope yt

Scott

KID COLTER...

WRONG END OF HIS GUNS

S cott C hristensen

Broken Spur Entertainment

ISBN:
978-0-9909829-0-6

DEDICATION

My many thanks to my family and friends that have inspired me and put up with stories as my dreams came together. This book is dedicated to all of you but especially my two boys, Chase and Colter. Thank you for your inspiration!

CONTENTS

ACKNOWLEDGMENTS

Special thanks to Janet Nielson, my editor and consultant.

Cover photography and design by

Scott Christensen

-Part I -

CHAPTER 1

June 1, 1863. A shot broke the silence of the morning and a bullet creased the crown of his hat. "Welcome to the war, kid... Now keep your head down!" a stern voice from behind advised as two more shots rang out. This was Winn Colter's first experience at nearly hit by a Union sharpshooter. He knew better than that and it wasn't the first impression he wanted to make with the men.

Colter arrived with the other recruits from Texas the night before and was now near Fredericksburg, Virginia meeting up with a large group of Cavalry riding under Jeb Stewart. The men were in a good position, on some high ground, with their horses tucked away back in the trees. Colter slowly walked forward to look over the field below. More shots were being fired down the ridge and bullets whined over their heads, ricocheting off rocks and trees. Even with the relatively few shots being fired, the smell of burnt gunpowder hung in the air. Most of the men still sat casually drinking coffee while a few picked up their rifles and moved forward to see what was going on.

Colter picked up his rifle and glanced over the field below while cautiously edging his way around the rock where he had just narrowly missed being dry gulched. Across the field and down the ridge, Winn could see a small group of Yankee soldiers scurrying along the tree line.

"Them Yankees been hunkered down there for two days and have them an ace-in-the-hole sharpshooter," Captain Harley Black explained as he walked forward holding his cup of coffee. He eased up to the edge of the hill by Colter, looking over at the field. "We've been waiting for you boys hoping you'd bring in supplies. We were down to about a hundred rounds for the entire Company. I'm glad those boys down there didn't know that," as he nodded his head towards the enemy line. The Captain raised the tin cup to his lips just as Colter saw a puff of smoke come from the side of a big rock about three hundred yards away. The sniper's bullet hit a rock a few feet away from Colter's head and ricocheted, knocking the coffee cup out of the Captain's hand.

"Damn that man! That was my only cup!" Captain Black peered over the edge. "I wish somebody would get that no account shooter! He's pretty good and has kept the men's heads down for two days. He killed Sherm Pickett yesterday doing just what you done, being a little careless and walkin' forward a little too far." He looked at Colter, who had hardly flinched with the shot, "You're lucky he didn't kill you when he hit your hat." Most young soldiers were scared out of their wits when bullets were flying. The Captain thought the kid must be too dumb to know better. He looked too young to have frontier experience.

Colter glanced down by the rock and could barely see the man's blue cap between two big rocks. He checked his load in the Sharps and started to bring the gun around. Very slowly, Colter edged around the rock to the left and pulled the trigger, kicking up rock and debris in the shooter's hideout. The man's head ducked for cover then slowly started to rise again behind his protection.

Colter ejected the fired shell and inserted another. Captain Black could see Colter was getting ready for another shot. "Don't bother Son. He's too far out and protected in those rocks." Colter slid his hat up on the rock to his left then carefully moved down to the right. A shot rang out and Colter's hat went flying; but while the hat was still in air, he carefully took aim and pulled the trigger. Colter got up and casually walked over, picked up his Stetson and brushed off the dust, inspecting it for damage. Colter could see Captain Black was right about the sharpshooter's aim; there were two holes through his hat. Had he been wearing the hat on the second shot, the bullet would have taken off the top of his head. Two bullet holes in his Stetson and it was only his first day.

Colter rubbed the hat carefully then slipped it back on his head. The Captain carefully peeked around the Boulder and saw two men running towards the rock where the sharpshooter had been hidden. Then he saw the soldier's body draped across one of the rocks. "By hell, you got him!"

Captain Black looked back at Colter walking towards the fire; saw him eject a shell from the gun and put in another.

The Captain looked back down the small valley and could see the two men dragging the lifeless body of the soldier back to the edge of the trees. He thought either the shot was lucky, or the kid was a damn good shot. It would be good to have a few more men around like that in the company.

*****

Rumors were going around the Company that General Lee would be sending the Texas Volunteers into Pennsylvania with Jeb Stewart and his men to face Major General Hooker. None of the men were familiar with the new recruits who rode in the night before, but they knew these fresh fish better be ready if they ever faced Hooker's force. Now was the time they needed men along that they could trust with their back when things got bad. It took time to build that trust. Captain Black knew even if the rumors of facing Hooker were true, orders change at a moment's notice and they could be off to fight other battles. They would wait for orders and see what General Lee had in mind for the Texans.

Colter was proud to finally make it to the war to serve the Confederacy as a Texas Volunteer. He waited two long, agonizing years from when he was thirteen, to join the fight, but he made a promise to his pa and waited to leave until he was fifteenth years old. Two of his good friends, Joseph and Thomas Keegan, left two years before and ever since, he was anxious to get to the war. Now Thomas Keegan was dead and Joseph was in some Yankee prison.

It had been hard to wait, but his father taught him a lot during the past twenty four months; everything from living off the land, to Indian fighting, He'd also been taught how to repair a gun in the field. All the training, he now realized, might actually be of some use. His Pa would never have walked to the edge of the hill as he just did. He'd been taught better than that and it nearly cost him his life.

Living on the frontier, some boys learned to shoot or hold a knife almost before they learned to walk. It was the way of life for survival in the west; but for some, even a gun may not be enough to face a pack of lobos or a bunch of Apaches. A man had to be savvy about his surroundings because in Texas, even the cactus seemed to jump at you if a rattlesnake or Indian didn't do it first. A man needed to know how to find water and food and see where trouble might be waiting.

Weston Colter, Winn Colter's father, was known as one of the top 'smiths in the territory who could fix or repair any gun brought to him. People rode for days to have their guns worked on by Colter even though his shop was located on the frontier in north Texas. As he inspected different gun designs, he learned more about each gun's strengths and weaknesses. He then designed a gun unlike any other using the best ideas of each. What he ended up with was a rifle that was way ahead of its time.

Growing up as the son of a gunsmith had its advantages and had put a gun in his hand at a very young age. Weston Colter had carefully taught his son Winn, how to shoot pistols and rifles, so that he was quick and deadly accurate. Winn was a natural shooter!

With rumors of trouble brewing back east, Weston was greatly concerned and hoped Texas would stay out of the mess. There were already enough troubles on the frontier fighting the Mexicans and Apaches, not to worry about other predicaments; but tensions were brewing and rumors were getting stronger. Then it happened and the Confederate States of America was formed.

Texas was the seventh state to join the Confederacy. They joined because Texans felt the Government failed to protect them from ongoing raids by Mexican bandits and Indian attacks. It seemed the Government was unwilling to make any effort to protect the southern border leaving a sour taste in the mouth of most Texans. Being tough fighting men, many Texans were more than willing to step up to the fight. Besides, the war was only expected to last three months...

The years of training from his Pa were good and now Winn was thankful for all he had learned. But on the morning of his fifteenth birthday, he did exactly as he told his Pa he was going to do. Winn gave his Ma a long hug then mounted his horse and rode away, headed off to war..

CHAPTER 2

June 12, 1863. General Robert E. Lee was in Virginia, inspecting his Regiments for readiness after some tough recent battles. Lee knew from the start the war wasn't going to be easy. The war had now dragged on for two long years. At this point, he didn't see how it could end soon unless something changed and the South found some luck.

As the General rode and met his fighting men, he could sense the despair in his troops. They were flat out tired. Some of these soldiers from Texas had been fighting from the start of the war. Thank God for Texas! They were tough fighters and many already had experience battling the Mexicans and Indians. Now they were all battle hardened, dedicated Confederate Soldiers and the future of the Confederacy rested in the hands of men like these.

Every one of these men had seen family or friends killed or wounded and some men just disappeared. These soldiers fought every day, ready to die if necessary. General Lee knew many of the southern men wouldn't live long enough to see home again. Win or lose, this would be one of the greatest tragedy of this war. The General respected these dedicated men and wanted to stay close to inspire them any way he could..

General Lee rode Traveler, his big gray horse, into the Shenandoah Valley finding his army battered but still holding strong. As the General rounded a bend on the trail, he heard a commotion up ahead. He cautiously rode out of the brush and saw three soldiers leveling their rifles at a feral hog scurrying for cover. It was well out of range and dust kicked up below and behind the hog as the shots missed. The General thought it was too bad. He knew the provision lines weren't the best and these men were probably hungry.

General Lee watched a young boy pull out his sharps and look at the escaping hog. He was about to tell the young soldier to stand down and save his ammunition but he fired a quick shot. Amazed, the General saw the running hog drop in its tracks. "That's a hell-of-a shot soldier," the General expressed, "What's your name?" Colter turned around to see the General sitting on his big gray horse, sided by two Majors. Colter stood up straight and said. "Private Winn Colter, Sir."

"That shot was impressive Private. Looks like you and your men will be living high on the hog tonight!"

"Yes Sir. Thank you Sir!"

General Lee looked back to the dead hog, "It looks like that shot was a good 300 yards, Son. Not bad for a quick shot."

Colter looked at the downed hog and knew it was farther out than 300, but didn't say anything about the range. He said, "Our men are pretty hungry, General."

Major Freeborn stepped forward seeing the General talking to Colter, "General Lee, Sir, care to join us for some pork and bean stew tonight? Private Colter just kept our dinner from getting away."

General Lee looked around at the soldiers. "I wish I could stay, but I need to keep riding to check on more of the troops." He looked back at the young soldier and was impressed by the stature of the young Texan. "Private Winn Colter. I'll remember that name."

General Lee edged his horse forward moving closer to the middle of the men and spoke up, "I've heard good things about this regiment. Keep it up boys!" The General turned to the men and saluted then looked at the young blond soldier packing a Sharps and a brace of Colts. It made the General think. He turned back to Major Freeborn, saluted then kicked Traveler forward. "Give 'em Hell boys!" The General looked one last time at Colter then put a spur to his horse and galloped away.

Only a few weeks before, General Lee and President Davis had been discussing an idea calling on the talents of a lone soldier for a special mission. This young Texan could be the soldier for that mission... Private

Winn Colter. He would have to talk to the President as soon as he could.

****

June, 21, 1863. Colter sat in the shade of a large oak tree and rubbed an oiled cloth over the barrel of his .45-70, then took out a kerchief and wiped the sweat from his neck and forehead. It was a relatively peaceful afternoon other than the faint echo of thunder somewhere and the sound of the creek babbling over some rocks on the far side of the meadow. They had been in the saddle for three hours riding north. Colter didn't know if they were in Virginia or Pennsylvania, but it was a miserable hot and muggy day, nothing like the dry heat he was used to back in Texas. Now that he was here with the other Texans, he wouldn't complain. In the time he had been with the company, Colter noticed that a few of the men were always complaining.

Every time the Company of Texans stopped, Colter busied himself cleaning or wiping his guns to make sure they were clean, dry and ready for action. That's the way his father taught him. He could hear his Pa's voice: "Keep your guns clean because your life may depend on your next shot."

Many of the southern soldiers brought their own guns when they joined the fight and Colter was better equipped than many of the soldiers he rode with. He was packing a Sharps rifle and a pair of short barreled Navy Colts with extra cylinders. He also carried a pair of saddle Dragoons in holsters mounted to the front of his saddle. He would be ready for almost anything if a battle erupted.

Colter noticed some of the men sleeping while others rolled themselves a smoke. The men had watered their horses in the small creek across the meadow and now were giving them a break from the heavy afternoon sun. They let the horses feed on the grass along the edge of the meadow. The men always made sure they took take care of their mounts. If a horse went lame or was shot and it couldn't be replaced, the man was transferred to an infantry unit. One thing about Texans, they knew how to pick a good horse and did whatever they could to protect them. No cavalryman ever wanted to lose his horse!

Colter had been in the Army for less than a month and right off had been sent to Virginia with thirty five other mounted recruits to fill in for the Texans killed or wounded during the battle of Winchester. The

13th Regiment of the Texas Volunteers was a mounted fighting unit and Company D was mostly from northern Texas with a few other toughs from Mississippi, Georgia and Arizona. This group of soldiers had been very effective in recent battles. Compared to other regiments involved in the fight, the 13th had come through the battle with less causality than other regiments in the fight.

No one could say Winn Colter, a fifteen year old boy with his blonde hair and brown eyes, looked like he belonged with the battle hardened regiment. At the battle of Brady Station, the men found out quickly Colter was every bit as competent, and as dangerous as any man in the Company.

Colter was assigned to Company D under Major Joshua Freeborn. The Major was a tall, lanky Texan who stood nearly three inches over six feet, had red hair and a graying beard. His uniform showed signs of wear and dust but it was impressive nonetheless. Freeborn was a down-to-earth leader who cared for his men and treated them all with respect if they deserved it. He was a tough soldier who expected orders to be followed precisely. He didn't like surprises and didn't take disrespect from anyone. One of the reasons the Company had been such a successful fighting unit was because the men followed orders and trusted the Major.

The sound of a horseman coming down the trail from the rear caught everyone's attention. Horses were pulled back in the trees and every rifle was ready. It turned out the rider was a courier trying to catch up with the Company with a dispatch for Major Freeborn. The rider had other dispatches to deliver and was gone almost as fast as he came.

The Major studied the dispatch for a minute then called for Colter to come to him. The men had scattered about 50 yards along the tree line to let their horses graze again while they could. "Colter! What the hell is this?" Freeborn asked.

Colter was worried that he had done something wrong still being the newest man in the unit. He jumped to attention. Freeborn paced back and forth while looking from Colter to the dispatch. He said "This here dispatch says" 'Private Winn Colter is to report to General Robert E. Lee in Richmond for special assignment'." Freeborn held the letter in front of Colter so he could see. "Look who this dispatch is from." The Major pulled the paper back so he could read it again to be sure he really read what he thought it said." Freeborn shook his head amazed at what he read "This dispatch is from Jefferson Davis, President of the Confederate States of America!" Freeborn couldn't believe it. "I never saw anything like this! How in the…?" Major Freeborn still couldn't believe what he was reading. He was taking big strides pacing back and forth, and then stopping to look at the message again. Men that were close enough to overhear were whispering back an fourth.

Colter thought for a moment then casually said "Major, I may be able to explain. You see, Sir, I met the President a long time ago. My Pa built a gun for Jefferson Davis 'bout three years ago when he was still a Mississippi Senator and I was just a twelve year old kid. I met him, but I thought he would have forgotten about me since he became President. I don't know how he would even know I'd joined and was with the 13th Regiment."

"Remember you, hell!" Freeborn called out, "This doesn't happen! Especially to a young, inexperienced kid two weeks out." Freeborn walked back and forth trying to think, shaking the paper in his hand.

Colter continued to explain, "My Pa's a gunsmith back in Texas and quite well known. His name is Weston Colter and I've heard other folks say he may be the best gunsmith in all of Texas." Colter could hear some of the men quietly repeating his father's name and whispering. "My Pa built a gun for President Davis and he had me shoot it the day I met him back home in Mesquiteville. Mr. Davis had taken a fall from his horse a few days before, injuring his shoulder, so he had me shoot the gun that day.

I knew Pa had been working on a Whitworth rifle to see why they can shoot like they do. For a muzzleloader, they are an incredibly accurate gun with their long slender bullets and hexagon barrel. Pa said a Whitworth can outshoot an Enfield three to one at a 1,000 yard target.

Pa had been talking to a lot of gun makers and he was designing a new kind of bullet using a brass case like the .50-70 Government. Pa thought his new design would shoot faster and farther than any other gun out there.

The gun he made for the president was a long barreled .32 caliber falling block that looked like a fancy .50-70 Sharps but it shot one of those long and slender bullets my Pa designed. I've never seen a bullet like it before. That bullet lead itself reminded me of the Whitworth bullet. It took

Pa some time but he did it! He worked on all kinds of guns and he could fix 'em all; better than new, and this one... there was nothin' like it I ever knew!"

The Major looked at the men who had gathered close to see what was going on. Some now had a questioning look on their faces. He heard Whitworth whispered between some of the men and Freeborn knew some about guns. He answered the question before it was asked, "The Whitworth is a British rifled musket that's known for long range shooting."

"At first I thought it must be a fancy squirrel gun for Mr. Davis's son," Colter said "but it was heavy and had a sharpshooter barrel that was longer than a normal rifle. It didn't seem like what a kid would shoot. That small caliber bullet wasn't what you'd expect a man to be shootin' in a rifle neither, but boy was I wrong!" Colter looked around and saw more men gathering in closer to listen to his story. Freeborn was waiting to hear more.

"Pa seemed nervous and was shaky that day with Mr. Davis watching. He asked me to shoot, but I wasn't sure that I could do it. I was just twelve; but Pa asked me to try. Pa pointed at a crow sittin' on top of a cactus out some 300 yards and told me to shoot it." A soldier named Jon Kennedy busted out laughing, "A crow at 300 yards? That's impossible!"

Colter looked at Kennedy's smirk and it gnawed at his insides to have the man talk and act like he always did. Kennedy's personality was generally disrespectful to everyone but especially to the new men, younger men or anyone he didn't like. That meant just about everyone.

Colter looked back to Freeborn and continued, "I thought the shot was impossible too but this gun was unlike any I had ever seen or shot. Pa talked with lots of 'smiths and gun designers before the war and was fascinated about all the new gun designs and brass bullets. He told me I would see changes in the guns people would want coming soon.

The big change in Pa's gun came after meeting a couple of German craftsmen that Pa invited to supper. They didn't speak good English, but that night they 'all went to Pa's shop talking about guns and bullets and swapping ideas all through the night. They talked about things I never heard of but it all had to do with brass bullets. Pa said after talking to Benjamin Henry and those Germans, he had an idea for a bullet and started to build a gun with a falling block design and a sharpshooter barrel. I never saw another bullet or gun like it."

Colter wiped some sweat from his brow. "Mr. Davis had a man bring Pa a German telescopic sight to put on that gun. When I got to look through it, I could see the crow's eyes blink. Pa loaded the gun with one of those long, slender bullets then handed it to me."

More than a dozen soldiers had moved closer to listen to Colter's story. "Pa made some adjustments, then threw a little dirt in the air, and watched the dust fall to the ground. He told me to put the hairs in the telescope on the top of the crow's head and hold steady. I did just as he said while the President watched."

Jon Kennedy spoke up again and asked sarcastically, "What happened? Did y'all get it?"

Kennedy was really starting to make Freeborn mad with his sarcastic taunts, interrupting Colter's story. Freeborn finally had enough and shouted at Kennedy, "Shut the hell up, Kennedy!" Kennedy looked back at the major and swallowed hard.

Colter added, "At the time, I thought I got lucky; I took the crow's head clean off with that shot!"

"Lucky?" Freeborn said, but after watching what Colter could do with his Sharps, the Major started thinking that if anyone could make a shot like Colter was describing, this kid would be the one.

" Pa said with a few adjustments to the gun, a steady shooter probably could do the same at 600 yards and consistently take down a man at 1,000 to 1,200 yards, maybe even farther. "

"President Davis patted me on the back and smiled when I handed him that rifle. Pa and he visited for a while then Mr. Davis came over and asked me how old I was, then smiled again. He shook my hand, then mounted his horse and left with the gun."

"Hey Colter," one of the listening soldiers asked, "Did your Pa make any more of those guns?"

Colter looked at the group, "Yes, he made eight total. The one for the President and then five more that went down on a barge crossing the Mississippi. Pa's shop was broken into while we went to get supplies and the other two rifles were taken! That was a month before I enlisted. Pa usually didn't spend much time on guns for ourselves because he was so busy, but he took the time and made one of those guns for each of us... but now they're gone. Whoever broke in took or broke his smithin' tools so he couldn't build another gun until he replaced missing equipment. He didn't have enough time or the tools to make any others before I left.

Winn made an agreement with his father that he could join the Texas Volunteers on his 15th birthday as long so he worked hard and helped with his chores and sick mother. The Confederate States didn't require service until boys turned eighteen but many younger boys volunteered to fight. Winn had been ready to leave when he was thirteen as a soldier dressed in gray came to Jacksboro asking for volunteers. Weston Colter could see it in Winn's eyes and knew his son was itching to go. With Winn's strong will, Weston knew his son would sneak away to join if he didn't give permission so he had to make a deal to keep Winn home as long as he could and hope the war would end soon. Even though Weston didn't like it, he had to support his son's decision to fight or they might lose him to running away at thirteen.

Weston took time from his smithin' to teach his son everything he knew that might help keep him safe. When the guns were stolen from his shop, Winn wouldn't wait for a new rifle to be built. On his birthday, Weston gave Winn his .50-70 Sharps and sat with him to talk. Weston looked at his son and said quietly, "I know I can't stop you from going but I don't believe it will be like you're expecting. I don't believe you will come any closer to Hell on earth than on a battlefield and I'll pray for you to come home." He was getting choked up and had difficulty speaking. "When it's time to leave, you'll know it..., Do it, Son! " After they embraced, Winn Colter said a final goodbye to his Ma and Pa before he mounted his horse and was off to join the fight.

As Weston Colter watched his son ride away, he knew this could be the last time he saw the boy alive and he quickly wiped away a tear from his eye. He knew this war was different from any other fought before. Gunpowder was more consistent and the new rifles with cartridge bullets were going to change everything. More men were going to die because guns were now more accurate. If more guns were using a conical design bullet similar to his design, even more soldiers would die. Men like Eliphalet Remington, Benjamin Henry, Samuel Colt and Weston Colter were changing the future of warfare with their gun and bullet designs.

Freeborn asked Colter if he had shot the gun his Pa had made for him, but he hadn't.

"I watched him test his rifle though and none of you will believe it," Colter declared. "I watched him hit a man sized target at 1,200 yards and saw him take down a deer at 800."

Kennedy jumped up shouting and accusing, "Colter, "you're a liar! That's 'most a mile and you're a crazy liar!"

Being called a liar, Winn could feel the fury jump inside him as the adrenaline filled his veins. Winn doubled up his fist and jumped at Kennedy so fast that Kennedy couldn't react because he wasn't expecting it, Winn's fist caught Jon Kennedy on the jaw with a solid left hook that snapped his head back. The quick punch surprised Kennedy and knocked him back two steps. Fury burst over his face. Nobody did that to a Kennedy let alone a damn kid!

Major Freeborn quickly stepped in and stopped the two and looked at Kennedy. "Talkin' like that, callin' him a liar is uncalled for Kennedy. Didn't you get no schoolin? That shot he was describing was near half a mile. We killed some Yanks at Fort Sumter farther than that but I always thought those shots were luck. I hear the shot was done with a Whitworth Rifle too."

Kennedy was still steaming mad. This kid had just hit him with a sucker punch and made him look like a fool! Kennedy hadn't even seen it coming, but it caught him solid on the jaw and set him back on his heels. Kennedy was thinking of what to do, but Freeborn interrupted his thought. "Kennedy, if you call Colter a liar again, I'll turn him loose with his Sharps and make you stand at 500 yards and give him a free shot. Do you want to call him a liar again? We've all seen him shoot and we've all been thankful we've had him!"

Kennedy tasted the blood in his mouth and spat on the ground then thought about the shots he knew Colter had made in the past two weeks. He had made shots that they all thought were luck, but there was no doubt he had made them. Kennedy thought to himself, for now, it wasn't wise to call this young Texan a liar. It was eating at his gut but he knew he had to back down and save it for later. "No Sir! No offense to his Pa," Kennedy snapped "but how can anyone shoot like that?"

"I don't know," Freeborn responded, "but if the President is sending for this boy, he must believe and I'll not dispute it! If I were you Kennedy, I wouldn't say words to a man, or a kid for that matter, that might pick you out of the saddle... a mile away!"

Kennedy thought for a moment of a bullet taking his head off and looked at this young kid with his fist still clenched, that he'd just called a liar. The taste of blood still lingered in his mouth as he studied Colter carefully. Kennedy noticed the kid was carrying two Navy Colt revolvers, butts forward. Few soldiers had one, let alone packed two pistols and even fewer would wear them butt forward. He didn't know this young hombre well enough to know what he really could do to anyone calling him a liar. Kennedy then recanted, "If your story's true then you and that rifle could shoot Grant or Lincoln and win this war!"

Major Freeborn looked back at the dispatch and again shook his head. "I know you can shoot," he said, "but If you really can shoot anything like your Pa, then I want you on my side! You sure impressed important people, Kid."

"Kid Colter" someone else repeated.

"Yea, Kid Colter." Freeborn thought of some of the shots Colter had made including that long shot on the wild boar when General Lee was watching. "Hope that lucky shot you made in front of the General doesn't get "Kid Colter" killed."

Colter could only respond with "Me too Sir." Freeborn looked at Colter and saluted him and so did the men who had listened to his story, except for one man. . . Jon Kennedy.

Freeborn handed the dispatch to Colter, "I may be a Major, but if you are receiving orders from the President himself and from General Robert E. Lee, I salute you!" Colter received a few handshakes and a few men came to look at the dispatch. Colter would leave the Company now and ride in the opposite direction to Richmond. Hopefully, he could get there without being shot or captured so he could find out what his orders would be from the General. What could this new assignment be? Winn wasn't sure but he knew for a dispatch rider to be sent looking for him, there was some plan in the works... and it involved him.

Colter mounted his horse and rode away from the Company of Texans. Having men around him had been a comforting feeling, but now he was alone with only his horse and rifle and the war was calling. Winn Colter put a spur to his horse and cautiously rode away up the trail headed toward Richmond, Virginia.

CHAPTER 3

As Winn Colter rode for Richmond, his thoughts lingered back two years to the day he first decided to fight. Winn had ridden into Jacksboro to pick up supplies from the Mercantile Store for his father when a group of cavalrymen rode into town. The lead rider stopped at the center of town and the bugler blew on his bugle. After waiting a moment for everyone's attention, a soldier stood forward to make the announcement. "I'm sure y'all have all heard rumors but now its official. Texas has joined the Confederate States of America and is now at war!" Winn heard a woman gasp and a few men cheered. The soldier looked around at the men that had gathered, "Texan's are being called to fight!" Winn hadn't thought much about what he said until the soldier looked squarely at Winn and said, "That means you too Son." Winn was only thirteen but he was convinced. He was going to fight for the south! His mind was made up.

Jacksboro was small and more men than not were against going to war. Now that the call came, men would go. Winn watched several men and some boys just older than him walk out to sign up and Winn followed. A table had been set up where one of the Cavalrymen was having men sign their names and Winn stepped forward. The man at the table looked across at the young volunteer with little regard, and a bit of annoyance. There should be more men stepping forward and this kid before him was wasting his time. He looked Winn up and down then asked, "How old are you Son?"

Winn said, "I'm thirteen."

"Why don't you go home to your Mama and let your Papa come

and fight?"

Winn snapped back, "I can shoot better than the last two men you just signed up." The man studied the young boy in front of him. If nothing else, the boy had guts. The soldier looked again, "We're only signing up men over sixteen. You're too young Boy!" Being told he couldn't do something made Winn angry. It didn't matter who was telling him what he could or couldn't do, if it was a teacher, a preacher or his mother, he always did as he wanted. Nobody could talk sense to him except his father. Winn made up his mind right then and there. He was going whether this soldier would sign him up or not!

Winn mounted his horse and quickly rode back home to inform his Ma and Pa that he was going to fight in this war. The sudden announcement didn't go well and left his mother in tears. Winn's announcement was painful to his father as well and it finally pushed him beyond his limits! He was proud of his son's determination, but he couldn't let him go fight, especially where he was only thirteen. Weston knew his son's willpower couldn't be detoured. All he could hope for a delay before he left on his own.

With some determination, Weston talked Winn out of running away by promising to support his decision to join if he waited 'til he was fifteen. Being such a strong willed boy before had really not caused any issues other than a few broken bones, some cuts and some burned fingers. Winn's personality had always driven him to be the best at whatever he did. This decision to go off to war had consequences that were a lot more severe and could mean a bullet or his life.

Weston secretly hoped the war would be over by Winn's fifteenth birthday so he wouldn't go. Rumor was that it should be over in three months, six months at the longest. Regretfully, the war had raged on for two years and had even gotten worse. As word arrived in Texas that two more of the local boys were in a Yankee prison, Winn's drive only became greater. He had made an agreement and promised his Pa, but there was no doubt he was going to fight for the South!

Weston knew the best thing he could do for his son was to teach and prepare him for what was to come. He taught his son everything he could about guns and shooting. Weston taught Winn about surviving and how to fight like an Indian. In Texas, a man had better know the Indian ways or he would probably end up dead. Weston had a great respect for the Indians and learned all he could about the Kiowa and Apaches and he had nearly lost his hair a couple of times. There was no doubt by any western man with any savvy that the Indians were incredible fighters. Weston taught his son to take care of his guns and to know what potential they held. He hoped the lessons would keep his son alive and safe when he was thrown into a life or death situation.

****

Weston Colter sat down the Patterson pistol he had just repaired and walked to the pot-bellied stove to pour a cup of coffee. He walked to the door and stepped outside of his shop to take a short breather from his work. He noticed Pepper, Winn's old dog, standing there wagging his tail looking back at him. Weston reached down to give the old dog a rough rub, the way Winn used to play with him.

Since Winn left, Pepper had either stayed in the shop at Weston's feet or stayed sitting in front of the shop looking down the trail to town, like he was waiting for Winn to come home. During the first few weeks after Winn left, the old dog made his way in to town every day sniffing his way around, then making his way back home. Weston took a sip of coffee and looked down the trail himself and said, "I miss him too boy," as he patted the old dog on the head.

It had now been over a month since he watched his fifteen-year-old son ride away from home with grand thoughts of fighting for the Confederacy. Weston was mad at himself for not being more forceful in changing Winn's mind about leaving to fight, but he knew there was no use. The boy was going and there was no stopping him when his mind was set. Now Weston felt he had lost the most important thing in his life, next to his wife Annabelle.

Of the couple's three children, two had died early of pneumonia before they were two years old. But their son Winn had always been as healthy as a horse. He had done well at everything he set his mind to, everything from his schooling to shooting. Annabelle couldn't have other children after Winn so as an only child, he was his parent's pride and joy.

Winn was his father's son and could be as stubborn as a mule. When he made up his mind, there was usually no stopping him.

Weston finished his coffee then looked down at Pepper to see that the old dog had his head down, but was still looking down the trail. He ruffled the dogs fur then went back inside the shop to work on another project.

*****

Arriving safely in Virginia, Colter met with General Lee as ordered and was later escorted to an official meeting with the President. As he entered the room, Colter wasn't sure if the President would remember him from his meeting years before with his father. Colter now wasn't sure how to act with Mr. Davis because even though he knew him, he was now the President of the Confederate States of America.

Colter respectfully saluted President Davis, showing his respect, showing the President he was a good soldier. As Mr. Davis walked into the room, he came right over to Winn with a big smile and eagerly shook his hand. He eyed Colter up and down, "You've really grown since I last saw you". The President's eyes still looked young but Colter could tell he was under great a great deal of stress. The President walked around his office nervously. He picked up his cigar then wiped the sweat from his brow; the President had reason to be nervous. The fate and future of the Confederacy rested upon his shoulders.

President Davis looked out the window for a moment with a faraway stare that a man gets when in deep thought. The streets were busy with military wagons transporting supplies, but the President's focus was on a buggy pulled by what looked like an older gray mare. It was some distance away, but the President could see a woman in the buggy. She looked like a fine southern belle wearing a frilly blue dress and a wide brimmed matching bonnet. She must be lovely because the President saw as she rode past three young men, they all turned back for a second or even a third look.

The President needed that, just a little distraction. Something to get his mind off of what was happening to all those brave soldiers not far away. The distraction was welcome but it was time to present an idea to Winn Colter that had only been discussed by a privileged few. A decision had to be made now on this idea that hopefully would change the South's success in the war.

The President turned back to Winn and his demeanor became serious. "Colter," he said, "General Lee told me he had found a young soldier that he believed had extraordinary shooting abilities. He called you a natural, and one of the best shots he's ever seen. Coming from the General, that's quite a compliment Colter."

The President had been sitting on the corner of his desk, but he got up and started walking again as he talked. "The General didn't mention your name, of course, or I would have already known what he said was true. He just said he may have found the man for an idea we've been discussing." The president stopped again and looked Colter straight in the eye, "General Lee said you made a hell-of-a shot with your sharps at a wild hog last week." Jefferson Davis wanted to study Colter's reaction as he talked about his shot. "The General said your shot at the wild boar was some 300 yards out... on the run no less!"

If the President was looking for a reaction, there was none. Colter's answer was matter-of-fact. "Well, yes Sir," Colter replied, "a bunch of our men heard the hog squeal as we rode along, so two of them went into the bush to flush the boar out. We hoped we could have him for supper, but the boys missed their shot."

The President asked how far the hog was out. Colter explained, "By the time the boar was out of the brush, it was nearly 200 yards out. We could all see that hog was on the run for the thicket and he just about made it. Another thirty feet and he would have been gone." Colter looked at the President thoughtfully, "The men hadn't eaten well for two days, Sir. I knew they were all as hungry as I was. We were all beginning to wonder if the rumbling and growling in our stomachs would warn the Yankee's we were coming!" Colter paused for a moment then quietly added, "That shot turned out to be some 350 yards, Sir."

Jefferson Davis chuckled, "I don't doubt your shot a bit. After seeing you shoot three years ago, I believe it!" After General Lee rode away, one of the men got off his horse and stepped it off. "You know, Sir," Colter said, "Pa being a gunsmith, I learned a lot more about guns and shooting than most men don't rightly understand and won't learn in a lifetime."

The President knew what Colter said was true. "I know your pa, and frankly, he's the smartest gunsmith I've ever known. If a gun can be improved, he makes it better and the gun he designed himself would match up with any rifle made in the world!" The president smiled, "Remember, I know how good your Pa's guns are because I have the one he made for me… I wish he'd make me a thousand! "

Colter could tell the President was proud to own one of his father's guns. Jefferson Davis imagined the shot at the hog that impressed the General, then remembered Winn's shot at the crow that introduced him to his gun. "Three hundred and fifty yards!" he said again. "Not many men can make that shot. Some might with luck, but with you, I don't even have to ask if it was luck".

"I don't think it was luck, Sir." Colter replied, "But I was aiming for the hog's head and the bullet hit him in the front shoulder. You could say I missed my mark, Sir." Colter winked feeling a little more comfortable now.

The President looked at Colter and smiled. "How old are you son? You don't look more than seventeen or eighteen now."

"I'm fifteen Sir." Colter could see the surprised look on the President's face. "Pa wouldn't let me join until I turned 15, but he kept me shooting and practicing." Colter looked more mature than his age. Colter said "I left home on my birthday and I just got with the regiment about three weeks ago."

Jefferson Davis looked at Colter's two holstered Navy Colts with his Arkansas Toothpick tucked in his belt. He stood five foot seven inches, but looked taller with his Stetson. Winn Colter was built solid, but it wasn't overly obvious. He had years to grow. His blond hair and brown eyes gave a deceivingly vulnerable appearance to a very capable and dangerous young soldier. As the President further observed, he could see his toned muscular body and keen eyes, observant and ready for anything. The President thought to himself that if he had more young men like the one standing in front of him now, the South would have already won the war.

The President looked at the butt forward pistols Colter was wearing," I see you're packing guns of a cavalryman for close quarters fighting."

Colter knew the President was meaning his Navy Colts. "Pa made sure I was set before I came. He balanced the cylinders and lightened the triggers making them dandy shooters." He added "Like they're meant to be in your hand, Mr. President."

Jefferson Davis knew that anything Weston Colter worked on was better than the original. "I can only imagine the guns if your Pa and Sam Colt ever worked closely together."

"Pa respects Sam Colt highly, but says even his guns can be made better. Pa's had me practice every day with my Colts. I could always shoot the rifles well but he made sure I would be accurate with my short guns. He wanted to make sure I would come home." Colter hesitated for a few seconds then said "I think Ma believes I will never make it home."

The President smiled at him, "I think you'll prove her wrong."

"I aim to Sir!" Colter agreed, "I'll keep my guns clean and ready to shoot." The President nodded his approval "I've heard The Texas Volunteers have a reputation for being a tough fighting unit. I've read reports those boys have been in some tough battles. What do you think of the Regiment?"

"Other than the officer that tried to take my Colts from me, Sir," Colter said, "they're a fine group of tough fighting Texans." Most are a lot older in their twenties and thirties but a couple are as old as my Pa." Jefferson Davis sat back on his desk and listened to Colter with genuine interest. He wanted to see how Colter reacted to his fellow soldiers and to see if he had experienced any battle.

Colter continued, "Major Freeborn is a good leader and, of course, some of the men are better than others." Colter looked intently at the President when he said, "Some didn't take too kindly to a new kid out-shooting them." The President was amused at Colter's perception. "Most the men accepted me and I think the Major was thankful to have me for my guns. Some still had a problem with me."

Colter thought about the newer replacements that had been sent with him to the regiment and knew they would have trouble surviving their first battle. "Some of the men don't have a sense for things that could get them killed. If they was back home in Texas in Indian country, well, they would have some trouble and probably be missing their hair."

President Davis looked Colter over again. From what he could see and knew of him, he believed Winn Colter would do just fine in what he was going to ask. "Colter, General Lee and I believe you are the answer to some mighty big prayers!" The President paused for a moment then walked over to a long wooden case in the corner of the room. He opened the lid and lifted out the rifle Colter's father had built.

Colter could see the gun had a new engraving of a pair of Rebel flags on the side of the stock but the engraving that gave him the most pride is what was prominently engraved on the barrel, "Colter Arms". Colter knew there was not another gun like it in the world as this gun was special made for the President and sported a long telescopic sight on top. He was proud to know that this gun was made by his Pa, Weston Colter.

The President said, "Did you know your father made six of these for me? He gave me this but the second shipment was lost as a barge sank in the Mississippi."

Colter looked at the telescopic sight, the fancy scroll designs etched into the metal and fine carvings along the stock. He knew this gun was unique with the gold inlay, customized for the President of the Confederate States of America. Colter remembered, "Pa actually made 8 rifles. One for me and him, but they were stolen from Pa's shop just before I left Texas." President Davis looked concerned thinking about the missing guns. "That's unfortunate to say the least." He walked over to Colter, looked at him respectfully and then gently handed him the rifle. "I've discussed this with General Lee and he had an idea... You are going to be that idea Colter." Winn was confused trying to figure out what the President was saying. "This rifle is one of the finest guns ever made! It has been built for long range accuracy unlike any other gun out there Colter. Your father built this special for me but I want you to take it now. We need you to take it!"

Colter looked down in astonishment at the gun in his hands. The President explained that his new orders had him working alone and answering to only two people, General Lee and himself. "I know what you can do with this gun in your hands. Some men might be trained, but you have extraordinary capabilities! In your hands, this gun can hit those long targets out five hundred yards or more. You probably know better than I. I've never had anyone with your natural ability shoot this weapon since you last shot it."

The President looked Colter in the eye very seriously, "Your orders are to target key officers, artillerymen and sharpshooters. Without leaders, armies fall apart. To be truthful, we may be winning some battles, but we have lost too many of our seasoned officers. I want you to turn that around." Colter sat and listened. The President explained "I only have two exceptions and this is important,"

"Yes Sir."

"Do not target General Ulysses Grant or President Abraham Lincoln. You may think taking them out could end the war, but after lots of discussion with General Lee and some of my other key military people, we have decided as bad as Lincoln and Grant are on the Confederacy, we believe the men in line as replacements would be much worse! Don't target either of these two men. Do you understand?"

Colter looked at the rifle then back at the President. "Yes Sir. Take out officers and artillerymen... and sharpshooters."

The president looked relieved and smiled... "Avoid bringing attention to yourself and you will stay alive longer, Colter." That was good advice that Winn would take to heart. The President added "You will be working alone. General Lee has drawn order papers so if by chance you are confronted by our troops, you won't be shot for desertion."

"I appreciate that, Sir." replied Colter.

Jefferson Davis looked a lot more relaxed than he did when Colter had first arrived. He continued "I understand you signed on for $11 dollars per month as a private. I'm giving you a field promotion raising you to corporal. You'll probably be the youngest corporal in the Confederate Army. Corporals normally earn $13 dollars per month but I'm going to authorize $20 dollars per month for you. That's more than a First Sergeant because I want you to know how important I believe your mission will be Colter!"

Colter thought in almost disbelief. Twenty dollars was more than he had ever had in his life and he was going to earn that every month. He would have to collect the gold or silver coins every month from the paymaster.

The President looked at Colter thoughtfully then cautioned him, "You may get shot for that rifle or your pay, so I would suggest you watch yourself. That includes some of our own men if you know what I mean."

"Yes Sir."

"Talk to my Assistant and he will get you anything you need Colter.

Take some bullets and get back to knowing her. She's an amazing rifle!" he said appreciatively.

Colter was almost choked up... "Thank you Sir."

He looked on the gun and it was just as he remembered it, sleek and balanced. He knew his Pa had made the rifle for President Davis. Exceptional care and focus had been crafted into every detail. This was not a soldier's gun. The President was right. There were men out there that would kill for a gun like this, a gun that could consistently put a bullet in a target at 500 to 1,000 yards and probably further.

CHAPTER 4

April 2, 1865. Winn Colter was in a position where he was deeply concealed amongst the rocks and debris just below the edge of the skyline. There were two huge boulders behind him that were situated so they created the illusion of a solid rock wall, but there was a small hidden gap between the two that allowed for a quick exit if needed. It was early spring and the vegetation below was thick and green. Some of the grass was already a foot tall and Colter could only imagine what it must look like in the pasturelands back in Texas. It was a quiet afternoon other than a few birds chirping in the trees below. Winn was thankful to have a small reprieve from the war even if it was only for a few minutes. It didn't happen very often.

Colter had always been very good when it came to moving undetected and finding this position provided an excellent vantage point of the valley. His father had taken the time to teach him well as a hunter in the ways of an Indian. He learned to be patient and move undetected while he was on the stalk hunting his prey. As a kid, all that was fun and games but in wartime, or against Indians, being able to remain undetected could save your life. Winn thought that his Pa would have never imagined him using those skills like this but maybe that's why he had spent so much time teaching him. He was preparing him for a life in the west.

Colter was relaxed in this position as he looked down into the small Tennessee valley below. The closest edge of the clearing ranged about 300 feet directly below where he overlooked the tops of a thick grove of trees. Winn could see the valley was only about 250 yards wide at its widest point but it was nearly a half mile long where it drew together from two canyons. The only previous evidence of man was what looked like a burned out line shack that had been destroyed many years before the war.

The entire area was surrounded by a thick wall of trees that kept the small valley hidden, but there was the trail that skirted the far edge. Winn noted it was getting a lot of use. This position was an excellent place with a clear shot from the hundred yards below to some 800 yards where the trail left the valley up one of the canyons. Winn had made many longer shots, some out to 1,500 yards so this position in the shadows, at the top of the ridge, was an excellent location and well within his comfortable shooting range.

Winn could see the trail had served as a light road; but because of its limited use, he knew there was a better trail or road behind the hill that led towards the town of Franklin then on to Nashville. During war time, the trail below was a dangerous, if not fatal; place to be if a sharpshooter was watching.

Colter had relaxed, but jerked as he found himself falling asleep. He hadn't realized it, but he was exhausted from several days of little or no sleep. Two days before he had a squad of Union soldiers stumble onto his hide-out and set camp not fifty feet from where he had been in position. Colter had been backed up against some rock with no way out so he held the muzzle of his horse all night to make sure he didn't make a sound. Although he thought it probably wouldn't have made any difference, because two of the Yankees snored so loud, he couldn't have gone to sleep if he wanted.

Now, through the exhaustion, Winn Colter found himself thinking about Texas and wishing he was back home. Winn had been away for two years fighting in this war and now everything he dreamed about it as a boy had changed. This wasn't anything like he ever expected. He lingered on all the things his Pa had said and taught him.

Colter wished this war was over because he was so tired! He was tired of all the killing, tired of the devastation and destruction of the land, and tired of seeing travesties against so many innocents caught in the middle. Colter knew that the fate of soldiers was one thing because they signed on for this duty. It was expected of them to follow orders and to die if necessary; but the women and children caught in the middle... many never to see fathers or husbands or sons again. Colter was grieved at what they went through and for all of their losses.

Colter had witnesses the horrific destruction and death caused by both Union and Confederate soldiers. He knew the war affected everyone but not many as bad as here in Tennessee. Towns and plantations had been burned to the ground and people had been killed. For what? Colter now couldn't even remember why Texas had got in to the fight in the first place. Yes, he was tired of all of it but still found himself stuck right in the middle of the Tennessee backwoods with no escape.

Colter could see the writing on the wall. The South had fought diligently for four years and won some decisive battles but nobody ever expected the war to last this long. Time was working against them and the South was losing.

Winn Colter was a good soldier and always followed his orders. He did his part as he selectively pounded away at the Union officers, artillerymen and sharpshooters just like the President and General Lee had ordered, but he had been doing this for nearly two years... It seemed like it would never stop. Colter had been at the battles of Chattanooga, Chickamauga and Vicksburg and had made many decisive shots; but as he put one Yankee down, there always seemed to be another two or three officers to step into place. The Confederacy was also feeling the loss of good leaders, but the South's supply of good officers was at a critical point and had started to dwindle. There was no doubt, the South was in trouble.

Colter had been in position on top of the hill waiting to see the Union troops move between the camps along the valley trail below. He was now just outside of Franklin, Tennessee where he had scouted this location several days before and knew it would be perfect to set up. With a few fallen trees and lots of overgrowth that created shadows, it was perfect for a sharpshooter's concealment. Colter was one of the best and had always worked alone. He always planned ahead with an escape route and this spot had one. Not like the rocks he got trapped against a few days before. This place was perfect! The biggest challenge facing Colter turned out to be his ability to hide his horse in a secure place.

Colter scouted around and found the main Union encampment about three miles northeast of this position, south of Franklin. He also knew there was at least one camp farther to the west but he hadn't actually laid eyes on it. He knew it was there because he had seen several small groups of soldiers and couriers traveling down the trail through this valley several times a day. There was no doubt, something was building based on the trail traffic both ways.

Colter wasn't interested in the Yankee couriers or the common soldiers who had been traveling below so he just watched them scurry back and forth like a bunch of blue ants. Sitting and waiting hour after hour left him time to ponder many things. Today he was thinking about what the war had done to the people of Tennessee. It had been particularly hard hit during the war. Families here had been torn apart with brothers fighting against brothers. Now, Tennessee was second only to Virginia in the amount of action seen. Battles were still being fought but Tennessee was now mostly under Union control with only scattered Rebel soldiers and isolated fighting units.

Colter had always stuck strictly to his orders. Careful scouting helped him identify troop locations and escape routes and had caused him to not fire on some occasions when he might be too close to enemy troops. The long range accuracy of his gun allowed him to stay at distances that no common soldier would ever imagine. That's why he believed he had gone untargeted as a sharpshooter for so long. Colter's actions had been very effective with many high ranking officers taken down. If the Union had known one man was behind the shootings, there's no doubt more effort would have been made to hunt him down and take him out.

Many times Colter's long shots were attributed to accident or just luck... bad luck in their case but what Colter was doing was devastating to the Yankees, especially their high ranking officers. Where he didn't brag or take credit for his shooting, the Union thought there was a squad of sharpshooters out there. That's why being alone was safer...Those were his orders.

CHAPTER 5

Colter blinked realizing he had dozed for a few minutes dreaming of his meeting with President Davis. It had been nearly two years ago. He had scrupulously followed orders doing exactly as President Davis had instructed. Now after all he had seen, Colter truly wanted the war to end, to move on. Colter remembered the words of his father when he had been so eager to go. "There is nothing good about war except when it's over." His father was right and spoke with wisdom that he hadn't recognized at the time. He now knew what his Pa meant. No matter how many officers he took out on his mission, there was always someone else to step into their place. The South had won many battles but it was losing the war. The end was near and could come down to a few select battle outcomes.

Colter heard himself say, "I want out... Did I just say that?" Colter felt done! He was tired, worn out and worst of all he was sensing the Southerners had taken about all they could. It's not that they were ready to surrender. In fact, many probably never would if it came to that, but the South was having a hard time. The southern states weren't as industrialized as the north and all kinds of supplies were now scarce. People were going hungry and having to do without in many cases. Plantations and cities alike were being burned to the ground. General Sherman and his army burned and ravaged everything in its path on his march to the sea. Sherman was one man Colter deeply regretted not putting a bullet into, but there never was an opportunity.

Colter felt the growing despair whenever he went into any form of civilization. Southerners were proud people but pride was about all they had left. For some, even that was broken. All other aspects of society were in a downward spiral. The South couldn't continue for much longer without its infrastructure falling apart. There were still those who truly believed the South could still rise to win the war, but balanced against them were the realist. This despair and gloom were the predecessors of defeat.

The war would be ending soon and Colter had heard what northern soldiers were doing to sharpshooters. Rumor was that even after the war was over, the Union army would search out sharpshooters. If he were discovered or even if they suspected that he might be a sharpshooter, he knew he would be killed.

Colter sighed and laid his cheek against his rifle. The smooth walnut stock was almost as comforting as a holding a good woman… better, he thought. What could he know; he had just turned seventeen and hadn't even kissed a girl. He had been told, "Hell hath no fury as a woman's touch," or something like that. That's what was said about his gun as well.

Colter's position was excellent with his escape route clear in his mind. From the enemy movement, Colter was sure something big was about to happen. Suddenly, Colter saw movement coming into the valley from an area he hadn't noticed movement before. Now he could see it, a small hidden draw where a line of trees offered concealment from the main trail. Colter looked closely through his telescopic sight. It was a fairly young man and a woman walking and pulling a large handcart. One of the causalities of war had been civilian stock animals. Many mules and oxen had been commandeered for military purposes or for food leaving many travelers on foot, pulling or pushing hand carts.

Colter could see the wheels were wrapped with cloth to conceal sounds as they traveled across rocky soil. It was easy to see that they didn't want any unnecessary attention from the Yankee camps. For some reason, this man had chosen to make his move now.

Colter curiously watched for a couple of minutes and was surprised at the speedy progress. This was no threat to him so he would just watch them pass and wait for a target. Sooner or later he was sure an officer would come. There had been too much movement between camps for it not to happen. He just had to wait. Then Colter saw it, movement on the main trail. Five… no six Union soldiers moving along the trail, but none were officers with enough rank to target. Colter could see the second the cart was spotted by a Union Sergeant as guns rose and the group of soldiers moved in on the handcart.

Colter watched carefully with his eyes focused back at the cart. Even at the distance of nearly 400 yards, he could see fear in the actions and movement as the couple pulled in close together at the front of the cart. The Union soldiers kept their guns leveled on the couple as they advanced. Sound traveled down the valley. He heard the man with the cart shout "We're not armed?"

"Why ye' sneakin' yella' Rebs!" one of the soldiers growled.

"No, No! We're not Rebs!" The man pleaded, "We're nothing… We're just trying to go through… We're trying to go west!"

"Go west? I think you're a Johnny Reb or spy, or a deserter!" A burley soldier was doing all the talking while the others stood close, like a pack of wild dogs. Two of the soldiers stood back away from the group, watching up and down the trail for any sign of movement.

"We're not spies," the man pleaded again. "And I ain't no deserter neither! We're settlers goin' west." His voice got a little quieter, "We're Mormons." The soldiers started to laugh.

"Mormons?… Mormons!" The other soldiers started to laugh louder. One of the soldiers said, "We hate Mormons worsen we hate Rebs!" The leader of the men, a big, rough looking soldier, lifted his Remington Army 44 revolver and put a ball in the man's right knee. Colter could hear the man's screams of agony echoing along the trees. Colter could see these travelers were probably done for. The woman had thrown herself across the man now and was screaming. There was nothing he could do…. He had orders…

A soldier pulled the woman away from the man then grabbed her dress and ripped the front open exposing her breast. For a moment all the men were staring then laughing. The woman's loose fitting dress had hidden her figure well, but now that she was exposed, all eyes were on her. Colter could see the woman was in big trouble. It would be a horrific death. She would be raped and beaten by six men. When they were done, they would kill her.

The wounded man was struggling to get to his feet and come to her rescue but a knife cut his left hamstring and dropped him to the ground again, his lower body completely useless. Screams of the man's agony echoed down the valley but he still tried to move toward the woman.

Colter couldn't watch. "Damn Yanks!" He knew what was going to happen. Colter put his hand across the eyepiece and bowed his head. It made him sick! He wanted to leave and get away, far, far away! Then the woman's screams changed and Colter looked back through the telescope and what he saw horrified him. One of the soldiers searching the cart found what looked like a young child hiding amongst the couple's belongings, a young boy.

"No. . . Don't hurt him!" The woman screamed "I'll let you all do anything you want to me just please don't hurt my baby!" Colter didn't know how but the wounded man attempted to get to the cart when the big soldier grabbed him by the hair pulling his head back and sliced the knife across the man's throat. The soldier just laughed as the wounded man's life blood poured out of his body. He then turned to the woman and said, "Oh, we're all going to have you over and over again if we want but I aint' doin' it with a Mormon Brat watchin." Colter could see the man had started to undo his breeches but then he lifted his blade and started moving towards the child standing on the cart.

This was too much! To hell with orders! That man was nothing but pure evil and Colter was not going to let anything else happen…. Damn Yanks!

Colter looked through the telescopic sight… Target! He pulled the trigger and saw the effect of his bullet as blood gushed from the man's head. Half his skull was now blown away. He was dead before his body hit the ground. Before it even registered in the minds of the other soldiers, Colter's second shot took the soldier closest to cover, entering his back and leaving an ugly hole ripped in his chest.

The woman yelled at the child to hide which he did by diving back under the items in the cart.

"Where the hell is he?" One of the soldiers was shouting as the big soldier ran over and pulled the woman in front of him, holding his Colt alongside the woman's head. Two other soldiers ducked behind the back of the cart for cover not yet grasping what had happened. By both men hiding behind the cart, they had lined themselves up to the shooter. One shot rang out and two soldiers went down, both grasping their chests. Both men lived long enough to realize they were going to answer to their maker in less than a minute.

Four soldiers were down, one hiding behind the woman and one behind a big rock. Colter knew all this shooting would draw attention and time was running out. He had defied orders in saving this woman and child and leaving them there might subject them to the same fate as before. Colter drew down looking close…no shot!

"Where is he? Show yourself ya yella Reb Bastard!" The soldier behind the rock lifted his Remington Army 44 and fired six shots wildly at shadows. Time was slipping away and if Colter didn't finish what he started, the woman and child were still likely to be killed.

Colter could see a toe of a boot sticking out beyond the big rock so he took aim and fired at the tough shot. Whack! The soldier came hopping to his feet immediately, the toe of his left boot exposing bloody stubs where three of his toes used to be. Colter took aim, pulled the trigger and then there was one.

The last soldier, the big one that had done all the talking in the first place started yelling, "I'll let her live if you let me go!" Colter doubted that. Between the woman's legs Colter could see the soldier's knee and he was pointing his Colt at every sound he heard. Because the target was so close to the woman, Colter wanted to make sure of his shot. He pulled the trigger slowly. The man's leg gave way underneath him and he was spun around from the impact causing him to drop his Colt.

The big man lay on his back screaming and bleeding. "Help me woman, I'm shot!" he demanded. Then the woman saw the big man's gun lying on the ground by her feet. She picked up the heavy gun and went to the man that had held her captive and had killed her husband. She pointed the Colt at his chest. He lifted his hand as if pleading for her to stop. She was thinking of him laughing as he shot her husband. She remembered him laughing after he slit her husband's throat! Anger filled her veins as sorrow filled her heart. She lifted the Colt in her hand and pulled the trigger sending a ball into the man's chest… He was done.

Colter stood up and moved out quickly with his horse from his hiding spot in the rocks. He moved toward the woman who had run to the cart and now held her child in her arms. When Colter got close, the woman whirled throwing the muzzle of the colt towards him. Colter stopped quickly and lifted his hands, "I'm the one who shot these men. I've violated every rule of my mission saving you, but I think we need to get you out of here… get you to safety. I would bet we have a squad of Yanks in here in ten minutes or so."

The woman was sobbing now. Her dress ripped, still hanging open exposing her breast. Colter looked at her closely for the first time. She was a fairly tall blonde, about five foot six, probably twenty to twenty-five years old and more beautiful than any woman he had ever seen. She ran and surprised him by throwing her body into his arms; her naked chest pressing against his and he could feel she was shaking terribly. She was gripping him so tightly that Winn thought she was like a scared child crawling into her father's arms, thinking a wolf was about to get her. Colter reached behind the woman and pulled her close to offer comfort, but this was something he wasn't used to and it was affecting him. Colter had heard of love at first sight, but this woman's husband lay dead only a few feet away.

He didn't have time for this! Colter backed up and warned the woman, "We need to leave now or we may never leave!" She got the point and ran to the cart, grabbed the child and an armful of clothing and items from the cart. Colter looked around quickly, "We need to go and we don't have much room for your stuff!" She looked at her arms then dropped the armful on the ground except for a man's shirt. Colter sat the child on the front of his saddle, then the woman, and then he swung up behind the cantle. Colter reached around the two, to hold the horn, to make sure neither fell off. Colter gave the horse some rein to get him moving quickly. The woman's bare chest occasionally brushed against his arm but neither seemed to notice or care. Other thoughts of pursuers were on their mind. The woman had put the shirt; she had picked up in the rush, around the child and had grabbed nothing else for herself. She still held the heavy pistol in her right hand and Colter wasn't going to take it from her.

They were on the move and safety was a priority. That meant they needed to make some quick distance. But with Yankees all around, Colter knew it might be better to hide out in good cover if they could. They may yet have another fight but he didn't want it, especially now. Colter thought to himself "I'm done! This war is going to end soon with or without me so I'm out!. He didn't know it but he was right. General Lee would officially surrender in two weeks.

Colter always remembered his Pa's parting words as he left to join the fight. "Lots of boys won't be coming home from this war Son. When you see it's time to leave, do it!" Colter hadn't really understood why he said it or what his Pa had meant at the time, but he did now. He could see things were getting worse... It was time. It ate at him every day knowing what his ma and pa would have thought about his actions but this was war and he was doing his duty. He prayed for forgiveness every night and prayed every night that this damn war would end!

No more orders. No more targets. Colter had made his choice tonight. His war was over!

CHAPTER 6

"Thank you," The woman whispered, "I thought they were going to..." she fell silent and tears began to flow. She made no effort to dry them. "I thought they would kill us." Her voice was shaky, almost a cry. It was too hard for her to get any words out so they rode in silence.

Colter could feel the woman shaking more violently as memories came to her of what had just happened. She choked, "That was my husband they killed." Her voice started to gain strength and get louder. "Why did they have to kill my husband? He never hurt nobody!" Colter gently raised a finger to the woman's lips. "We need to stay quiet; we're still in a great deal of danger." As he said that, her body jumped and became tense looking back over her left then right shoulder.

It was late afternoon and the sun was falling. There was no sign of darkness, but it would be coming soon. Colter put a gentle hand on her shoulder and she turned and looked into his deep brown eyes. He said, "I'm going to get you out of here. I'll protect you." Something about his eyes showed this man was full of confidence and it gave her comfort. She had nearly been killed and had lost every single thing important in her life... except her son. She turned back forward, wrapped her arms around the little boy and held him tight. The feeling of this young man's arms around her should have bothered her. After all, she had just lost her husband, but the look in the young man's eyes and the feel of his arms holding her gently only offered solace. There was something good inside this man and she needed that right now.

Colter knew he needed to get away from the main trail and get the two to shelter. He had found a spot a few weeks before as he searched for a sharpshooting location. The spot looked like an excellent hiding place but he had avoided it because there was only one way in and out. To a sharpshooter, that was not acceptable. However, Colter believed this was a case for hiding and the location had water, some grass for the horse and a rock overhang that would offer protection if the weather changed.

As they rode close, Colter put his hand on the woman's shoulder, "There's a spot up ahead where we can lay low and hide. I think it's too dangerous to travel right now and I sure don't want another gun battle with you riding in front of me." She nodded. "We have to be extremely careful going around this next tree because there's a huge hornet's nest hanging from a branch by the trail." She nodded again and Colter swung the horse wide around the tree. As they moved forward along the trail another two-hundred yards, Colter got down and led the horse off the trail to a fallen tree. He cautioned her, "Hang on!" as the horse carefully stepped over the tree and slowly maneuvered his way up an ancient trail, almost lost to the vegetation. Colter led up through the brush on the narrow trail to a huge boulder that had cracked in half. It was a tight fit but he urged the horse through the opening. On the other side, the ground turned sandy and grassy. He led the horse to water then helped the woman and child down from the horse. He pointed to the overhang while the woman carried the child over and waited for Colter to finish.

Colter loosened the cinch, then pulled the saddle off the horse to give him a breather. While the horse ate, Colter grabbed a handful of grass and gave the horse a rubdown. Colter knew it would be dark soon so he reached in his saddlebag and brought out a candle, some matches and a small bone needle. He also grabbed a small snare that he used to catch rabbits and tucked that in his back pocket. He unhooked his bedroll and blanket and brought it over to the woman so she could better cover herself. He handed her the needle and thread. "I hope you'll be able to fix your dress."

"Yes, thank you." She answered now realizing how exposed she had been. Her dress was more torn than she realized. She attempted to cover herself, now very embarrassed. She looked at his eyes and they were looking straight back into hers. She saw this young man held no disrespect or sideways glances. She could tell he was a kind and decent man by just watching his actions. She had found not many men were that way. Did he know she was a Mormon? Would it have made a difference? She didn't want to chance it and decided to keep that concern quiet. Then she realized she hadn't even told this man her name. She looked back at Colter and introduced herself, "My name is Courtney-Mae Montgomery...and the boy is my son Chase. I'm sorry. I hadn't told you." She looked at him then ducked her eyes.

Colter took a moment to look at this beautiful woman in front of him, and then he too ducked his eyes hoping his stare into her eyes didn't frighten her. "Well, Miss Montgomery and Chase, my name is Winn Colter. Nice to officially meet you." Colter was now feeling urgency to check their back trail. "Pardon my manners, but I need to slip back outside to take care of a couple of things to help better our chances of getting out of here. I think its best we don't have a fire since they are probably looking for us now. We can't chance the smell of smoke to give us away." Courtney thought about what he said and understood.

Colter pointed to his saddle, "I have some jerked beef in the saddlebags if you're hungry. You can eat that, and if you're thirsty, the spring over there's good."

Colter looked at the rock overhead and explained, "The only reason I found this hidden pocket was I saw that black on the rock up here." He pointed to the soot on the rocks. "I took some time to see what was up here." Miss Montgomery looked under the overhang at the black on the ceiling where travelers had built fires in the past. The blackened ceiling looked like it had been many years since the last traveler was here.

Colter cautioned Courtney, "Stay quiet, I'll be back in a while. If you see the horse lift its ears and look like he's going to whinny, walk over and rub his nose and talk quietly to him. He won't bother if it's only me but he's kind of lonesome and may try to whinny at other horses. We can't have that."

Colter cut a small branch to use to wipe away any sign of their trail. As he came through the boulder at the entrance, he worked quickly eliminating their sign where they left the main trail. He then moved quickly back to the hornets' nest and studied the surroundings.

First, Colter picked up and moved a fallen tree branch to the edge of the trail where it wouldn't allow a rider to make a wide pass away from the hornet's nest. He then laid another small tree across the trail that looked like a recent fall. This tree was big enough that a horse had to step over, but small enough that a traveler wouldn't be concerned and would keep his eyes on the hornet's nest. This is where he set the snare.

The snare was attached to the base of a stick that Colter carefully leaned to the side of the hornet's nest. If this worked, the horse that stepped into the snare would jerk the stick causing it to poke a hole in the nest setting off a flurry of angry hornets. Colter was betting his life... or rather three lives... that the riders would be frantic to get out of there. Some riders would race over their trail and some would whirl and race back the way they came. The commotion would cause hours of delay and hopefully end the search for them. Give it a day or two and hopefully they would be able to slip out and away and put many miles between them and the large Union camp.

CHAPTER 7

Major Winston Black was getting angry because he had been waiting for his brother to show up with medicine from the other camp, and he was late! His feet were killing him and, by hell, if Nate wasn't his brother, he'd court martial him or at least beat the hell out of him when he came. Winston knew Nate was an ornery, loud mouth bruiser but he was his brother and their father had asked him to watch out for Nate. How could he do that? Nate didn't follow orders. He had been accused of raping a plantation owner's daughter and had killed who knows how many Rebs, prisoners that were all trying to escape, of course. Winston had looked at some of the dead prisoner's bodies and noticed more than one had been shot in the knees or had brutal knife wounds that looked more like someone had been tortured.

Winston knew his brother Nate was out of control, usually drunk, and looking to punish these Rebs! He overheard Nate telling his "buddies" the Union should just wipe these southerners off the map and start over. "Kill 'em all!" he said… Where the hell was he?

In the distance, Winston heard a shot. That was nothing unusual in this country with some soldier shooting at something for food or maybe a shadow. He wondered if it could be his brother pissin' around. Damn him!

Winston walked over to the fire and poured himself a cup of coffee. As bad as his feet hurt, the coffee was about the only thing that offered a way for him to relax for a moment. Winston heard another sound but couldn't tell where it came from. He could hear voices in camp and a few men were moving around. He decided the sound was just somebody in camp. Winston stepped away from the camp with his coffee in hand hoping to get out to where it was quieter so he could listen. He asked a private walking by, "Did you hear something... a shot?" "No Sir." The soldier replied.

Winston stood still and listened. With such a large camp, there were so many sounds but ... He heard the report of six quick shots sounding like they came from a pistol.

"Private," Winston ordered, "Saddle my horse quick and get ten to twelve men who will ride with me. Tell them I'm going to check out some shots." The Private scrambled and moved towards some of the men resting in their tents. Winston again heard one then two more shots. What's happening out there? "Private, Hurry up!"

Winston stood on the edge of the camp. There was too much noise behind him with the rustle of horses making it difficult to listen. He thought he heard another shot followed by yet another. That's a different sounding rifle out there. Something's happening and they needed to get there. It had to be his brother!

The horses left the camp on the run heading up the main trail towards the larger Union camp five miles ahead. They had been waiting here for days, waiting for orders to root out and attack the small Rebel bands that were scattered across northern and eastern Tennessee. There had been no reports of Rebel troops gathering anywhere right now and the Union had planned to use superior numbers to devastate any Confederate bands they came across.

The union was winning the war but it had been a slow and hard fight. Major Black had taken a bullet at Gettysburg, but his brother had drug him back to the doctors and held one at gunpoint to make sure his leg wound was treated and not amputated. No one could say the Reb's were a pushover and General Lee had been a formidable opponent.

Major Black needed to get to his brother. It had to be him! What trouble had he found out there this time? The Major topped the ridge and looked down into the valley below. He pulled his telescope from his pocket and could see a cart... and blue clad bodies scattered on the ground. "No, No, No!" The Major yelled as he went galloping down the hill with disregard for his own safety. "Nate! Nate!" he called as he came up close. There was Nate lying in a pool of blood... with his leg dangling at the knee, barely attached. He was dead! No doubt about that. Winston was beside himself. Oh God! How was he going to tell his father?

Winston was supposed to look out for Nate who really didn't want his older brother giving him orders. When Winston and his father signed Nate up for the army at seventeen, he was a big boy hanging with the wrong crowd . . . a dangerous crowd. To Winston, the army looked like a safer place for Nate than the crowd back home but now here he was in Tennessee, dead at nineteen.

Major Black got off his horse and looked around. A handcart with cloth wrapped wheels... "Sneaky bastard!" He looked at the young man lying to the side of the cart. A bullet wound in his knee, a slice across the back of the other knee and a gaping slit throat. The Major could see the man had drug himself several feet leaving a blood trail to where he lay next to the cart in a larger pool of blood.

The Major looked at the cart with items thrown around like it had been searched. There lay a woman's belongings along with a dress and a child's toy. He stood and looked around again then asked "Is there a woman ... or a child?"

"They're not here, Sir." one of his soldiers offered.

Major Black pointed to a group of trees fifty yards away, " Our men must have been ambushed from over there. "

"No, Sir" a young soldier responded, "We've already checked and there's no sign. Nobody's been in those trees." As he pointed to the ground "The only sign is this one horse coming in on the run and stopping quick here. And those boot prints show one person with small feet."

"One person?" Winston got angrier. "One damned man did this? Killed them all... Where from?" The soldier, looking at the sign pointed, "Look at the bullet marks and blood by the rock where this soldier lost his toes. And see your brother's..." the soldier paused then looked up at the Major and swallowed hard. "Go ahead." "See the blood there and the bone chunks from your brother's leg. Those shots all came from that direction." The soldier was pointing at three tree stumps seventy yards away. He didn't pay attention to the rock cliffs behind them that were 350 yards away.

"You can see your brother was also shot point blank in the chest while he lay on his back. There's his knife with blood on it but his pistol scabbard is empty." This boy, a young Captain, could really read sign. Winston could almost see the whole incident, remembering the sounds of shots he heard at the camp. Winston walked back to his brother's body and studied the angry look on his face. "Still ornery even after you're dead," he said talking to his dead brother. "I can see what you were doin', trying to rape some woman after you killed and tortured her husband. And somebody done killed you for it." Winston glanced around, "Killed all of them! I'll get revenge Brother! You don't deserve it, given what you were doing, but it's what Father would expect from me."

The other men were gathering the dead and bringing their bodies to the cart. They could rig the cart to be pulled by a horse and make it fairly easy. The Major would send two men back to organize a burial detail while the rest went after the shooter. It was obvious. This was a dangerous man they were pursuing. If this man was part of a rebel unit, he could get all of his men killed. This was personal!

Major Black considered for a moment then sent all of the men back to the camp except himself and the Captain. The two of them would have the best chance to hunt this Reb down and then get back to the Union camp within a day or two. It was time to say good bye to his brother if there was any chance of catching the shooter.

The Major looked at his brother's face. Despite his bad habits, he had turned out to be the best fighter in the unit. When he was younger, he got mixed up with gangs in New York and became a street thug. But something happened in the gang, something to do with a prostitute that the gang leader favored. The prostitute ended up dead, several of the gang were beaten, two were shot and Nate ended up stabbed three times. That's when he joined the army and left town with his brother to escape the wrath of the gang.

Winston had been promoted to a Major but his brother Nate couldn't get above the rank of Corporal. The drinking, the fighting, drugs and that accusation of the plantation's daughter. If she hadn't been a Reb, Nate would have been hanged. It was always something and Winston pulled every string he had to keep Nate from being court-martialed.

Now it was time. The major stayed with his brother for a moment, talking to him. "I'll tell father you died in battle. He'll still be mad but at least he'll think you died with honor, not in some New York City brothel with a knife in your back."

Winston turned back to the tracker, "Captain! Help me find this Reb son-of-a-bitch that killed these men so I can personally kill him!" The Major looked at the pile of bodies and said to himself, "If he doesn't kill me first."

The two rode out following the tracks of the big horse. To the trained tracking eye of the Captain, he could tell the horse had taken on additional weight but it hadn't slowed the horses long pace. He must be a good mount. "We need to move quicker as we're losing ground. We'll lose 'em at dark." The Captain realized they needed to pick up the pace, but he also remembered the grizzly scene behind them. All those dead men, very capable men including one of the Union army's most notorious thugs,-- Nate Black, Major Black's little Brother from New York City.

Stories had made it around about Nate Black killing prisoners. Not many cared about that until when he raped that young girl. Even if she was a southerner, some of the soldiers were ready to string him up themselves! But because he was the brother of a respected Major and partly because many of the men were scared of Nate Black and the thugs he surrounding him, soldiers turned away with disgust, but dared not do anything about it.

If this chase was all to avenge the death of Nate Black, then he had no desire to be riding point after what he saw of the six dead men. However, one thought that kept running through the Captain's mind was that it looked like one man had done all the shooting. If it was one man, the thought kept bouncing around his head that it might be Kid Colter, the Reb from Texas who killed thirteen men when he was cornered by union troops. That's the story he had heard. Colter had thrown his knife into the nearest man, then killed the rest with his Navy Colts. The Kid supposedly had killed more than seventy men, but the Capt. supposed many of those were probably any death that couldn't be explained. The Captain heard the government had offered a reward for the man who killed Kid Colter. $500 would be nice… or how about a $1,000? He didn't know how much or if it was even true but it would be a nice way to leave the war with saddlebags full of more money than he had ever seen!

Every time the Union thought they were closing in on the Kid, he disappeared. Some of the Kid's legendary kills were hundreds of miles away from each other... on the same day. The Captain was sure this kid had killed at some time, but he couldn't be as bad the stories described him. The dead soldiers behind them did count for something. He better be careful.

The Captain moved forward with the Major seeing the general direction the tracks were heading. He noted "This Reb is heading up the trail that will run him into Johnston's Army. Two miles and he will be in the middle of five hundred Union Soldiers. There ain't no Rebs for ten miles that we're aware of."

"And I want to get him before he gets there!" the Major said, "With all our troops in the area, he can't be moving too fast."

The Captain had to remind him, "And if we move too fast, we could ride into a bullet."

"Listen Captain... I want him! Point me in the right direction and I'll lead." The Captain looked at the trail. "He's gotta be heading up that trail. That's his only option." The Major jerked his horse and took off on the run, palming his .44 Remington. He rode now like he was chasing the devil! The Captain thought if they was chasin' Winn Colter, they may just be doing it!

The Major rounded the corner and kept his horse at a trot, gun raised looking for trouble. There was a hornet's nest ahead. Major Black slowed down to a walk; he didn't want to make a nest of hornets mad. The Captain rode up close and had the same thoughts. Ten or twelve steps and they could bring the horses back up to speed. The tracks they followed had never picked up to a trot or gallop. "If I knew I had riders coming behind me, I'd be moving quicker," the Captain commented, "I'm starting to wonder if he's waiting for us to catch up. This could be an ambush!" With that, the Major ducked his head and went to ride around the hornets' nest but as he did his horse took a step over the fallen tree. The front foot stepped to the side of the snare, but the back foot went in. The Captain saw the Major's horse take a step and jerk the long stick.

The Captain rolled off his horse waiting to hear the rapport of a gun but it didn't happen. The Major's horse felt something pull its leg and heard the stick fall, then it jerked and poked the horse in the shin. The poor horse didn't know if he had a snake or animal biting him so he lunged to the side and started to buck, throwing Major Black in the air. The unexpected leap had thrown the Major off balance. He was unable to gain control or grab hold because he held his gun in his hand, and he flew head first straight into the hornet's nest. The crash broke it open and dropped thousands of hornets right on top of him and his horse. Immediately the hornets were swarming and attacking everything around them.

The Major's horse let out a scream and took off bucking and kicking running up the trail with a swarm of hornets all stinging and buzzing as the horse ran. The Captain's horse was getting stung as well and took off after the Majors horse gaining speed until they both were at full run going down the trail. Colter's snare hadn't worked as planned but the effect was more devastating.

The Major was completely engulfed in the swarm and was swatting the stinging hornets. He had dropped his gun but didn't care. Hornets were under his shirt, sticking to his neck and face and now he felt stings on his buttocks and in his groin. They were everywhere. The pain was overwhelming! He was sure it had only been a minute but his eyes were starting to swell. As he took a big breath, he inhaled a hornet through his mouth and it stung him in his throat. As he coughed the hornet up, he looked at the back of his hands. No fewer than twenty of the ornery insects were attached to his swelling limbs. It was becoming harder to breath and now he couldn't see out of his right eye. There was no getting away! Major Black saw his pistol lying on the ground and he bent down and grabbed it. His whole body hurt and he was struggling to breathe with hornets even going up his nose. He tried to say something but couldn't... He lifted the gun and placed the barrel under his chin. He thought to himself, "See you in hell, Nate" as he pulled the trigger.

The Captain had taken off running trying to get some distance away from the fallen nest, but he had been stung over twenty times on his neck and face. He whirled, swatting but could feel them crawling on his back and chest and stinging repeatedly. He couldn't get away quick enough! The Captain had just left the Major when he heard the gunshot. He didn't want to look back because he knew what the Major had done. He had problems enough of his own and he knew that. Men stung as many times as he had been sometimes died.

The damn things were under his clothes! He started to rip his shirt and pants off and throw them to the ground swatting every new sting he felt. His eyes were closing; he felt tightness in his neck. He'd even been stung under his pants. All his parts there were swelling too. There was a creek ahead. He staggered forward until he reached a small muddy bog where he laid down and rolled in the cool mud covering his entire body. The mud finally offered some relief.

The Captain lay in the mud, his dreams of reward now gone. His only thought was wondering if he was going to die here in the cold mud. He felt sick. He rolled on his side and puked then lay back down. If he had to die, he wished it wasn't this way. He wished he wasn't alone. Then fear caught him as he saw eyes looking back at him as a young man walked forward.

"Sorry, I didn't mean for it to turn out this way..."

The Captain looked up. He couldn't move. He asked, "Are you Winn Colter?"

Winn was completely surprised that the man knew his name, "Yes... I'm Colter... My old Indian trick was supposed to stir up the nest, but get you moving down the trail and lose me."

"Good trick, Kid." He just lay there in the mud, trying not to move.

Colter paused for a moment, then said, "You know, those soldiers killed that man back there and were going to rape the woman and kill her kid. They were all bad men."

The Captain laid there listening, knowing what Colter said was true. Half the Union army knew it was true. "I know that's true. That big one was Major Black's brother. He was a thug and deserved what he got. You did the world a favor!" The Captain was amazed at the quiet demeanor of the blond haired young man looking down on him. He glanced up and saw the two Colts in the holsters, but the man acted like he wasn't concerned at all.

Colter uncorked his canteen and gave the Captain a drink. "I wouldn't wish this on anybody," he said, "I hope you'll be ok." That surprised the Captain again. This soft spoken boy with a Texan drawl was not what he expected from a man with a reputation as bad as "The Kid."

The Captain asked, "How many men you killed Colter?"

"I never count, but I hope I don't have to kill another. The war's over for me. I can clearly see the South is losing and the war is going to end soon. Nothing I do will change that. I can feel it." Colter paused for a moment and looked back down the trail. "Those men back there killed this woman's husband and I'm going to make sure she gets where she was heading."

The Captain was puzzled and asked, "Why would you do that?"

"I have this feeling like it needs to be done," Colter answered. "There's something about her that tells me she won't turn back or have anything to turn back to for that matter. If she goes on by herself, she will die. I heard her husband say they were Mormons before that big soldier shot him in the knee... He killed the man right in front of his kid. Slit his throat and laughed and was going to kill the boy... I stopped it."

The Captain thought for a moment. This didn't seem like the cold-blooded killer everyone said Kid Colter was. "I hope this war ends soon so we can pull our country back together. You done fightin?"

There was no hesitation with Colter's answer, "Yea, I'm done. From what I hear the Union is planning to execute me if I'm caught. Even if I didn't do most of what they say. What I did do, I was following orders, just like every other soldier out there... except the bad ones."

The Captain' thought for a moment. This man could have killed him but Colter actually seemed concerned with his condition and even gave him water. He felt better now that the stings were covered with the mud. Even his throat felt a little better.

The Kid walked away for a minute then came back with the Captain's clothes and sat them by the edge of the mud laying his revolver on top of his clothes. "When the pain goes away, roll into the creek and wash yourself off. I'm sure the swelling will last a few days and you will feel sick but you look like you will live. I hope you understand that I don't want to fight no more. I want to see our country come back together too. Work out our differences. The bad men are like those men back down the trail, I hope you agree. There are bad men on both sides."

The Captain had thought the same thing. "I'd be court marshaled for saying this, but good luck. I hope you can get that woman out. Get goin' or you'll have riders right on top of you soon. Johnston's Army is over the hill. You might want to avoid them. They won't be as understanding as I am."

Colter looked back down the trail, "Your horses are gone. I'll bet they made it back to your camp. I suspect someone will be looking for you, but it probably won't be till after dark." Colter nodded, stood up and turned on the run heading over the bank of the creek and he was gone. The only thing the Captain could do was to wait for help. He didn't know how long but he hoped it gave Colter time to get away from this place. The Captain thought to himself... What was he thinking? That man was the enemy. Colter surly wasn't what he'd expected.

The captain thought of what Colter had said about the happenings back down the trail. Colter could have turned away and let the woman and child get raped and killed. He could have even left after the shooting, but he didn't. The Captain thought of his own wife and two kids back home in Vermont and now felt ashamed. Colter was doing something that he knew he would have walked away from and now he was ashamed of himself. The kid did a good thing! Right now it didn't matter which side he was on. The Captain respected what Colter was doing for the woman. Even though Colter was just a boy, the Captain thought, he's quite a man... Not the man of his reputation.

CHAPTER 8

Colter made his way back to the hidden pocket careful not to leave any tracks that would indicate the direction he was heading. He probably should have killed the man back in the mud with the hornet stings. Now Colter hoped he had made the right choice. The hornets being so effective actually surprised him. He would have never dreamed that a rider would have been thrown into that nest, but it worked. Now he needed to get away.

They were in a hell of a fix! Alone he had full confidence he could slip away but trying to sneak a woman and a child out this mess made it extremely dangerous for all of them. Winn thought for a minute then decided all his chips were on the table. He would hide here for a day and watch any troop movement. Hopefully the Yanks would come, do their usual search and be gone within hours. But if they found the opening to this little pocket, Colter would have to fight like he never fought before and he would still probably lose.

The next twenty-four hours would demand every skill of his body and mind to slip out of this mess. He thought he should take the woman, Courtney-Mae, back to Texas then take her northwest along the Old Spanish Trail to New Mexico or the Utah territory. After Colter thought for a minute he decided it might be comforting for Courtney Mae to visit with another woman for a few days and knew his Ma would enjoy it as well as. Then he could take her and her son north to some Mormon village or if he had to, all the way to Utah.

Colter had been gone for quite some time and now his mind and body were reminding him that he had only a few hours of sleep in the past two days. He was extremely tired and recognized his body needed rest. He made his way back to the overhang and saw the woman and child wrapped in his bedroll sleeping. Looking at them lying there Colter was sure the events of the day must have been exhausting for them too.

There was no doubt, Courtney Mae was a beautiful sight. Colter almost felt guilty looking at her knowing her husband was dead and probably still warm just a few miles away. The soldiers probably gathered up their dead but what would they have done with the Mormon's body? Colter hoped they took care of him just as they had for their own.

Colter took one last look then quietly moved to a darker part of the overhang and leaned against the back wall. It would be dark soon and he would need to go back out to survey their situation. Even though the weather had turned off cool, the safest option for them tonight was to not have a fire. Another big concern Colter had was he knew they had to keep the young boy quiet. With little or no wind today, the sound of a crying baby would be heard a long way. Come to think of it now, Colter had not heard a sound from the little boy. He was either extremely well behaved or had other issues that kept him silent.

Colter's eyes were heavy as he leaned against the rock wall, blinked and went to sleep immediately. Western men found they had to get sleep when they could. A man needed to rest but sleep light because he may need all his wits to avoid a bullet or to keep his hair. There may be trouble just around the bend and being rested with a keen sense was the western way. It sure had saved him a few times.

Courtney Mae heard Colter take a deep relaxed breath. She looked up and behind her to see him leaning against the rock wall with his eyes closed. She asked herself, "Why did they have to kill my husband? her eyes began to glass as tears again filled her eyes.

As hard as it was for her to admit, her husband was an idealist. He may have had wondrous ideas, but the reality was that he was a city kid who knew nothing of the western way... or how to deal with thugs either. Maybe in time he could have learned what to do but his time was cut short. What was she going to do?

Before any thoughts of her future, Courtney knew they were all in a bad situation and she couldn't figure how they were possibly going to get away. She and her husband had walked into the wrong place at the wrong time. But for her and her son's sake, Winn Colter happened to be in the right place at the right time. Courtney also knew with the soldier's killings, there would probably be a search looking for the man or men who had done it. She hoped this young man was as capable as she thought because she knew all of their lives depended on his abilities.

Colter awoke after being asleep for a little more than an hour to find Courtney-Mae sitting up and looking straight at him with her penetrating green eyes. He could see she had been crying because of the redness of her eyes, but she had stopped crying now. He thought she would turn away but she didn't. She kept staring into his eyes wondering where this young man had come from. He was her protecting angel ... and avenging angel all in one. Without him, she and Chase would both be dead. Courtney-Mae had a feeling in her heart that was strange. She hadn't felt it with John, even after being married to him for two years. She sure felt it now looking at Winn Colter. Something about this young man sparked a feeling in her heart that had been missing since she met her first husband.

Courtney's first husband had died on a ship crossing the Atlantic Ocean as they were immigrating to the United States from England. She was pregnant at the time and the rolling of the ship had her sick the entire voyage. Her husband's death was a surprise. On the 20th day of their voyage he got sick and he was dead three days later. She had to bury him at sea.

Her second husband, John Preston Montgomery ,was another passenger on the same ship and was also from England. He had been disowned by his family when he announced he wanted to go to America to join a Church. He had listened to a man... a missionary telling this story of a young boy named Joseph Smith who was the leader of a new church. The missionary told John that Smith had been visited and taught by an angel when he was fourteen years old. Smith later translated a book from golden plates given to him by the angel. Smith was killed, but the church continued to grow.

John Montgomery told his family he was going to America to join that church. His father kicked him out with only enough money for a ship's passage. He didn't realize he would be dropped off in the middle of the American Civil War. The Utah territory was actually still considered part of Mexico.

John befriended Courtney-Mae just after her husband died. She had been desperate not knowing what a lone woman might have to face alone in America. She wouldn't have guessed, but she and John were married a month later.

John worked as a stableman, carpenter, and cook and even in the ship yard trying to save enough money to buy a wagon so they could go west to the Utah Territory. In the meantime, their son Chase was born and growing. With the war in full swing, cash was hard to come by and the worse things got for the South, the less their Confederate dollars would buy. It had taken John two years to get enough money to buy a wagon but he still didn't have enough money for mules or oxen. They were impossible to get. If they wanted to get out before the Union army invaded Richmond, they had to go now. The only option left to them was to buy a hand cart and leave. John and Courtney-Mae left and were heading west. That's when all this dreadful mess started. They were caught by those Union thugs... when that soldier killed her husband .

She searched for answers in Colter's eyes. Before her sat this young man who was tough enough to live and survive in the west. It was crazy the way she was looking at him and feeling a flutter in her heart. Was she only feeling this way because she was now alone or was there something more? Courtney looked at Colter and said: "I didn't have the proper chance to say 'Thank you' for saving me and my son's life."

"You're welcome, Miss Montgomery, but we're not out of this yet. I hope we're not in for a hell-of-a fight." Colter realized he had just sworn in front of a lady, "Pardon my language ma'am. I'm not around many people, sorry."

"You don't have to call me Miss Montgomery," Courtney said, "You can call me Courtney Mae or just Courtney would be fine. And your language reminds me of my father. It didn't offend me. Of course, my father didn't have your Texas drawl." With that Colter smiled. "Well then, you can call me Winn but lots of folks call me Colter."

Winn could see she had sewn her dress back together and did a fine job. He didn't know if he brought it up, if he would bring back memories of its being ripped in the first place. He thought it best to leave that one alone. Winn didn't know what to say so it was time to change the subject. "I need to be getting back out there to check on things to see if we're hunted. Hopefully they've given up, but I wouldn't bet on it just yet. I set a diversion down below that didn't quite work as I expected. Now there's a dead man back there and one lying in the mud with forty to fifty hornets stings. I talked to the man and felt sorry for him. He was in bad shape with all those stings but I think he should make it."

Courtney asked, "You talked with him?" Winn could see a bit of panic in her eyes. "It wasn't the wisest thing to do, but I did. I felt sorry for the man. I only meant to spook their horses to get them away from our trail. It would have worked fine but this man sensed a trap and bailed off his mount just as the other horse stepped into my snare. The rider was thrown head first into the hornet's nest and the whole thing landed right in his lap. I bet he was stung more than a ten times."

Courtney Mae thought for a moment then cringed. "That must have been bad."

Colter continued, "I told the soldier down there what those men were about to do to you. I told him the big soldier drew his knife and was going to kill your baby." Courtney remembered the horrible thoughts of losing her baby. She was so scared that the man would really do it. "I told him I was going to get you out because those soldiers killed your husband. It may have been that I had the drop on him but he acted like he understood and wished us luck."

Colter had to make a decision now, to gather up Courtney and Chase to run or take a chance to wait it out for a day before they left.

Courtney looked at Winn with growing appreciation. There was something about this young man that she couldn't put a hand on yet. He presented a confidence in his manner that was comforting to her. Even the way he treated his horse when they first stopped, caring for the animal before he even took a drink of water for himself. Not many men would do that. Then a vivid memory returned as she thought about the way those soldiers were falling dead all around her and her son Chase. The feeling of relief it created was overwhelming and the thought drew her to him.

Courtney knew she was older than this man in front of her, but she wasn't sure how much. She was twenty four years old and guessed Colter look to be about twenty. In reality, Colter was only seventeen. He portrayed himself with confidence far beyond his age.

Before any thoughts of her future, she knew they were still in a great deal of danger. Courtney couldn't dream of how it would be possible to get away. For all her husband's precautions, they had walked into the wrong place at the wrong time. Now for Courtney and Chase's sake, they were lucky that Winn Colter happened to be in the right place at the right time.

Courtney knew the killing of seven soldiers wouldn't go unanswered. With Tennessee under Union control, it would probably instigate a coordinated search to look for the man or men who did the shooting. She hoped Winn Colter was as capable as she thought he was because she knew their lives depended on it.

Colter looked at Courtney and instructed, "Just do as I say and I'll get us out of here." Courtney looked at the confidence in the young man's eyes. There was no doubt Winn Colter thought he could get them out. Looking into his eyes, she would trust him even if she didn't have to. She could feel he was right.

Colter left with his rifle and moved to a higher position up the face of the hill. He needed to work his way to the top of the small cliff so he could see the clearing below and the entrance to the hidden pocket. He eased to the edge and carefully looked over.

The cliff was really nothing more than a pile of huge boulders, but it did offer a view of the small clearing below. Colter could see there was a group of about thirty infantry solders walking around the clearing but all were staying wide of the fallen hornet's nest. The Major still lay where he went down but the hornets still buzzed around the area as if they were assessing damage to rebuild their nest. The bottom of the nest still lay below his feet and no man was willing to step forward to remove his body at this point. The Captain was sitting up on a rock with a blanket wrapped around him and someone had rolled him a smoke. His clothes still sat by his side with the pistol lying on top. Through his telescope, Colter could see the man kept the mud covering his swollen body. That was the best thing he could be doing to relieve the pain and swelling.

The soldiers hadn't taken a lot of interest in pursuit and must have thought that he and Courtney had continued down the trail. Six soldiers were right at the entrance to the hidden pocket. One was looking at the ground and pointed at something. Colter got nervous that his hideout was found. A second man walked up and started to shake his head in a negative response then turned to walk away. The first pointed again then slowly turned looking defeated and fell in with the other five soldiers.

Colter had a feeling that things were starting to look better unless someone accidentally stumbled into their hiding place. Colter now felt their chances of escape were double what they were three hours ago. The soldiers would eventually clear out after retrieving the dead Major and would head back to their camp. Then Colter could wait until dark and move out to catch the trail that led to his planned escape route.

CHAPTER 9

Colter thought about every possibility concerning their situation. To the west there were probably over 1,000 men at the large camp he had found in the grassy valley less than a mile and a half from where they hid. The other union camp had to be close to the town of Franklin, Tennessee not more than four miles away. Colter thought of what he knew of the area and decided the camp was probably on a plantation by the Harpeth River. Two Union forces of that size, that close together, had to be preparing for something, but Colter could only guess. He thought it had to be something big and soon with all the activity between the two camps.

This entire area was now crawling with Union troops because of the killing of the Major and six troops. Pushing his horse too fast would be dangerous at this point. That had happened before his running into a wandering group of soldiers. He might run into a desperate deserter, or a squad on a specific mission. A single man was hard to detect and you didn't know what to expect from the smaller groups. A lone desperate man was the most dangerous because he might be willing to shoot you for your gun, money, your horse…or even for a woman.

Colter thought about his worst experience of his accidental encounter. He didn't wear a uniform, so at a distance, he could possibly pass as a local. He could also be mistaken for a deserter himself. A close observer might see the twin Navy Colts and know he was a dangerous man. His long range sharp-shooting success had been kept very quiet, but the story of a shootout or one of his escapes had become legendary. Regretfully, the stories had given credit to the right man.

Several months back, Colter had set up just below a hilltop near Spottsylvania, Virginia. The Confederate troops were getting ready to move on a position that was defended by the Union Army's Sixth Corps. He shot a union officer, a Major General by the name of Jed Sedwicks who was giving orders to his regiment. The men were keeping low and jumping at every sound they heard, ducking behind any cover they could find. Two of their commanding officers had been put down by a sharpshooter in the past two days at the very spot. The men could feel eyes on them. It was true; Colter had been watching them; taking appropriate targets of opportunity.

Jed Sedwicks stepped forward scrutinizing his men and chided, "What? Men dodging this way for a single bullet? What will you do when they open up fire along the whole line?" He berated them, "I am ashamed of you men! They couldn't hit an elephant at this distance." With a squeeze of a trigger, Jed Sedwicks was dead from Colter's bullet from 1,200 yards away.

Colter could see artillery being shifted to his direction. He didn't think they had any idea where he was, but they did know his general direction. Because of the shots a few days before they knew the shot came from a long ways away. If, by chance, they were searching for a sharpshooter with a telescope and saw the muzzle flash or smoke from his rifle, they could possibly know where he had taken his shot. Colter didn't want to chance an exploding cannon ball. It wasn't likely, but the Union cannons could get in a lucky shot. Colter decided it was time to make a quick exit.

As Colter rounded a blind turn on the trail, he faced ten Union soldiers who were obviously out searching for the sharpshooter that had only fired minutes before. Colter saw every soldier had guns leveled and ready with the closest man no more than fifteen feet. The farthest man out was back about forty yards. When they saw Colter's rifle they would surly execute him on the spot. Soldiers hated sharpshooters and felt that it was a cowardly way to fight unless the shooter was on their side.

Colter's pistols were clearly visible but there was no chance to get them with all guns pointing at him. "Drop those pistols slow and careful," the third soldier ordered. This was a fix! Ten guns leveled on him. He slowly pulled out the Colts and tossed them to the ground, but the soldiers hadn't seen the two .36 caliber saddle Dragoons.

As the soldier got closer he hissed, "Get off your horse you Damn Reb!" From behind, Colter heard the eight Union Howitzers going off in succession. The first shell exploded some five hundred yards back down the trail behind him. The second a bit closer and the third hit a tree about one hundred and fifty yards away. The Union soldiers all heard the artillery and knew more exploding shells were in air. Now, he and the soldiers could only guess the shells were coming straight at them all. Men were ducking and looking for any cover.

As Colter slid out of the saddle, he used the distraction to pull his two saddle Dragoons. A rifle shot from his right hit one of the soldiers in the thigh. Between the artillery shells raining down on them and this new threat from their flank, the remaining nine soldiers didn't know where to hide or who to shoot. Colter didn't hesitate and the two .36's lit up, dropping the three closest soldiers. An artillery shell then exploded fifty yards out that killed the farthest soldier.

Colter rolled to his left as bullets smashed into the ground where he had just stood. One bullet left a hole through the crown of his Stetson. Colter stood up straight and blazed away left and right with the short barreled Dragoons dropping soldier after soldier until none was left standing. As the smoke cleared, the adrenalin still filled his veins as he searched for additional targets. He saw the damage he had caused. He hadn't even heard the remaining artillery shells coming in. One had landed about 90 yards behind him, and the rest went harmlessly into the trees back to his left.

In the distance, Colter heard, "Coming in, don't shoot." He was surprised to see his former commanding officer Major Freeborn with his troops coming from the trees, amazement on their faces. "Colter... By God you're alive!" Freeborn barked as he moved forward.

"Yes Sir, I'm alive." Colter answered. He lowered the two Dragoons and stuck them in his belt. Colter's horse had jumped and was some thirty feet way with head held high and nostrils flared smelling the blood and smoke. Colter picked up his two Colts. He inspected them, spun the cylinders, and then put them back into their holsters. He pulled each Dragoon and replaced the empty cylinders.

Colter looked at his old commanding officer and breathed, "Major Freeborn... Thanks for saving my neck!"

Freeborn walked close and looked Colter over. "It's Colonel now," he said. "It was Johnston here who fired that one shot, but we were too far out to help. Johnston had the best chance but even he was out 'bout 200 yards through the trees."

"But I only nicked that one Blue Belly" Johnston said "You killed them all… 'cept that one killed by the artillery shell. Even the one I nicked in the leg."

Another voice came from the group of soldiers, "We were just trying to get in position when that shell exploded and all hell broke loose from your guns. Never saw nor even heard of anything like it!"

Johnston said, "One 'gainst ten. You should be dead Colter!… You should be dead!"

Colter looked around at the eyes of the men facing him. He could see the looks, some respect, some fear and one definitely glared with contempt.

Colter asked, "Could you men keep this under your hats and not tell anyone about this? It would hurt my mission." Of course, they all agreed, but Colter knew men witnessing such an incident couldn't help but talk. One of them would get drunk and word would spread about "Kid Colter." Reputations killed men sometimes with a bullet in the back. Colter didn't want to have a reputation and had done everything he could do to avoid getting one. Now he needed to disappear to keep his mission successful. After all, stealth was his best weapon, and that is what General Lee and President Davis expected from him.

This incident was just bad timing and he was lucky everything happened as it did. Colter looked around at the group of Texans. There were a lot of new men but still some familiar faces riding for Colonel Freeborn. It had been a little over a year since he received his orders from President Davis. Colter looked at Freeborn and asked, "Can I talk to you privately, Colonel?" They walked a short distance from the group of soldiers to talk.

"What is it, Colter?"

"Remember when I left last year? I had orders from the President.

Secret order that I can't reveal to anyone… Not even you Sir. I have orders from General Lee and I only answer to two men." The Colonel studied the young man's face before him. He knew what Winn Colter could do… what he was capable of. The fierceness he had seen as they rode forward moments ago was replaced with a kind and friendly personality, two very different men in one body.

Freeborn thought about what Colter had just said and remembered the dispatch… It was good enough for him. He said, "Good to see you, Colter." The Colonel then saluted him, " Good luck on your mission." Colter saluted back then nodded. "Colonel." Colter walked to his horse, picked up the reins, stepped into his saddle and rode away.

Kennedy was watching Colter ride away when a Private walked up to him and asked "Who's that?" "That's the Colter Kid," Kennedy said, "or rather Kid Colter. He was in this unit for a couple of weeks last year, but he left. I thought he must have been killed or deserted. The Kid was only fifteen and shouldn't be here!"

"We'll . . ." the Private Said "Kid Colter just put a bullet in the head or heart of nine men. May God have mercy on the soul of any man that crosses that boy. Thank God he's on our side!"

Kennedy's mind was racing. He was thankful he didn't have to face Colter like he almost did a year ago when he called him a liar. Now he was jealous of Colter's abilities. Colter was what Kennedy wanted to be. He wanted the reputation of a bad man. He wanted respect from all the knob head, hard back soldiers that looked down on him. He wanted them to say "Jon Kennedy's got sand… he is the rankest gunman in all of Texas!" Kennedy reminded himself that he never wanted to meet Kid Colter on the wrong end of a gun.

Kennedy looked at the private and said, "He's good, but without us, he'd be captured or dead now. Don't forget that!" He thought for a moment then spoke up again, "Those Yanks must have been new recruits. Anybody can shoot fast… I can shoot that fast!" The Private chuckled then quickly walked away. Kennedy's face turned red and flushed with anger. He didn't get any respect, even from new Privates. Kennedy thought about Colter, "A bullet in the back if I had to. No chances!" Even through his anger he had to respect the "Kid." He may have even been a little scared at the thought. Someday, he may have to put this kid in his place. Like it or not, Winn Colter was one of the fastest and best shots he had ever seen.

There was one thing that bothered Kennedy more than anything else, the Kid never mentioned how many men he'd killed. He never boasted how fast he was, almost like he didn't want credit for the kill. Kennedy had killed eighteen men during the war and had shot the horse out from under a Yankee General. He would have killed him too, but a big soldier stepped in front of the General to protect him and took Kennedy's last three rounds. He watched the General get up, and was hurried to safety by the soldiers around him.

For Kennedy's own protection, he had always surrounded himself with new recruits. He let them be the first target and to take the bullets. This had kept his kill count low, but he had taken credit for a few of the kills other soldiers had made before getting themselves killed. Now the Kid had made him look like a fool. Someday Colter would pay... Some day!

****

The story mushroomed just like Colter thought. Soldiers were drinking and started to tell the story of how Colter faced ten men. The rumors spread of how Colter killed nine out of ten soldiers that had the drop on him. Some thought it must have been an exaggeration, but the story of a kid gunning down nine men with a pair of .36 caliber Dragoons was amazing! Kid Colter they called him!

Kid Colter was known not just by the Confederate soldiers. The stories spread through the saloons from the locals to the Union army as towns were occupied and prisoners were captured. "Kid Colter was becoming known for his pistols. Luckily the story of his rifle remained a secret but many questions were asked about where Colter was assigned and to what unit? It was known he had been with the Texas Volunteers, but now was he just a rogue deserter who would kill anyone in his path? No one knew. Now he was getting credit for about any unexplained death, both Union and Confederate. The only thing that they all agreed on was no one wanted to be on the wrong end of Kid Colter's guns.

Reputations killed people and that's why Colter had tried so hard to avoid taking credit for those he killed. It was a haunting thought that this was exactly what President Davis had warned him about when he received his orders. It had been good advice that Colter lived by. It was advice his Pa would have given. His Pa knew more than he thought and explained why Weston Colter had always taught Winn to avoid trouble when he could.

It all made sense now. He realized that his Pa really knew what he was talking about when he tried to discourage him from sneaking away to join the army. It was why his Pa had been so insistent on teaching the Indian ways. How to see and not be seen. He thought his Pa was scared and just wanted to save his hair. Winn could clearly see now Pa was not afraid, only wise. Some of the very friends Colter had wanted to run off to join the army with were now dead. His Pa had warned him they didn't have the wilderness skills to survive and he was right. Pa's teachings had saved his life from some renegade comancheros back in Texas, but now here he was again hiding from people who wanted him dead.

Winn thought about Courtney. She was a Mormon! To be truthful, he didn't really know what a Mormon was but he knew from talk, it was legal to kill a Mormon in Missouri. Governor Boggs had issued an extermination order on Mormons in the Missouri territory so they must be devils! Courtney didn't seem evil. In fact, she seemed like a kind, strong woman. She seemed to be the kind of woman that fit right in Texas.

Colter had always been a good judge of character and he could tell this was a good woman, the kind he hoped to someday marry and take home to meet Ma and Pa so he could settle back into his Texas life. It took him getting into the middle of a mess to see that. When he got back home, he was going to thank Pa. The training had saved his life many times. Someday, Colter would teach his son what his Pa had taught him. To do that, he had to get back home. He was going to get back home!

Now Colter needed luck to get them all out of this alive. Alone, he had no doubt he could slip away; but with two passengers, one of those a being a small child, he may have to leave them … Now he didn't know if it could be done. On the other hand, Colter didn't think he could just leave the woman and child. He remembered Pa saying that at times he would get a feeling inside, when it was the right thing to do. That feeling was telling him to help the woman. Was there something else? He knew he wanted to protect the woman even if it meant doing so with his life. If that day was now, may God have mercy on those men who tried to stop him.

CHAPTER 10

In the light of the moon, Colter led his horse down through the broken boulders into the clearing below. He checked the saddle and lifted Chase and Courtney back on his horse. He slowly and quietly led the horse down the heavily traveled path for nearly two miles. He finally reached the opening to an old Indian trail he had marked with a pair of rocks. Most of the troops stuck to the main trails so the ridge top trail was hardly used except by game.

It was a long night as Colter carefully walked on. At times the vegetation became so thick that Courtney and Chase had to walk as the horse worked its way through dense growth and fallen trees. Given the circumstances, they made good time. Even in the dark, the old trail bred horse made his way like he knew where he was going. The three had only one encounter with soldiers, but Colter sensed a campfire and they stayed wide of the camp not knowing if they were Union or Confederate.

Colter kept the horse pushing for most of the night and continued through the next day only stopping to give his horse a chance to chomp some grass and drink from a spring. Colter was satisfied they had put close to twenty miles between them and where the shooting had taken place. With so many troops in the area, he felt lucky they hadn't run across any more men. The ancient trail had served its purpose and Colter was thankful he had stumbled across it months before. He had ridden it when he had to check in with a quartermaster and send in his report to General Lee.

The young boy had started to fidget. For the first time, Colter heard him cry but Courtney quieted him quickly. Colter realized the only thing any of them had eaten in the past day was a handful of jerked beef. A mile or so farther down the trail was an abandoned farmhouse and partially burned smokehouse back in the trees well hidden.

As they cautiously approached the old farmhouse, Colter left Courtney at the edge of the small clearing while he checked to make sure it was safe to move forward. After a quick inspection, he was satisfied the place was not occupied so he went back and led the horse beyond the old house and picketed it out back. Colter had stopped here many times and had left a slab of bacon hanging in the smokehouse the last trip through. There were also some carrots and potatoes still growing wild close to the house. This would be a place to rest and eat!

Chances of escape were looking better and Colter knew just what had to be done. It was going to work! Courtney and Chase sat by the edge of the trees as they watched Colter unsaddle the roan. He rubbed down his back with a hand full of grass and let the animal loose in a small hidden corral.

Colter disappeared for a few minutes then returned with a handful of carrots, potatoes and onions washed and ready to fry. He then walked to the smokehouse and emerged with the bacon and a great big frying pan he had dug out of the house on a previous stop. Colter built a small fire, fried some bacon, potatoes and onions and made coffee. There were still a lot of Union and Confederate troops wandering the area, but if he was careful, Colter would get the three of them to safety. The food was satisfying and Colter was amazed to watch Chase and Courtney eat like they hadn't eaten in a week which they probably hadn't. He thought for a moment about their situation then said "I'd like to take you to North Texas with me where my Ma and Pa live. Then if you want, we can take the Santa Fe Trail up to a place in New Mexico or to the Utah Territory where you were headed."

"You would take me there?" Courtney asked. Something inside her burst and the tears began to flow.

Colter thought to himself that offering to take her into New Mexico or Utah would make her happy, but all it did was make her cry. What is it with women? Colter was completely confused! Did she or didn't she want him to take her to Utah? Now he wasn't sure. When it comes to women, he knew as much about their emotions as a hog knows about Sunday school. Carefully Colter asked, "Did I say something wrong to upset you?

Courtney came to him and gave him a great big hug and kissed him on the cheek. "Now what was that for?" He just couldn't figure out women. It seems that's just what his Pa used to say about his Ma, "Can't never figure them out." The ride to Texas was going to be a long one. Hopefully he would be able to untangle a few questions by the time they got there.

CHAPTER 11

Before they started, Colter explained the importance of the next few days to Courtney. Their escape depended on their ability to remain unseen and unheard by the many thousands of Union troops in Tennessee. There were a lot of soldiers scattered along the back trails between Germantown and Memphis and along the Mississippi River. Traveling with a young child would make this, more difficult, but with luck and a lot of prayers, they hoped to be able to do it.

The Union controlled many of the cities including Memphis and Germantown and had built forts to protect the rail lines. Tennessee was mostly under Union control, but that didn't mean there wasn't still support for the south. Nearly a third of all able-bodied men in Southwestern Tennessee were the first to answer the call to fight. Now four years later, they still had a lot of men out fighting. Many were dead too.

Colter thought more about getting a second horse. If it ever came to a fight with the three of them on one horse, there was little doubt he would lose. If he was lucky, he may be able to buy a horse for $15.00, but a saddle was another thing. A saddle could cost him closer to $50 dollars in gold. He now had over two hundred dollars in his saddle bags so he had the money If he could get a horse.

The second horse would make their escape much easier once they got away from the mass of troops near Memphis. Colter decided their best option for escape was to go south into Mississippi then get across the river into Arkansas where he hoped they could move faster.

The worst thing about traveling by horse during wartime was it always drew plenty of attention. Cavalry units drew less attention than a single rider or even a pair of horses. A lone man was always at risk of getting his horse commandeered by the army or just flat out stolen. He had to be extra careful that he didn't end up dead over a good horse.

There were nearly 5,000 Union soldiers in Memphis. Colter estimated they outnumbered the Confederates as much as 3 to 1 in the surrounding area. If the Yankees ever saw the guns he was packing, Colter knew he would be sent to prison or more likely shot on the spot. On the other hand, Colter knew there were some Confederates just as bad. A fine horse could be pretty tempting to any soldier. Still, the best thing he could do was to find a second horse for Courtney and Chase to ride to Texas.

After a day of rest, Colter restocked his saddlebag with grub and moved out covering another 30 miles without any incident. The idea of a second horse was becoming more appealing. At times Colter rode behind Courtney and Chase, but he also walked a good deal to give the horse a break. Given the number of soldiers in the area, Colter realized they couldn't go much faster until they got to Indian Territory. There, they would have to move fast.

Colter had ridden through this area two months ago. About three miles ahead, he had sat down with a man and his wife in a small farmhouse for supper. The farmer and his two sons had joined the army for a three month enlistment thinking they could pocket some quick cash to put into their small farm. Both of the farmer's sons were killed by an exploding cannon ball and the farmer lost his left arm in a battle near Nashville. That was the end of their family's dreams.

Colter could see the farmer was functioning quite well for missing an arm, but the Yankees had taken his mule so he couldn't plow his farm. Besides the mule, they had taken two hogs, all their chickens, half their flour and all their salt. The Yanks missed the farmer's milk cow that was stashed up in the trees and the farmer had been wise enough to hide his seed for the coming season.

Colter had just shot a wild hog so he gave most of it to the farmer. He then hooked up his horse to the man's plow and turned the soil so he could at least try to plant a crop to survive. He also gave them $20 to buy some supplies. With nothing to live on, this couple probably would starve to death during the winter.

Though his gift to the couple had been minor in his eyes, the farmer and his wife looked at it differently. They would never forget what Winn Colter had done for them. They told Winn that he was always welcome in their home. That is what he hoped for now, a place they could get a good night's rest, at least, for the woman and child.

The skies darkened and Colter could smell rain. As they rode down through the creek bottom, Colter noticed boot prints and fresh horse tracks in the mud. He could see it had rained there in the last two hours so he knew the tracks were fresh and he went on guard. Colter had chosen this path because it was the least likely for someone to take. From the tracks, it looked like it had to be two people. The horse didn't follow the tracks of the boots like you'd expect to see with a man leading a horse.

Colter heard a gunshot come from not far away. It could have come from the farmhouse where he was headed that was now less than a mile away. He slipped off the back of the horse and pulled the rifle from its boot and led the horse off the trail. "Wait here. There may be trouble," he warned. Before Courtney could question him, he was off on the run. Another four hundred yards out, Colter came to the edge of the farmhouse clearing.

The creek wove its way across the meadow coming from the canyon behind the farmhouse. Colter was breathing hard, but he could see a horse tied to the farmer's hitching rail. He was a long ways out, but a tree stood with a deep V in its trunk just off the trail. Colter laid his rifle into position to see what was happening.

Through the telescope, Colter could see what looked like a Confederate soldier in a beaten and battered uniform. He was standing over the farmer who was laying on his back against the doorframe of the farmhouse with his one remaining hand held up high.

The soldier looked like he was holding a Remington Army revolver which was unusual for a Confederate soldier. Colter could see the farmer was pleading for his life. His wife was standing half way behind the door obviously crying and also pleading for her husband's life.

Colter couldn't see the second soldier, only the one standing over the farmer. This was a long shot, longer than he was comfortable with especially after running for some distance. This had to be close to 1,200 yards but there wasn't time to get closer. He quickly made adjustments to the telescopic sight. Normally he would throw a little dirt in the air to determine wind, but it was all mud right now. He looked at the grass, but it was wet and didn't move with the wind. He only saw slight movement from the trees and grass. Colter had to guess and hope his shot would hold true.

The man on the porch was waving his gun back and forth taunting the old farmer and his wife. Even though this man was a Reb, he was a bad man and looked like he was going to kill the farmer… for what, his milk cow or money? Colter slipped a bullet in his gun and took a long breath and then eased it out allowing his scope to stop shaking… If his aim was true… It seemed to take forever for the bullet to get there, but when it reached the target, it caught the man a little high and right. A miss to the heart but Colter knew this was a shot to the lungs. The Soldier flew back against the wall of the farmhouse and his gun discharged but missed the farmer. His revolver dropped to the ground, but the man staggered back to his horse.

It surprised Colter that the man got to his horse and mounted up. The horse took off on the run with the man barely able to hold on.

A running horse with a slumped over man at 1,000 yards was a tough target and Colter didn't think it could be made so he held the shot. Colter looked around and still couldn't see the second man. The farmer had gotten up with help from his wife and now held the Remington. After standing on the porch for a few seconds, he ducked inside the house with his wife.

Colter ran back to his horse with Courtney and Chase and mounted behind them. He moved the horse at a rapid pace until he came to the farmhouse "Hello in the house!"

"Who's out there?"

"It's Winn Colter and some friends. Can we come in?"

Before he had finished speaking, the door flung open and the farmer stood with a look of relief. "Thank God for you Colter!"

Colter asked, "Are you ok, Sir?"

"Just a little deef from that gun blasting by my head."

Colter looked around the yard and saw why he hadn't seen the second man; there he lay dead by the barn with a pitchfork in his back.

"That one" the farmer indicated, "had me down pistol-whipping me when my wife stabbed him with that fork. They's deserters...The worst kind! The farmer spat on the ground, "stealing from fellow Southerners! When I told him we had nothin', he knocked me down and started to kick and beat me. Didn't seem to matter I lost my arm fighting for the South or that the Yanks already stole everything we had. I think those two would have killed us!"

Colter's attention turned back to the horse that had run away. "Mr. and Mrs. Duncan", he said, "This is Ms. Montgomery and her son Chase." Colter wanted to act formal for these people. "Ms. Montgomery, these here folks are friends of mine."

"Mrs. Duncan, I need to go after that rider. Can Mrs. Montgomery stay with you while I go after that man?"

Mrs. Duncan reached up and took Chase, "Come down dear," she said to Courtney, "Let your man do his thing." Colter looked at Courtney a little sheepishly. He didn't correct Mrs. Duncan on her statement; he just ducked his head and rode away on the run.

Courtney caught the statement as well. She really hadn't thought of Colter as "her man" until that statement. Yes he was young but something inside her burned with desire, and it felt right to her. Winn Colter was proving to be as much... no, more of a man than either of her two husbands. She asked herself, what would he think of her?

Colter turned his horse and took off fast making up ground on the horse that ran away. As usual, he was cautious looking for ambush locations. This man on the horse should be dead but somehow he kept going, Colter couldn't figure other than it might be adrenalin. There was a lot of blood on the ground, but the light rain was washing it away fast. He was already two miles out from the farmhouse as he rounded a turn where he found the soldier lying face down in the mud.

Colter cautiously approached the man and saw no movement or breathing. He was obviously dead. His horse was another fifty yards up the trail in a dry spot under a tree. Colter could see the animal was still tense from the run and the smell of blood. He needed that horse!

He dismounted and slowly moved forward with his own horse, both sniffing the air for the scent of the other animal. As he reached the horse, Colter slowly touched the bay on the rump then slowly moved to the neck and picked up the reins. The saddle was covered with blood as was the horse's neck. Colter walked the two animals over to where the man lay. The sky was dark because of the overcast and rain fell harder now.

Looking at the soldier's clothes, Colter could see this man wore an infantry uniform. From the looks of the battered cloth, he must have been in some tough battles. That Remington he used earlier must have been taken from some dead Union officer, maybe the prior owner of this horse.

No matter how he ended his life, Colter wanted to treat the man's body with respect. He was a former Confederate soldier.

Colter tied the two animals to a tree and after a quick search of the man's belongings, found a small blue porcelain pan in his saddlebags. With that, he dug a hole in the mud that was a little more than a foot deep, much harder than Colter expected. Colter dragged the man's body into the depression and pulled mud up over him. He then gathered some rocks and placed them on the grave. Working in the rain was not easy, but he got it done.

Colter fashioned a small cross with two sticks and a torn piece of cloth. He stood over the grave and thought for a moment. "Lord, I don't know what drives a man to do what he's done. Lookin' at this man's uniform. Maybe he's seen or done too much. Please forgive him Lord of his transgressions and forgive me for putting him in the grave. Amen"

Colter walked to the horses and noticed the rain had washed away most of the blood except some still on the saddle pad. It was raining quite hard now and the saddle was soon clean. Colter had been gone for several hours. It was time to get back.

As Colter came to the farmhouse, he could see a fresh grave behind the house with a spade still sticking up from the ground. Colter rode to the barn and led the horses in. He was soaking wet but he took off each saddle, picked up some straw, and gave both horses a good rubdown. Colter looked at the new animal. The horse looked as if he'd been ridden hard for a thousand miles and neglected. He wasn't a great horse but he'd be ok. Looking at the horse's condition, Winn considered riding back out there, digging up the man and shooting him again for the way he neglected his animal. Then again, he may have just found or stolen the horse himself. Burying the man had tired him. Colter was sure that everything else including his bedroll, would be soaking wet too so he left it. "Take Care of that later," he thought to himself. He picked up all of his guns and made his way out of the barn. He walked to the house knocking then asking permission to enter.

"Come in my friend!" Mr. Duncan said. The smell of food cooking almost brought him to his knees. " My wife's cooking up some beans and pork. Fresh biscuits will come out of the oven shortly and there's a fresh cup of milk there for you." Colter hadn't realized how hungry he was. He wanted to run to the pot and eat but that wouldn't be proper manners. Then he saw little Chase wrapped in a blanket asleep by the fire, some of his supper still stuck to his face.

"I saw the grave out back. If y'all had waited, I would have buried that man for ya."

Duncan said "I didn't bury that man, your lady did. I only dug a few spades full before she pushed me out of the way."

Colter corrected Duncan this time, "She's not my lady, Mr. Duncan, she's…" Just then Colter saw Courtney wrapped in a blanket, her bare shoulder exposed. Her hair was still wet and curly but those eyes looking at him stopped him in his tracks. Colter could see her wet clothes and under things were hanging by the fire.

Duncan saw Colter's face, "There's a boy in love" he thought. "If he's not, he should be."

Mrs. Duncan looked up at Colter and saw the water dripping off him making a puddle on the floor. "You need to take those things off before you catch a cold."

Colter was stupefied still looking at Courtney and barely heard Mrs. Duncan.

"Take off… No, I can't, nothin's dry."

"That's what I said, you need to get out of those wet clothes and dry off." With that, Mrs. Duncan walked into the next room and brought a quilt. "Take 'em off here!" pointing to the corner, "I'll not have you muddying up my bedroom floor."

"No... I, I,"

Courtney and Mr. Duncan laughed. "Might as well do it Son," Duncan grinned. "I know better than to cross Mrs. Duncan." With that, Mr. Duncan moved quickly and ducked away from his wife's reach before she hit him.

Courtney offered, "Mr. Duncan and I can hold up the quilt. Nobody will see anything."

With some hesitation he thought arguing with two women would be pointless. He had learned that from his mother.

Mr. Duncan and Courtney opened the quilt and lifted it high. Colter hesitantly started to remove his soaked clothes. He kept a close eye on Courtney making sure she wasn't peeking, but what she forgot was she herself was naked in a quilt. Courtney held the quilt with her left hand, her right holding onto the top of her own, but her leg was coming out of the quilt, exposing herself to just above the knee.

Colter had never seen legs as nice as what he was looking at now. He was down to his wet skivvies and started to slip them off when Courtney turned quickly to tease. She saw more than she intended, seeing his muscular chest and long legs. She really wasn't trying to do it, but it happened. She saw him as he jumped for the cover of the dry quilt. He was embarrassed but it felt so good to be dry. He didn't care.

Courtney and Mr. Duncan let go of the quilt and Courtney covered her leg. Now both were a bit embarrassed.

Mrs. Duncan called out, "Dinner's ready," and the smell of the food diverted everyone's attention. Courtney felt so good, comfy, warm and dry in this little cabin. Dinner was wonderful! Mr. Duncan had used the money Colter left on his last visit and bought beans, flour and salt. Mr. Duncan had also smoked the wild hog Colter had given them. There was no doubt that Mr. Duncan was an incredible meat smoker and Mrs. Duncan a great cook.

Colter tried to avoid it, but every time he looked up, Courtney was looking at him. She quickly diverted her eyes but she was looking at him nonetheless and he could feel it. Colter didn't know why, but it made him feel good. She seemed happy visiting with these folks and that felt good too.

Mr. and Mrs. Duncan enjoyed the company. Colter's last visit was good but this visit with Courtney and Chase felt like their sons had come home. Everything felt like it was starting to fit together. Mrs. Duncan held Mr. Duncan's hand and she smiled. She could see this young couple was meant to be together.

Mr. Duncan felt a tightening in his chest. He looked at the two young visitors and expressed his gratitude. "My sons were taken away from us during this war, and now God brought you here to us ... I would be pleased to consider you as my son if it don't offend you. I can't think of anything more right than you two before me here tonight."

Courtney looked at Colter again and she knew she definitely wanted this man. Every sense in her body needed him. She just hoped that he would choose to be with her when the time came. She barely knew him, but she knew she had fallen for him.

CHAPTER 12

When Courtney woke up at dawn, Mrs. Duncan was already up and cooking some pork for her guest. "Ah, did you sleep well, my dear?"

Courtney picked up her dry clothes and was slipping them on. "It is so nice to sleep on a bed." She said, "It's been some time. I slept really well."

"Your son woke in the night," Mrs. Duncan said, "but I took care of him. It's been a long time since we had any little ones in the home."

"Sorry, I would have…"

"No, no, no," Mrs. Duncan exclaimed, "It was my pleasure! It was nice to have someone sleep in that second bed. Nobody has since my sons…" Mrs. Duncan voice trailed off as she remembered they were gone.

"I'm sorry Mrs. Duncan." Courtney replied with concern in her voice.

"Those boys all thought it was going to be just a big adventure." Mrs. Duncan said, "Be gone three months and make some extra money…" Mrs. Duncan fell silent for a moment. Courtney's mind was somewhere else. Mrs. Duncan could sense what Courtney was thinking. "You love that boy, don't you?"

That caught Courtney off guard and she started to blush. She looked at Mrs. Duncan who had turned to look at her as Courtney tried to turn away. "I have no right to, but I think I do."

Mrs. Duncan smiled, "I could see it from the first time I saw you look at him. The way you watched him ride away after that soldier. And he looks at you too." Courtney was surprised at Mrs. Duncan's insight. She was a very perceptive woman. Mrs. Duncan added "He may be young, but Colter looks like a good one. If'n you want him, you better grab him, else someone else will."

Courtney smiled but didn't say anything; she knew she wanted Winn Colter. Even Mrs. Duncan could see it.

Mrs. Duncan was a feisty lady at forty five years old. Her red hair was now streaked with grey, but it didn't make her look old. Courtney liked her. She was amazed Mrs. Duncan could read both her and Colter. Mrs. Duncan had been standing there with a smile, then turned to Courtney with the grin still on her face and said, "I saw the way you two was looking at each other over supper... I was scared you two might jump right up there on the table."

"Mrs. Duncan!"

She just laughed and turned back to work on breakfast.

Outside Mr. Duncan went out to the barn and peeked in. Colter was busily working on the saddles trying to make sure the contents of the saddlebags would dry. He had left after supper to go to the barn to clean and dry his guns. Mr. Duncan walked in to see an assortment of guns that astonished him. There were three small caliber Dragoons, two Navy Colts and a Remington Army 44. There were also four spare cylinders. Two of the cylinders he could see for the Colts and the other two he wasn't sure, but Duncan's focus fell on an incredibly engraved rifle with a tube attached on top that ran almost the entire length of the gun. "I ain't ever seen anything like that."

Colter turned to look at Mr. Duncan. There was a kindness in this old man's manner and Colter liked him. "She shoots like you wouldn't believe," Colter commented as he finished cleaning and started putting everything away. Before him sat fourteen $20 dollar gold pieces. He turned to Mr. Duncan and handed him seven. "I found these hidden in a hollowed out compartment in the soldier's saddle tree. It'll give you something to live on."

Mr. Duncan was astonished..."I can't take these from you."

78

"You said those Yanks stole your Mule and things. Think of this gold as payback." Colter replied, "I think the soldier may have had it and didn't even know it was there. I think he probably killed the rider and took the horse looking to go home."

Duncan thought about what Colter had said and pulled the coins back in his hand. He looked at Colter and with broken up voice confided, "You know, I meant that last night, claimin' you as my son. I'd be proud!"

Colter could see this meant a lot to Mr. Duncan. "I'd be honored sir."

Mr. Duncan slipped the coins in his pocket then moved forward to shake Colter's hand. As he did, Mr. Duncan pulled him closer and gave him a hug like a man would do with a son returning home. Mr. Duncan thought about his sons and wept. Colter stood there not really knowing what to do or say but partially understanding what must be going through his head. Thinking about his sons.

Mr. Duncan backed up and apologized. Colter just waived it off.

Mr. Duncan responded, "You take your woman and boy and get away from this war. It's destroyed my family!"

Colter looked at Mr. Duncan, "Mrs. Montgomery's not my…"

Mr. Duncan interrupted with a wave of his hand, "If she ain't, she sure has somethin' for you. She said your name three or four times last night in her sleep. That woman's smitten with you! And I saw the way you looked at her too."

Colter was now embarrassed and his face started to redden. He ducked his head and started shoving belongings back in his saddle bag. To change the subject he said, "That horse looks like he sure traveled a lot of miles."

Mr. Duncan turned back to Colter, "You'd have to travel lots of miles to try to find another woman like that! When we's digging the grave, she told me how you saved her and her son from those Yanks. Don't matter she had a husband last week Colter. It may be destiny. You might do better, but you surely could do worse."

Courtney was a fine woman, but he thought he needed to get Courtney to Texas, to meet his Ma and Pa. Then he could decide what to do. He had the approval of Mr. Duncan, but he wondered what his Pa would think?

"We'll see, Mr. Duncan... We'll see."

After two nights, the horses were rested and now saddled and ready to go. Mr. Duncan directed Colter to his cousin who owned a barge that could get them across the Mississippi. From there they would travel through Arkansas and then into Indian Territory. And then, if all went well, they could cross the Red River into Texas.

Courtney sat down with Mrs. Duncan and held her hands. "Thank you Mrs. Duncan for letting us stay in your home. It means more than you will ever imagine. We'll never forget. Can I ask what your first name is... so I know?

Mrs. Duncan smiled. "No one's called me by my fist name for more than five years... it Laura, but everyone around these parts just knows me as Mrs. Duncan.

"We'll then, Mrs. Duncan, thank you from the bottom of my heart!" Mrs. Duncan got up and gave Courtney a big hug. She was choked up. "Remember what I said about your man." Courtney quickly glanced around to make sure Winn didn't hear. She smiled at Mrs. Duncan and gave her one more hug.

As they left the Duncans standing on their front porch, Courtney and Chase were both crying. These fine people had accepted them in their home and become close friends... Family. Colter tipped his hat and wasn't sure, but he thought he could see both Mr. and Mrs. Duncan with tears flowing down their faces. They were watching another son riding away that they might never see again. This time, their son had a beautiful woman riding by his side. This time their tears were full of hope!

As he rode away, listening to Courtney and Chase crying, Colter also felt tightness in his chest. Mr. and Mrs. Duncan were fine people who had gone through a lot. Colter looked back one last time. They were still standing there on the porch. He lifted a hand and they waived back. Colter knew he would never see the Duncans again. Riding away from home two years ago didn't bother him, but it did now. He thought to himself, "Audios amigos." Goodbyes are hard..

CHAPTER 13

They made good time traveling across Arkansas as it was under Confederate control, but Colter still tried to avoid troops whenever possible. He avoided towns except to buy a few supplies. They had followed the advice of Mr. Duncan and crossed the Mississippi on a steam barge several miles below Memphis and had no problem except it cost him a double eagle. Mr. Duncan was a spittin' image of his cousin except the cousin still had both hands. Apparently, he had been smuggling Confederates back and forth across the Mississippi and had made a killing! He could make more in a day than a soldier could in a month.

Chase was handling the ride well. Colter was still concerned because he knew there were a lot of miles to travel and they still had to ride through Indian Territory.

It would have been faster to travel down the main trails, but his Pa had always taught him to ride the secondary trails as they were safer with fewer travelers. These back roads and trails shouldn't add more than a week to their travels and it would be a lot safer. Colter was observant and was constantly looking for any sign on the trail for likely ambush locations. So far, nothing had happened.

It was time to give the horses a break so Colter and Courtney were off their horses walking. Chase sat high in the saddle proud that he was riding on his own. Courtney enjoyed walking by Colter. His close presence was always comforting. By chance their hands bumped and it scared both of them, but nothing was said. Both could feel the pressure building in their chest but both were too scared to act. Colter thought maybe another chance bump. He timed the swing of his hand and bumped her again. Those bumps had sent shivers down her spine. Her entire body tingled. She saw a stick ahead on the trail and acted as if she didn't see it. As she stumbled, Colter reached down and caught her as she fell. Holding his hand she didn't let go. She couldn't take the torment any longer. A woman's feelings needed to be fulfilled.

Courtney stopped Colter then stepped in front of him and leaned forward giving Colter a tender kiss. So much for him being aware of his surroundings... Colter had never been kissed like that before and he liked it! It was better than he imagined. Colter leaned forward and kissed her again. Then from behind them they both heard a little giggle and a laugh. Colter didn't know what Chase knew, but he knew enough that seeing a kiss was a funny thing.

Courtney and Colter looked into each other's eyes and they both laughed too. What else could they do? They continued to walk hand in hand down the trail. A bunch of Comanche's could have ridden right up on them and Colter wouldn't have seen them coming. You can't do that in Comanche country and he knew that. Letting your guard down for a moment out west or in Indian Territory could be fatal. Colter knew he had to get his mind back to matters at hand which meant getting them through safely.

As Winn and Courtney mounted up and rode on, Colter optimistically explained, "We may cross into Texas today. Within a week, I could be introducing you to my Ma and Pa."

Courtney was excited for him but scared that his Ma and Pa would look at her as an "old maid." She still hadn't told Colter how old she was and she hadn't asked how old he was. She was in love just like Mrs. Duncan had said and was scared she might lose her new love. Courtney knew she was a possessive woman and wanted one man. She was scared of coming home. Maybe he had a girl before he left to go fight in the war. She was terrified! Now that she knew she loved him, she couldn't share him with any other woman! But what if she did lose Colter? What if his parents shunned her? Would she have to marry some old man with several wives? She couldn't do that. No, she knew she would have to do whatever it took to have this man... Winn Colter. She was in love!

Colter thought of what just happened. That kiss was the best thing he had ever experienced and he wanted to kiss Courtney again. He would be proud to introduce her and Chase to his Ma and Pa. Hopefully they would see what Mr. and Mrs. Duncan had seen. He prayed they understood. He wanted this. His Ma knew he always did what he wanted. It was his Pa that he needed to convince. He glanced back at Courtney and saw her eyes looking at him. Yes, Courtney is who he wanted. Though he had only known her for a very short time, he thought she was fine as... no, better than any woman he had known in Texas. If this was love, he wanted more.

The question would be if he and Courtney could stay in Texas. If the Army considered him a deserter, they would want to hang him. Then again, if the Yankees ever found out he was a sharpshooter, they would come looking for him too. The best thing would be to see his Ma and Pa then take Courtney to the Utah territory like he had planned. Get away from Texas and all the bad men that would be coming home from the war. With his reputation and those stories going around about his killings, it was only a matter of time before some Texan decided he wanted to test his speed, or sneak up from behind and shoot him in the back. Hopefully those Mormons would be accepting. If they found out he wasn't threatening and kept his gun skills quiet, maybe he and Courtney could have some sort of normal life. Colter was willing to try anything to get away from his reputation, but first things first. He had promised his Ma and Pa. He was coming   home.

-Part II-

CHAPTER 14

It had been a year since Weston received any word about his son. All he knew was that Winn had been sent to Virginia to meet with President Davis and General Lee, and then he was gone. Weston didn't know if Winn was dead, alive or maybe in a Union prison. Weston heard the Story of Kid Colter and a shootout, but he thought it was exaggerated as most stories went. Winn... if it was Winn, was an excellent shot, but nobody would have shot it out with ten men and not got his self killed or at least took some bullets. That was just not likely!

Weston knew Winn was good with guns. When it came to shooting, he was a natural! Weston had taught his son the best he could and it was a lot more than just shooting a gun. All you can do is teach someone right and hope they remember when they get out on their own. Now it was up to him. Weston hoped the lessons and the many hours of practice had done some good.

Weston realized he had been daydreaming again thinking about his son. It was time to get back to work. He walked to his shop and started to work on a Volcanic repeating rifle that had a broken firing pin. The Volcanic was an ingenious piece of work that his close friend Benjamin Henry took and re-designed to shoot a better bullet, the Metallic 44 Rimfire. Weston thought if Henry had only designed his rifle around a bullet like his own, then Oliver Winchester would have gone back to selling shirts and Benjamin Henry would have owned the company.

As Weston finished up his work on the rifle, he glanced out the window and noticed four riders coming towards his shop from the west.

Most riders came to the shop from the east, from the direction of town. Still it was nothing unusual as people come from all around to have broken guns repaired.

Weston was giving the Volcanic a final cleaning when the door opened and three of the four men walked in to his shop. "How can I help you men?" Weston always made it a point to be cordial to customers since the men were, after all, coming into his shop with guns.

The Kennedy brothers glanced around the gunsmith shop to see Weston Colter cleaning a Volcanic repeating rifle. There were two windows in the shop, a small one that looked out towards the house and a larger one that faced towards the town. Westlee, the oldest brother, stepped forward with Jon on his left and Preston on his right. Preston asked, "You the gunsmith?"

"Yes I am. You got a gun that needs fixin?"

Westlee looked around the room then said, "I need some bullets for a gun I got."

And what kind of gun do you have. What caliber?"

Westlee calmly sneered, "I need .32-70 brass bullets!" He wanted to see if the mention of the caliber caused any question but the gunsmith didn't seem to even blink.

Immediately Weston knew he had trouble standing in front of him. The.32-70 was the caliber that he had developed and he had only made eight guns in that caliber. One of them went to President Jefferson Davis; five supposedly went down on a barge crossing the Mississippi. The other two were stolen from this shop two years ago.

"You got that gun? " Colter casually said, "I'd like to see it." Weston picked up the Volcanic and started to rub the barrel and action with a cloth.

"You got some bullets or not?" Westlee demanded.

"I can make you some," Colter replied, "but it might take a week." The sweat started to bead up on his forehead and he could feel sweat start to roll down his back.

"I don't got a week. Westlee snarled, "I need 'em now!""

Weston kept rubbing the Volcanic then picked up a few of the .40 caliber Rocketball cartridges that were lying on the bench top. Innocently he fed the shells into the magazine of the rifle, but Weston saw the look on the men's faces. Two of the men got nervous and reached for their pistols. Weston quickly levered a shell into the action and spun the Volcanic on the lead man.

"Who the hell are you?" Weston demanded. He had them under the gun and the men couldn't move.

"Whoa now, mister! "Jon Kennedy tried to calm the situation. "We're from down south in Grayson County. We're the Kennedy brothers. We don't mean you no harm. My brother just needs some bullets made. That's all. You don't need to be pointing that rifle at us."

"I don't need to have my gun on y'all?" Weston said sarcastically, "That caliber you just asked for is real uncommon. Fact is, I'm the only one that builds a gun in that caliber!" The nerve of these outlaws... to walk in his shop asking for bullets for his stolen guns... Weston couldn't believe their nerve! He said, "I only made a few of those guns and I know where all of them are. Five are at the bottom of the Mississippi River; President Jefferson Davis has one and the last two were stolen from this shop. So which ones do you have? Y'all don't look one bit like Jefferson Davis, so that gun is out. You don't look like fish, so I doubt you have any of those guns that went down in the Mississippi. As far as I see it, that only leaves two possibilities, one I made for my son and one for me!

Weston Colter felt the adrenalin surging through his veins. He couldn't tell if these men were common thieves or just plain stupid coming in here asking for bullets for the guns they stole from him out of this shop!"

Jon and Preston stood by their brother with their hands on their pistols. Jon had taken two steps to the side to make for a more difficult target just in case the lead started to fly. Weston knew he needed to be cautious. He knew he only had two bullets in the Volcanic with three men standing in front of him. He couldn't forget, there was still one man that was still outside. "You try anything and your brother here in the middle will get a bullet between the eyes!"

That's when Jon Kennedy said something that caught Weston off guard. " I just returned home to Texas. I've been fighting with the Texas Volunteers. I served in the 13th regiment with Kid Colter... That's your boy, right?"

"Kid Colter... You mean Winn Colter?" Weston had waited for any news of Winn and even though it was coming from outlaws, it was enough to distract him from the trouble he was facing.

"Yea," Jon said, "that's him... Winn Colter... I knew him. "

"Knew him?" Weston's mind wasn't where it needed to be in this situation, "Did something happen to Winn?" Weston's focus was broken. The distraction pulled his attention toward the man on the left... the one claiming to know Winn. Weston hadn't heard anything from his son for so long that terrible thoughts had been running through his mind. Day and night, Weston wondered if his son was dead or alive. He had been waiting for any word at all. Weston's finger eased off the trigger as he waited for more information about his son from this outlaw.

Weston let his guard down and a shot rang from outside! The bullet hit the window sending shards of broken glass flying through the air, but the bullet held true and slammed Weston hard in the right shoulder. The impact of the bullet spun Weston around to the right. His natural reflexes caused him to pull the trigger.

Preston Kennedy was standing just a little too close as the Rocket ball viciously tore along the side of his jaw and through his right ear. The room was full of smoke and the echo of the shot was deafening! The wounded outlaw grabbed the side of his face and started to scream as blood quickly dripped heavily between his fingers.

Weston never hesitated. He levered the second bullet into the Volcanic, but as he started to bring the gun back around, Westlee grabbed the barrel and held it out pointing at the ceiling, making the gun useless. Preston Kennedy could feel the pain and could see his blood flowing to the floor. His ears were ringing bad... so bad, that he couldn't hear anything but the ringing. The pain in his jaw was almost unbearable, but then he touched the hanging flesh that used to be an ear.

Preston was furious about getting shot. The pain was becoming so intense that he pulled his pistol from its holster and put three bullets dead center into Weston Colter's chest.

Westlee whirled on Preston. "What the hell you do that for Brother? I needed him to make some bullets!"

Preston said, "I can't hear you Brother... Do you see what he did to me? I'm bleeding all over the place!"

Westlee was mad and had to practically scream for Preston to hear what he was saying. "Another inch to your left brother, and that Volcanic would have taken your head off! At least then Colter could have still made me some bullets!"

Jon asked Westlee "What's so good about that gun?"

"I've never saw one shoot like it, Brother!" Westlee bragged, "I've killed a Mexican soldier at 3 to 400 yards and maybe a couple of Rangers at that distance too. Search around the shop, Brother! Maybe he has some bullets around here for my gun. Take anything you want and we'll burn the rest!

The three brothers were ransacking the shop when Will Kennedy, the brother that stayed outside, noticed a woman slowly walking towards the gunsmith shop with a basket in her left hand. She had tears flowing down her cheeks but her eyes never veered, never blinked as she moved forward towards him. He didn't notice a short barreled Dragoon in her right hand hidden by the cloth of her dress sleeve.

Annabelle Colter had watched the men ride in and saw three go inside her husband's shop. When she heard the first shot, she turned to see a puff of smoke and the rifle of this man before her, pointing into her husband's shop. The shots inside the building told her what must be happening and she suspected her husband was dead. Without Weston or Winn... she had nothing to lose.

Weston kept a short barreled Dragoon by the door of the house and had taught Annabelle how to shoot for her own protection. With trembling hands, she picked up the gun and walked out the back door. The man was still standing by the horses in front of Weston's shop. She thought again about her dead husband inside. Tears were flowing down her face as she walked toward the man before her. He was looking into Weston's shop and hadn't noticed her walking from the house. When she was within ten feet of the man, he finally saw her with a look of surprise on his face. But that look almost instantly turned to one of gloating over what he had done. He had just shot the gunsmith and saved his brothers!

He smiled at Annabelle revealing ugly crooked teeth, but as he did, Annabelle lifted the short barreled Dragoon. Will Kennedy's look of gloat changed to shock as he realized what he was facing.

Annabelle pulled the trigger of her dragoon sending its .32 caliber ball into the man's skull. The bullet hit him just under the left eye and he was dead before he hit the ground. The horses he was tending jumped, but only moved a few feet. She continued to stare at the dead man lying on the ground by her feet.

The shot outside brought Jon Kennedy running to see what was going on. He saw his brother lying face down, blood running from his body. He turned to look at the woman when she realized he was standing there. She started to turn her dragoon toward the man when his right hand flew up and she saw flames come from his gun. She didn't feel any pain but she felt tired. She couldn't hold the dragoon any longer and it fell from her hand. She saw flames twice more and then she saw Weston. He was waiting for her with her two darling babies. She reached out for him and felt his touch. She was at peace.

Jon Kennedy felt sick. This was not the way he'd expected the day to turn out. One brother dead; one with a bullet hole through his ear and now he had killed a woman. Not just any woman, this was Winn Colter's mother. Kid Colter! What had they just done?

Westlee Kennedy came back to Texas from the war to heal a bullet wound, but instead of returning to the fight, he went back to his outlaw ways. He had stolen some guns while Jon was still off fighting for the South. Jon was killing Yanks while his brothers, Westlee and Parker, were rustling cattle and stealing horses. Jon was only back in Texas for a week before Westlee had the four brothers riding north towards the small town of Jacksboro, along the Butterfield Overland Mail Route.

Westlee Kennedy had told his brother Jon he had stolen some guns, but Jon had no idea they were Weston Colter's guns. Jon Kennedy had witnessed Kid Colter face down ten men by himself... where he got his reputation! The Kid scared him now that he wasn't drunk on Tequila. "Dear God!" he thought to himself, Kid Colter was going to kill them all!

Not just them, but the whole lot of saddle bums who rode with them. Jon needed to tell his brothers they had made a mistake. .. Westlee needed to get rid of those guns!

Jon Kennedy went back inside and broke the news that William was dead and the woman outside was dead too. Kill a man in Texas and you may get away with it, but kill a woman ... If the law didn't get you, the other outlaws might! Jon told his brothers, "We need to get rid of anything that ties us here! We need to burn it all! This is Kid Colter's Ma and Pa." Jon was panicking and wanted to distance himself as far away from this place as he could.

"Kid Colter... The one we heard those stories of?" Westlee asked, "I heard he was a tough hombre, but he couldn't have killed those fifteen Yankees with his knife and pistol!"

Jon corrected Westlee."He killed nine men in under three seconds with a pair of .32 caliber Dragoons! I saw him do it and every bullet was in the head or heart!" Jon swallowed hard, "I hear he's even better with his Navy Colts and he's deadly with a Sharps!" Jon was perspiring profusely as he kept recalling the day he watched Colter take down those nine Yanks. Another clear memory was the look in the Kid's eye as they rode in... It was the look of death!

Jon felt bad for his dead brother but Will was plumb weak north of the ears! Preston watched out for him and Westlee always had him along. Jon was still amazed William had lived this long. Ever since he was a kid, he was simple and never had much common sense.

Westlee asked, "Did you say the Kid's name was Winn, Brother?"

The question brought Jon out of his thoughts. "Yea, it's Winn Colter."

"That name's engraved in the stock of my rifle. The other rifle had "Weston" engraved on it.. I traded that gun to Frank Baxter for a bottle of tequila and a poke with his woman afore I knew how the damn thing could shoot, else I would have gave it to you or Preston. I only had twenty bullets, but now I'm out. That's why we rode up here, to get more of those damn bullets and Preston done keeled the gun maker!" Westlee bragged, "I keeled me a pair of Rangers in El Paso last year with that gun; one I keeled out of the saddle near a quarter mile."

"You would be better off to throw that gun in the fire," Jon said, "cause if Kid Colter tracks it down, I won't be standing by you, Brother!"

Westlee was starting to get mad, "Are you yellar, Brother?"

Calling anyone yellow was fighting words, but Jon only let it go because it was his brother. "No I'm not yellar, but I'm not pickin' a fight with that hombre if'n he's all hell-fired up because of his dead kin. I seen the Kid's guns a blazing. He's no greenhorn, believe me, Brother! I don't want to be on the wrong side of his guns... and we done killed his Ma and Pa. I'd just as soon skedaddle from here fast!

Westlee finally agreed, "Ok brother, let's burn it down! Drag the woman in the house and set it on fire. I'll check the shop one last time and set it afire too. Without bullets, that rifle's no good to me anyways. I'll throw it in. Your brother Preston's bleedin' all over with that ear. Get him on his horse and we'll take William away from here and bury him."

Jon Kennedy ran out of the shop and dragged Annabelle Colter to the house. Inside he saw how well kept everything was. He looked around. There sat a tintype photograph of the Colter family probably done just before Winn Colter went off to war. Jon thought the photograph was haunting, all of them were looking right back at him... especially the Kid. What had he done? Jon had never felt fear like now. He needed some tequila.

In the shop, Westlee Kennedy took one last look at the body of Weston Colter lying on the floor. As he turned he glimpsed a black canvas bag sitting on a shelf way in the back. He reached up and pulled the heavy bag down where he could see what was inside. There were nearly two hundred rounds of .32-70 shells. With that many shells, he better get back that other gun from Baxter and give it to Preston. He thought that would be fair since Preston already paid for it with his blood.

Westlee took the bag of shells and slipped them into his saddle bag. After all, this is why he came. They were more costly than he anticipated but William really was an idiot .It's hard for a brother to say, but Will didn't have nothin' under his hat but hair. The family was probably better off without him.

As the brothers rode away, Annabelle Colter's house and Weston

Colter's shop were engulfed in flames. Hopefully all the evidence would be gone and nothing could tie the Kennedys to this tragedy. Jon Kennedy kept thinking of that photograph. It was like the Kid was looking back at him. Like the Kid knew.

CHAPTER 15

Colter realized just how excited he was to be coming home. The town had changed its name from Mesquiteville to Jacksboro not long before he rode out to join the fight. Mesquiteville, before the war, was a small frontier town settled in the pasturelands and located on the Butterfield Overland Mail Route. It was the farthest Texas settlement to the North at the time.

The first settlers in the area ran cattle, had to survive Indian raids, and cleared away mesquite brush to make their town site. It was latecomers who decided to change the name to Jacksboro and the new name never did set well with Weston Colter. He was stubborn about accepting the name change and never called the town by its new name.

The Colter homestead and smithin' shop were just south of Jacksboro where his Pa still claimed the name would remain Mesquiteville. If it meant the town's boundary ended at the Colter property line, then so be it. For the town to really grow, it needed to see some change. The biggest reason the town hadn't expanded to its potential was because of continued attacks by Kiowa and Comanche. Now two years later as Winn Colter rode closer to home, he hoped the Indian attacks on the town had become fewer since he left. He hadn't heard anything since he went on his mission for the President. Even his rides to see the quartermaster or to meet with General Lee offered little information about what was happening back here in Texas. Now that he thought about it, Winn didn't remember if he'd ever asked anyone about home since he left two years ago. Now he was looking forward to surprising his Ma and Pa. Their boy was coming home!

Colter noticed the closer they got to the pasturelands, the more they were seeing sign of cattle. Colter had noted a few branded steers, but most of the longhorns were still running wild. It took a good cowboy to chase these moss heads out of the mesquite, but a lot of those Ace high riders were still off fighting the war.

Two friends of Weston Colter, Charles Goodnight and John Adair, were planning to build a ranch not far from Mesquiteville. Their hopes of gathering wild mustang and longhorn cattle would make them rich, but the Kiowa attacks had made more than one man change his mind or part with his hair. Colter hoped Indian depredation had lessened since he left but he still didn't know.

The area before them was a series of rolling hills covered with live oak, juniper, yucca, and mesquite. They were close to the pastureland that brought the first settlers to the area. He hadn't realized it; but after two years away from home, now the homesick was setting in. Colter started seeing landmarks he recognized, and he knew he had less than thirty miles left.

Courtney was worried now more than ever about losing Colter, She didn't want that to happen. Winn Colter had been such a gentleman this entire time that she and Chase had been with him. She was so pleased the way Winn had treated Chase, teasing and playing with him. Chase had really taken to Colter and Courtney couldn't have been happier. Suddenly Colter reigned up and his smile disappeared as he looked to the ground. It was very evident something was wrong and concern was written all over his face.

Chase had been riding with Colter, but now he pulled up as Courtney came to their side. Colter passed Chase to Courtney and slipped her a .32 caliber Dragoon. "We may have trouble," he warned, "I was so excited to get home, I lost my focus". The pony tracks in the sand were unshod and fresh and Colter knew they were in extreme danger. "Looks to be about a half dozen Indians." He said quietly, "Where we are, I suspect they could be Comanche or Kiowa. Either way, we need to get off the trail and away from here. Stay behind me!"

Courtney suddenly realized the danger they were facing and wrapped her arms around Chase and held him tight. She looked at Colter and nodded that she understood.

Colter looked around quickly then broke across the grassy flat trying to put some distance between them and the trail. Colter rode quickly but not too fast to stir up a lot of dust. Courtney put her full trust in Colter and stuck right on his horse's tail. Had Colter missed the tracks crossing the trail, they would have ridden into an ambush where the trail made a sharp turn to cross a small ravine.

The Kiowa had seen the pair of horses for nearly an hour and could see the boy rode a powerful animal. Better than any of the horses they rode. The boy was careless with his actions, not looking for danger. They would have those horses soon and kill the boy.

The Kiowa had positioned themselves for an ambush by the edge of a ravine where there would be no chance of escape. They all saw that one horse carried a blonde-haired woman and a small child. After they killed the man, they would each have the woman many times before they killed her. They may kill the child or take him as a prisoner. They could decide that later. Blonde young women were a prize and the Indians were excited to see her riding towards them.

The Kiowa knew their tracks had given them away when the horses whirled and dove off the trail just before they got to the ambush. Now they would have to chase the pair of horses down. Maybe the boy wasn't as stupid as they had thought. Four braves rode fast after the riders that now had quite a lead. Two of the braves turned back down the trail to flank the riders as they tried to get around the Indians farther down the wash.

There wasn't a lot of cover, but enough to stay out of sight of the pursuing Kiowa. Courtney had stuck right behind Colter as he chose the path to get them through. She was holding the reigns with her left hand and wrapping her other arm around Chase, with the Dragoon held tightly in her hand.

As Colter ducked around a juniper tree, Courtney tried to take a quick glace to see if there were Indians behind them. As she turned back around, it was too late. Juniper branches caught her and Chase and knocked them out of the saddle to the ground.

Colter heard the sound and whirled with his Colt in hand thinking the worst. He was relieved it was only a juniper that had caused the fall. He quickly grabbed the loose horse's reins and quickly returned to Courtney and Chase who were now crying with fear. They were both scared and unsettled from the fall, but otherwise ok. Courtney looked up. She was terrified when she saw the four Kiowa warriors coming in fast. There was nowhere to hide! Colter pulled the rifle from its scabbard and quickly loaded a shell. "Courtney, Get Ready!" With the warning, she pulled Chase in close and lifted the Dragoon.

The Kiowa could see the three had nowhere to go so they raced their ponies toward the woman. Colter quickly took aim and fired but the movement of his horse threw off his shot which gave the Indians even more encouragement. Colter slipped the rifle back in its scabbard and whirled his horse back towards the charging Indians. He pulled his Navy Colts and charged strait back at them. Colter took aim at the rear Indian first which was an impossible shot for a pistol but he pulled the trigger. The slug caught the Indian in the center of his chest, then rolled him off his horse backward. The first three wouldn't have known except for the release of air as the warrior hit the ground.

The Kiowa leaned low behind their ponies necks and returned fire with Winchesters they had just taken from a group of blue soldiers a week before. They hadn't lost a brave in that attack on the soldiers, but now one of them was down. Horses were running towards each other, closing distance fast. In just a few seconds, they were within 30 yards. Colter shot the lead horse, killing it instantly and sending the rider rolling into a prickly-pear cactus where he screamed in pain but came up running. The second horse had to jump the first fallen horse and the rider had to sit up or be thrown to the ground. As he lifted his head, Colter put a bullet between his eyes.

The last mounted Indian ducked down low and as he and Colter passed, they both fired shots that missed. But now Colter's attention had to be back on the grounded warrior still running straight at him. Even though he was full of cactus quills sticking out of his chest and face, he picked up his tomahawk and pulled his knife and was coming at Colter's horse screaming a war cry. Colter shot him in the chest but the brave kept running. Colter shot him again and again and bullet after bullet slammed through his chest but he kept coming. The brave leaned back for a swing with his tomahawk and Colter fired one last time hitting the Indian between the eyes. The tomahawk swing never came forward as the Kiowa warrior fell dead at the horse's feet.

The last Indian hearing all of the shooting behind him, focused on the woman as she pushed the crying little boy behind her. The Kiowa warrior came off his horse on the run flailing his tomahawk. Today was going to be a good day to die: but before he did, he would bash in the head of this man's woman and child!

Courtney was so terrified she forgot to shoot and just stared at the screaming Kiowa warrior coming down upon her. She closed her eyes and ducked, holding Chase waiting for death from a blow to her head... She realized she had heard a boom! She opened her eyes and saw the haunting stare of glazed eyes looking back at her. Dead only a few feet from her. She turned to see Colter still kneeling with his rifle pointing her direction. He had saved their lives again. She held on to Chase and cried.

As Colter approached leading his horse, he had no sooner put his rifle back in the scabbard than Courtney knocked him to the ground. She flung her arms around him as she kissed him affectionately then started to cry again. She squeezed him so tight, pulling herself into him, he could hardly breathe. Winn thought to himself if he had to die, this wouldn't be a bad way to go. He could feel her body still trembling with fear as the adrenalin wore off.

Courtney looked into his eyes and knew she loved him. She kissed him deeply... affectionately ... again. There was that familiar little giggle and laugh from behind them again. Chase thought these two were acting so funny!

The remaining two Kiowa warriors had heard the shooting. They could tell the fast report of a pistol or pistols and the odd sounding rifle. It had made the last shot. A raven cawed overhead. What did this mean? A transformation... deaths of the warriors. This boy must have great magic to beat four Kiowa warriors. Today was not his day to die. The two Kiowa would have to go back to tell Chief Santana that the crow had warned them that the magic of this boy was strong. His pistols fired fast and his rifle talked differently than other rifles. They would remember the sound of that rifle and know death would find those who attacked the boy.

The crow cawed again. Today would not be a good day to die. The Kiowa turned their ponies and rode away to the north.

Courtney and Colter heard the giggles and laugh and all they could do was kiss again and laugh with him. Chase ran and jumped on top of them and the three hugged each other. But passion was building between Colter and Courtney. Both could feel it and both wanted it. Courtney had vowed to herself that they wouldn't let things go too far until she could see the reaction of his Ma and Pa. She'd do anything to keep him. She loved him!

The light in the sky was starting to disappear and Colter knew they would have to make camp one more time before they arrived at his boyhood home just beyond Jacksboro. Courtney thought to herself… "Mr. and Mrs. Winn Colter… Courtney Mae Colter," she liked the sound of that. She was truly in love with Winn Colter who now had saved her life on three occasions. She thought to herself if Colter came to her tonight, she wouldn't be able to resist. Who was she kidding? Winn had better resist or she was going to take him! Her desires were killing her!

One more agonizing day and she thought she would know, know if she could fully release her desires on this man, or live the rest of her life not having what she wanted more than anything in the world. She could only pray that her choice was right and hoped their lives could be together forever. That was one of the things the Mormons believed, families could be together forever. This was the man she wanted. From his kisses, she believed he wanted her too.

CHAPTER 16

Colter had a sleepless night. He sat up and cleaned his guns in the dark using only moonlight knowing there still might be Indians out there after their scalps. Colter had allowed them to have a small fire for a few hours, but later moved camp to protect them from another attack. Colter cut the trail of the two Kiowa warriors, but they definitely looked like they were pulling out of the area. Nonetheless, even one Kiowa within a half day's ride made the area dangerous and Colter would not let his guard down again.

The night was colder so Chase was wrapped up in a blanket. Colter made one last sweep of the area and checked the horses. They were standing calmly. He paid close attention to his horses. They would let him know if something or someone was trying to sneak up on him from the shadows.

Colter turned around to find Courtney waiting for him. The night was cool but beautiful and the moonlight danced across the desert. A coyote howled in the distance and two others answered back. Courtney was sensing everything out there. It was peaceful; but after today, she knew the desert could be filled with danger. She looked at Chase wrapped in the blanket lying between the saddles then walked quickly over to Colter who was looking at the moon and the stars. As he turned to face Courtney, she could feel her heart beat faster. She was sure that the only thing keeping him from hearing her heartbeat was the night sounds of the desert.

He smiled and reached out to pick up her hand. She was trembling so he pulled her in close and put his arms around her trying to warm her.

She looked at the moon and snuggled in close. There was no place she would rather be. Her will was broken and what would happen tonight she didn't know? She had never felt her body ache with desire as it did now, but all he did was hold her hand against his chest. The feel of his heartbeat was comforting through the night. Her hand on his chest pushed his will to the limit. It was a restless night for both of them. Neither of the two got much sleep.

Colter was up early and had the horses saddled and ready to ride well before daylight. He sat there quietly wondering what might have changed at home in two years. He felt guilty that he hadn't thought much about home for nearly two years except on Christmas. Now he couldn't wait to see his Ma and Pa... he would be home before noon.

Courtney got on the horse and Colter handed her the still sleeping boy to ride across her lap. Last night was rough on Colter. Courtney's hand on his chest made him want so much more, but today's desire to get home, to see his Ma and Pa, was almost as strong. He hadn't realized that he was homesick until this moment.

They rode out into the pastureland, seeing lots of unbranded longhorns. With the lack of cowboys to push or gather cattle, they were as thick as ticks on a deer! Closer they got to Jacksboro; they started seeing more and more cattle, mostly branded with the Goodnight brand and John Adair's JA. Colter could see both those two ranchers had been busy the past two years rounding up and branding these wild longhorn mossbacks. Both of these men were respected ranchers in the community and had been part of the first settlers who moved into the area.

After riding for three hours, they finally made it to the edge of Jacksboro. As they rode, Colter could sense something was different. Something was wrong and the townspeople were giving them strange looks as they rode into town. He wondered if he had changed so much that the townsfolk didn't remember, but he decided that couldn't be. Colter knew some of the boys who left to fight came home missing an arm or a leg. Some hadn't come home at all. Now, here he was coming back home, riding in with a woman and a child. However, Colter was getting an odd feeling that something else was very wrong.

Colter rode on through town headed towards his family's homestead. Mr. Goodnight recognized him and rode straight over. "Good to see you, Winn!" Charles Goodnight had been a Texas Ranger since 1858, but he was also building a ranch and had some mighty big ideas.

"Mr. Goodnight, It's so good to see a friendly face," Colter smiled, "We just crossed the pasturelands and I see y'all been working the wild ones.. Got many branded?"

"You could tell? " Goodnight smiled with a sense of accomplishment, "We've branded About five hundred in the past three months." Goodnight paused for a moment then a solemn look came on his face. "Winn, have you been out to your home. "No sir," Colter replied, "just heading out that way now."

Goodnight looked serious and tried to figure how to express himself. He looked at Winn and said, "Your Pa's a good friend of mine, you know that Winn. I'm afraid I got bad news for y'all that need tellin' before you go out there."

"Bad news?" Colter questioned... He had a pain hit him in the chest and drop into his gut.

"Yes Winn," Goodnight admitted. "I don't know how to say it other than to outright tell you." Goodnight looked somber. He paused for just a moment..."Your Ma and Pa are dead, Son. Whoever done it burned your house and your Pa's 'smithin' shop."

Colter couldn't say a word. He was sick thinking that his family was gone. If he hadn't been sitting on his horse, he thought he may have fallen down. Then Colter got angry and questioned, "Are you still a Texas Ranger Mr. Goodnight? Who did it?"

"Yes, I'm still a Ranger, and we don't know yet who done it. There was no evidence. Nothing but some blood. Your Pa must of shot one, but nobody ever knew. Usually somebody gets drunk at a saloon or cantina and talks. That's how word gets around who done it. Somebody will talk and the Rangers will go after them."

"When did it happen?"

"Bout six months ago." Mr. Goodnight then paused...He wanted to say this right. "Nobody knew where to send word. We heard...Well, we heard a lot of things and I bet most ain't true. Fact is, I even heard you were dead a time or two. This war's taken a lot of good Texas boys, but I'm glad you ain't one of them, Winn!"

Colter thought about what the Ranger had said, then asked, "It's been that long and nobody's talked?"

"Not yet but they always do. We believe it was four of them did it. Townsfolk heard shooting but you know that's common from a gunsmith's shop. We all saw the fire and went to help, but it was already too far gone. We buried your Ma and Pa behind the house." Colter didn't say anything.

Charles Goodnight wanted to comfort Winn the best he could, "Your Pa was the best gunsmith in Texas, and was truly respected by all the Rangers. Nobody knows why anyone would do what they done."

Mr. Goodnight looked at Colter then at Courtney riding beside him with a little boy. "Y'all got a reputation Son and true or not, it'll follow you."

The news of his Ma and Pa's death was sinking in, like somebody just kicked him in the gut. Colter felt the gentle touch of Courtney's hand on his thigh and he glanced at her quickly. Tears were flowing down her cheeks. She could sense what the news had done to him and could feel his pain. The news hurt her too. She had lost too many people in the last few years.

Goodnight paused for a moment when saw the woman's sad and gentle reaction to the news. He could see the concern in her eyes as her tears began to flow. "Let the Rangers figure out who done it, Winn. Suddenly Goodnight realized, "Forgive my manners Ma'am." He took off his hat and asked Colter, " Is this your lady Winn?"

Colter looked at Courtney who was looking back at him waiting to hear his response to the question.

"Yes Mr. Goodnight. I'm sorry. This is Mrs. Montgomery; Courtney Mae Montgomery and her son Chase." Mr. Goodnight could clearly see her reaction to Colter saying "Mrs." as she pulled her hand back off his thigh.

"Courtney, this is Mr. Charles Goodnight. He's a Texas Ranger. and a rancher. He's been a friend of my Ma and Pa for as long as I remember."

Colter looked back at Courtney then turned back to Goodnight, "Courtney's husband was killed by Yankees and they were going to…" He paused, "It's not the way any woman should ever be treated. Had I left her there, I'm afraid they would have killed her and her son."

"Sorry to hear about your husband Ma'am, but I'm not sure if you could be traveling with any better company, Winn Colter's a fine young man… A fine Texan!"

"Thank you Mr. Goodnight. I've already found that out." Courtney looked at Colter with a slight smile, but his mind was lost in thought. She could understand why after just finding out his family was dead… murdered, and nobody knew who or why.

"I wish meeting you was under better circumstances, Mrs. Montgomery; but I'll still want to welcome you to Texas." Goodnight thought for a moment. He really wanted to talk to Winn to find out how he'd been. "Why don't you three come out to the ranch and we can put you up for a night or two. I know my wife would enjoy some company besides the ranch hands and the kids."

Colter took him up on his offer. "Thanks Mr. Goodnight. That's a mighty fine offer and we'd appreciate your hospitality while I look things over." Courtney seemed pleased to be invited to stay at the Goodnight Ranch.

As they rode through the town, Colter started seeing more people he recognized and a few he didn't. He bypassed the family home for now and rode with Mr. Goodnight towards his ranch. Colter was impressed and could see the Goodnight ranch was growing and looking to be in good shape. Mrs. Goodnight walked out onto the porch to see who was riding in with her husband.

"Hello, Mrs. Goodnight" Colter said in a slightly deeper voice than when he left two years before. Even though it was deeper, she recognized the voice, but not the face of the boy she had known. "Winn Colter! Get down off that horse so I can give you a hug!"

"Be careful Son!" Mr. Goodnight warned, "Her hugs have been known to squeeze a steer so tight that it keeled over!"

"Hush! George!" Mrs. Goodnight was embarrassed, "It was only a calf and I was hanging on for dear life!" Mr. Goodnight chuckled. He loved to tease her about the calf. Mrs. Goodnight looked at her husband again as he sat there snickering... She pleaded, "You know that calf was stuck in the corral gate. I just pulled it out and it took off!" Now Colter and Courtney were picturing the scene and were smiling. Mrs. Goodnight kept trying to explain because of the laughter. "The calf stumbled and fell or it might have drug me into the pastures!" Mrs. Goodnight's face grew red with embarrassment. Trying to change the subject, she ordered Winn again, "Get down here, Winn Colter!"

Colter knew that when Mrs. Goodnight gave a command, it was hopeless to resist. He stepped out of the saddle and she grabbed him before his feet hit the ground and squeezed him in a bear hug. Colter heard his back pop three times. He wouldn't admit it, but she squeezed so hard, he couldn't breathe! Courtney had to laugh seeing the expression on Colter's face as he gasped for air. Mrs. Goodnight was a buxom five foot five inch woman with dark hair and jovial eyes. Courtney was sure not a man on this ranch dared cross this woman, let alone her Texas Ranger husband.

"Winn Colter, let me have a look at you!" Mrs. Goodnight stepped back to have a better look at the young man before her. "You've turned into a mighty handsome young man, Winn. If I was ten years younger..."

"Hey now!" Mr. Goodnight smiled knowing what Winn had just endured.

Mrs. Goodnight turned to Courtney's horse. "And who might this be?"

Colter turned to introduce them. "Mrs. Goodnight, This is Courtney."

No offense, Miss Courtney, but I was asking about the fine young man riding in front of you."

Courtney smiled and said, "This is my son Chase." Chase glanced back at his mother with a look of horror. He had just seen this woman try to kill Colter. His mother wouldn't allow her to squeeze him. As Mrs. Goodnight came closer to the horse, Chase was practically climbing his way around behind his mother. Mr. Goodnight laughed at the sight and Courtney smiled too.

"Chase, are you hungry, Boy? Do you want something to eat?" With that, Chase's fear of death left him, and he was more than willing to go to this lady if it involved food.

"Come in!" Mrs. Goodnight said, "Food will be on the table in a moment. There's enough for all of you."

Mr. Goodnight turned to his wife, "I invited these folks to stay with us for a few days... If that's all right with you? A couple of days should give you time to spoil that little boy some."

"Of course they're welcome! Winn's like family. You know that!" Mrs. Goodnight acted genuinely excited to have them and it made Courtney feel at ease. " This will give me some quality time with Courtney too." Mrs. Goodnight added, "It's not often I get to have the company of a woman!" Courtney felt good about this woman who was willing to open her doors to a stranger. She seemed like the kind of woman that could keep a Ranger on his toes.

Colter went out to remove the saddles and give both horses a good rub. Dinner had to wait as Colter did this every day after their long ride. The smell of the food was wonderful as Colter entered the house. Everyone was sitting at the table waiting when Winn came through the door. Courtney had had a moment to freshen up and she looked incredible to Colter.

"Well don't just stand there, Winn!" Mrs. Goodnight announced, "supper's ready!" Colter jumped at the order and sat down by Courtney where they all enjoyed a wonderful supper of beef, potatoes, biscuits and coffee. Afterwards, Mr. Goodnight and Colter went outside and watched the sun falling in the west Texas sky. Colter pondered, "I sure missed that... the sunsets. Virginia, Tennessee and Georgia all had pretty sunsets, but there's something about Texas."

Mr. Goodnight thoughtfully looked at Colter. "What's your plan with that woman in there?" Colter was caught off guard by the sudden question, but answered quickly, "I think I'm going to marry that woman."

Goodnight looked at Colter and thought for a moment. "You know Winn, I thought the world of your Pa. I would love to have you stay on to help with the ranch, but I know what happens to men with reputations. Either the Rangers get called to face the bad ones or some hombre thinks he can make a name for himself and picks a fight. I know your Pa trained you to shoot but the stories that have made it back to Texas said you were a ruthless gunman." Colter looked at Mr. Goodnight with shock at what he was saying. "Knowing you, I didn't believe those stories for a minute, Winn; but some do." Colter sat quietly and listened.

"I'm afraid if you stay, some hombre that's heard of your reputation, will try to pick a fight. Or worse, someone could sneak up and shoot you in the back. A man with a reputation will get blamed for robberies or killings that can't be explained." Colter though about what Mr. Goodnight was saying. It was the same thing President Davis had warned him about.

"I think you should rest here on the ranch as long as you like, and then take that fine young lady up to Santa Fe or Denver. You may even go up into Wyoming. Go somewhere that you can lose your reputation."

Colter knew that was good advice. "Do you know anything about the Utah Territory?"

Goodnight thought for a moment. "That might be an even better place for you to disappear. But there's lots of Mormons there." Goodnight knew the Spaniards explored the Utah territory and brought back a lot of gold. They searched for the lost cities of Cibola and Eldorado, but never found any of them.

"I've ridden as far north as the Grand Canyon, but that's all. That's the biggest canyon I ever saw! I met an old Mountain man that told me about the red rock mesas along the Colorado River that he said reached half way to the sky. He also said the Mormons have established settlements all across the territory in the past few years. Some of it's real nice country, but lots of it is just desert."

Goodnight thought again, "Winn, I think Utah might be just the place to get away from your reputation. Find yourself a place where you're not known and build yourself a ranch or a shop like your Pa's." Colter knew Mr. Goodnight was sincere and looking out for him. It was good advice.

"The Spanish Trail goes right through Santa Fe. Catch the Trail and it'll drop right in the middle of Utah with all them Mormons. If y'all don't like it, follow the trail to California." The more Goodnight thought about it, the better he felt. "I think you should find a little place that's nice, and homestead. There is lots of grass, trees, wild game and good people. Most of them Mormons are good people. I'm sure they have some wild and dangerous ones too. Just like everywhere else."

Mr. Goodnight was somber for a moment before he said, "Winn, let the Rangers sort out this killin affair with your Ma and Pa. I won't give up on them. I promise you that!"

Winn knew he had to leave, but he still needed to go home to fulfill his promise. "I need to go look around my house and shop one time before I go. I'll be leaving home possibly for the last time. I need to see."

CHAPTER 17

Winn Colter and Ranger Goodnight rode up to the Colter homestead just after daylight, but there wasn't much left to see. Winn felt like he had been gut punched. He knew this was going to be hard, but actually being here was harder than he had envisioned. Winn looked around at his boyhood home, but there really wasn't much left besides the remnants of the charred buildings..

Goodnight watched Winn's reaction as they rode up to the burned-out home. He knew this couldn't be easy but he understood why Winn had to do it. Ranger Goodnight said, "I'll tell you what I know, Winn." The chimney still stood and there were a few charred timbers. For the most part, everything was gone from the house except for the stove and washtub and some other metal items. Colter noticed shards of his Ma's prized china plates and a spoon lying where he figured their table use to sit. Now it was only blackened earth.

Colter rode over to his Pa's shop and saw it had fared a little better, but not by much. The hitching post was still in place so both of them got off and tied their horses to the rail. The pot-bellied stove still stood in the middle of the charred timbers which had stopped burning at about waist level. Colter and goodnight stepped inside.

"The fire did a lot of damage," Goodnight said, "Your Pa was inside." Mr. Goodnight hesitated before he continued. "We think who done it took some guns. We found a few in the rubble, but I know my Volcanic was gone. Your Pa was replacing a broken firing pin. And Joe Barton brought home a Spencer rifle from Virginia that your Pa was fixin' the barrel. It was gone too. "

"Stealing broken guns?" Colter said, "That don't make sense unless they had already been fixed."

Goodnight explained, "There were two empty .40 caliber Rocketball cases in the shop by your pa's body. That's the bullet my Volcanic shot."

Winn thought about what might have happened then asked, "Ranger Goodnight, Remember, Pa's shop was broken into just before I left? They stole some guns including the ones Pa built for me and him. Did the Rangers catch them that stole those guns?" Mr. Goodnight ducked his head. "Never a word 'bout those guns of your Pa's. We followed four horses to the south, but lost them when some Comanche's came after us."

By noon, Winn had looked at about everything he wanted. It was tough trying to figure what had happened amongst the destruction six months after the fire. Colter had walked circles around the yard, around the shop, and in the house. He was confident Ranger Goodnight had done a thorough search and was telling him everything he knew. "Mr. Goodnight, what about the cash box?"

"Cash box?" Goodnight looked confused. "Your Pa kept his money in a drawer by his work bench didn't he? What was left of the drawer was across the room. I didn't know anything about a cash box."

Winn walked over to the stove in the house and reached down into debris in the bottom of what was left of the firebox. He moved a flat stone and there sat a heavy metal box. Winn pulled it out with Mr. Goodnight watching. As Winn opened the metal top, he could see a Patterson revolver with a scorched grip and some scorched Confederate dollar bills.

Mr. Goodnight shook his head, "We'll I'll be! I'm amazed anything survived the fire." There was one hundred and twenty Confederate dollars but the surprise was 62 Double eagles!

Colter said, "Pa kept a few dollars in the shop but he stashed this box under the firewood. It looks like he done well after I left."

Goodnight was amazed…"Your pa's given you a good start there Winn. You could stay and rebuild but who knows what to expect with the wars end. The more I think about it, the better the Utah Territory sounds."

Winn agreed, "I'll have to decide soon."

Goodnight said, "I don't think ya'll go wrong with that young gal back at the ranch. She's a handsome woman and carries herself like a Texan! If I didn't have the Mrs.; I'd sweet talk that lady myself!" Winn looked at Mr. Goodnight who had a big smile on his face.

Colter smiled, "Y'all better be thankful Mrs. Goodnight don't hear you say that. I think she would grab you like a wild calf and crush you in a death grip!"

"That she would my boy." Mr. Goodnight said, "That she would!" Mr. Goodnight ducked quickly, and then glanced over both shoulders knowing his wife wasn't there but he still had to look to make sure.

The two made their way back to the ranch after wandering out to look at some of the cattle on the pastureland. Goodnight commented, pointing at the cows, "There's my future Winn! Long as those Yankees don't come down here and try to shoot us or the Mexicans don't decide to try taking back Texas!"

"I wouldn't believe it!" Colter said, "Not as long as the Rangers are around!"

Goodnight looked at Colter again, "There's not as many Rangers as you think. Besides, we got us enough troubles with Indians and banditos. We don't need the Union or Mexican Army here."

CHAPTER 18

After supper, Winn asked Mrs. Goodnight if she could watch Chase for a while so he could show Courtney his home. He didn't know it, but Courtney had already talked to Mrs. Goodnight about watching Chase for some time. She had all but told Mrs. Goodnight how her desires were eating her up and how she needed time alone with Winn to discuss their future.

"Sure Winn. Take your time!" Mrs. Goodnight said "We're not goin' anywhere and I'd love to have that boy to spoil for a while." She gave Courtney a wily smile and a wink. Courtney ducked away, trying not to smile back.

Winn and Courtney rode out together with some good daylight remaining in the late afternoon. As they got closer to his boyhood home, he rode close to Courtney and reached out to take her hand. Courtney glanced at him out of the corner of her eye; her whole body tingled at his touch. As they reached the burned out buildings, her senses came back to her.

"I love this place. I love Texas, but..." Colter ducked his head almost ashamed of what he was about to say. "You've seen me shoot... The problem is, so did a group of soldiers in Virginia when I was in a tight spot. I don't even remember how it happened." Colter took off his hat and stuck his finger through the hole in the crown of his Stetson to show Courtney. "That's how close I came to dying that day. One inch lower and it would have taken off the top of my head. Stories got told, and exaggerated. Now I have a reputation as a shooter... a bad man." Colter looked at the ground thinking Courtney would think less of him. "The

Yankees might come looking for me after the war if I stay here. Because of stories, they even offered a reward for killin' me." Colter kicked a rock, "The stories ain't true... most of them anyway." Courtney listened intently.

"Mr. Goodnight reminded me something else could happen. Somebody that wants a reputation could come hunt me down. Maybe shoot me in the back just to say they killed "Kid Colter." I didn't want that reputation and I kept it quiet, but men talked and got the stories wrong. Mr. Goodnight and I discussed his concerns this morning. We both agreed it would be wise for me to leave Texas."

Winn pointed out behind the shell of the house, "We need to go over there...There's my family." He was choked up for a moment. They dismounted and Winn could see there was a wildflower growing by the side of the house. He hesitated, but bent down and picked it to give to Courtney. She looked at his eyes because he didn't say anything. She couldn't tell if he was still choked up or didn't know what to say.

Winn led on taking her to the side of the graves that were set back under an oak tree. Two fairly-fresh graves of adults and two older graves of children.

Winn turned to face the graves. With his hat in his hand he said. "Ma and Pa, this is Courtney Montgomery... I think I love her..."Courtney turned to look at him. "I do love her." Courtney felt uncomfortable at first but holding his hand, she moved in closer. He looked into her eyes and put his arm around her as she laid her head on his shoulder. Courtney saw tears flowing down his face.

"Mr. and Mrs. Colter," she spoke to the graves "I love your son... And I hope to marry him. You should be very proud of your boy." Winn could feel his heart pounding. This woman really had an effect on him. Something came over him and he felt himself kneeling in front of Courtney.

"I don't know if this is the right time, but I need to ask... here." Courtney looked at Winn and tears began to fill her eyes. Every sense in her body wanted him to ask. She almost couldn't wait for him to say it. They moved under the shade of the oak as Winn talked before he went back to his knee. He could now see she was eagerly waiting for the question so he drug it on for a while longer, but this question was too important to leave hanging. He looked deep into her eyes and took a deep breath. "Courtney" he said. She could hardly take it! She leaned forward and kissed him. He pushed her back. "Courtney, I love you"… She came forward again kissing him. Passion was burning her up inside… He pushed her back again, forcibly having to hold her back. "If it's not too soon, I'd like to marry you." This time she knocked him off his feet as she aggressively moved in to kiss him. He again tried to say through her kisses, "When you're ready."

Her emotions were exploding! Never had she had feeling like this before and it had been building inside her for a couple of weeks now as they came all the way from Tennessee. She said "Now… I mean yes!" Her kisses were passionate. Her touch became light and gentle, but she had full control. And her eyes… her eyes could melt a man's heart. She kissed him deeply again. Now Winn thought of Chase. No little voice laughing at them this time. "I guess we best be getting back for Chase," he said, " Mrs. Goodnight…"

Courtney teased. "Mrs. Goodnight said we have all the time we want." Courtney's eyes never flinched. "She won't let Mr. Goodnight come looking for us 'till after breakfast." Winn was embarrassed to think that women would even talk about that. He looked at Courtney and swallowed hard. She looked at him with that wry smile. Winn thought he knew what was going to happen tonight but he never could have imagined what was in store for him. It was the start of the rest of his life… No, he could tell this was start of the "Best" of his life!

****

George Goodnight sat in a chair holding a sleeping boy. He looked at his wife who was smiling. "What?" Mrs. Goodnight kept smiling. "Where are they? I didn't think they would be gone this long."

"Oh, I wouldn't worry just yet my dear. There's young love out there."

George started to question when he finally got the hint. He looked down at Chase then back at his wife who just smiled back at him. He said, "I hope she's not like you or she might squeeze that boy to death!" He got a hard look for that. "But," he said, "If I was going to die, my dear, that's how I'd want to go." Mrs. Goodnight came over and gave him a kiss on the cheek. The boy in his lap, he realized, probably just saved his life!

George Goodnight thought about Winn and Courtney. She seemed a few years older, but there was no doubt, Winn Colter was a fine man and he deserved some happiness. Utah could be a nice place for Winn to get away from his reputation. Surly none of them Mormons would have any idea about Winn Colter, his reputation, or his past.

CHAPTER 19

Mr. Goodnight took Colter on a ride in the pasturelands to look at cattle and to have another talk with this young man. Goodnight explained, "These Longhorns are out of control here, Colter. John Adair and I've been talking. As soon as we can, we're going to push a herd of two, maybe three thousand head of longhorns up to a railhead in Kansas; when the war ends. The way we figure it, we'll ship cattle all across this country and get rich! That is if the price comes back up."

Colter thought about that many cattle and wondered how successful a drive that far would be. "Have you ridden that trail up to Kansas?"

"Before the war," Goodnight replied, "but we didn't have cattle like we do now. Hell, folks are killing them for their hides. There are a lot of hungry people out there and we can feed 'em. Bring the country back together."

"And make some money?"

"That's right," he said, "make a lot of money!" Goodnight got somber for a moment "You know Winn, I wish you were staying. I could use a good man, but your names known by a lot of people. Stories of your shooting are being talked about by the rough crowd in the saloons and cantinas. Some want to ride with you and others want to shoot at you. I heard the Yanks had a price on your head." Goodnight looked at Winn thoughtfully. "You've got every Union soldier lookin' over his shoulder for the Texas Devil with guns blazing!"

"I hear that too." Winn said. His tone became more somber." I also hear they're hunting down sharpshooters to kill 'em. If they find out where I am, they will be coming for me."

"I figured they would have you sharp shooting," concluded Goodnight, "After seeing you shoot when you was young, I have no doubts. Your Pa said you were a natural shooter, the best he ever saw. It worried him. You know Winn," Goodnight conjectured, "if the Union army did come lookin', there's a lot of Texans that would stand by you."

"I know and appreciate that, but there's some Texans that might shoot me in the back for a reward. I've seen some men that are pretty hard up and a reward might be tempting." Colter paused for a moment... "We're losing the war, Mr. Goodnight."

Goodnight pondered for a moment. "I think we've all figured that out. Whether we accept it or not.... It wouldn't surprise me if the war's over in six months." Colter thought of what he had seen the last few months across Virginia and Tennessee. "It wouldn't surprise me if it happened within a month."

A half dozen longhorns scurried out of the mesquite brush and across the trail in front of them. "There goes $12.00..." Goodnight said, "Before the war, it would have been closer to $90." The longhorns were so thick that even at $12.00, Goodnight still stood to make a fortune if he could push the steers to a railhead like he planned.

Goodnight suddenly smiled as he remembered something, "I've got someone for you to meet." The two turned their horses and rode back to the east at a gallop watching wild longhorns scatter in the mesquite like a bunch of jackrabbits. They rode through the arroyos and looked at hundreds of unbranded cattle. They didn't see any with the Goodnight brand until they were nearly back to the Ranch house. Colter said "looks like you have lots of work runnin' around out her." Goodnight agreed "I can have our branding fires burning every day and it won't amount to a hill of beans compared to number of moss heads out there.

Goodnight turned his horse and ridding past the corrals and the bunkhouse and rode until they reached the chuck shack. As they got closer, Colter could see a curl of smoke coming from the chimney and watched an old man, bent at the waist, step outside with a cup of coffee in one hand and a big spoon in the other. "We've found he's a hell-of-a cook!"

116

Goodnight explained, "All I know is that he goes out to gather roots and herbs from the wild and adds it to his food. He makes the best tasting grub any of us ever tasted! He's cooking longhorn stew today and there's no question it's the best in the pasturelands. Every longhorn we've seen the past two hours has made my mouth water just knowing what was cooking back here in his shack, but that's not why I want you to meet him."

As they rode forward, the old man stood up straight for just a moment then started to slowly inch back down until walking nearly bent in half looking at the ground. As they rode up, Goodnight called out "Hola Mi Amigo!" The man turned with a big smile. "Senior Goodnight... I take it you are hungry, No?"

"I've been thinking about your stew since yesterday! Two bowls and some coffee, Juan!" The old man struggled to stand straight. The old man was bent in half again before he made it to the door. "When I found him a year ago," Goodnight said, "he had an Apache arrow sticking out of his back and he was next to dead. Even after I got the arrow out, I thought he was going to die, but he didn't. He's a tough old buzzard!"

"We brought him back to the bunkhouse and kept him there until he could get up and moving again. To thanks us, he cooked me and the boys supper. We've had him as our cookie ever since." The old man came back out of the shack with the two bowls of stew and handed them to Goodnight and Colter. Colter caught a whiff of the stew and could tell it was going to be good.

Goodnight introduced Winn, "Juan, this is a friend of mine. He's heading up north to the Utah territory." The man's eyes lit up. He now held up two tin cups and poured coffee. After tasting the stew, Colter agreed it was the best he had ever tasted. Goodnight looked back over his shoulder then said quietly "Just don't tell my wife we ate out here or she'll be mad." He rubbed his belly, "I've been eating an extra meal about four or five times a week. I put on some extra pounds like a fatted steer and can hardly fit in my trousers!" Colter laughed. Goodnight continued, "You'll learn boy. Some things are better left untold." He rubbed his belly again.

Colter turned his focus back to Juan as they sat back to enjoy their coffee and let their food digest. The old man looked to be in his late 60's and Colter had noticed that he could only stand straight for a moment. Then very slowly as pain in his back took control, he would begin to bend over until he was back in the position of almost looking at his toes.

Goodnight continued "Juan's told us of a lot of interesting experiences he's had. Only a fool argues with his cook, so we listen. I expect some of his stories are true and I won't be the one questioning." Colter nodded in agreement. Goodnight said, "After that arrow in the back, Juan's had to live with the pain. He told me his back was bad before the arrow, caused from working in gold mines down in old Mexico. But I know that arrow didn't help his back none!

Juan spoke to Colter and asked "You been to Utah Territory before Senior?"

"No," Colter said, "I'm taking a woman there to settle… to get away from Texas. My Ma and Pa were killed just down the trail so there's nothing holding me now."

Juan looked at this young man before him and saw how Senior Goodnight treated him. Juan said, "Let me tell you a story amigo about when I was a Chico." Juan went on to tell the same story he had told to Mr. Goodnight many times. When he ran into the Apaches, he was headed north to explore areas where his father had taken him as a boy. The old man excitedly told stories of the lands they now called the Utah Territory. It was all still part of Mexico at the time.

The men Juan's father had traveled with were all heavily armed though their weapons were very old. Five of them, including his father, wore their father's or grandfathers Conquistador metal breastplates and helmets. They packed ornately decorated matchlock and flintlock rifles and pistols and carried large Spanish swords. They were all fierce fighting men as well as miners.

These men had made this same trip many times to mine gold and silver and had explored farther north at times. The miners told Juan of two grand lakes at the base of a mountain that his father said looked like a sleeping woman. One of these lakes was fresh water and full of fish. The second grand lake was larger than the first and was salodo…salty and dead. Juan had only heard of this and other fantastic sites farther north and wanted to explore them before he died.

Juan explained that when he was nine years old, his father had let him travel with the group of men as they went north to mine gold and silver just as they did it every year, but the expedition would end in tragedy.

Juan realized now with his back injured, he could never make that ride again as he had hoped. He was happy here cooking for the ranch hands and Mr. Goodnight had welcomed him to stay. Juan didn't know why, but he told this young friend of Mr. Goodnight's some details he never shared with anyone. He explained how the group traveled through Santa Fe then up through the Taos Valley into the San Louis in Colorado. The miners then turned west into what is now Utah across the Rio Verde and the San Rafael . He talked about the "Rio Severo" or the wild river that flowed north.

Juan talked about everything like he had just been there last week, but it had been more than fifty years. Juan described the abundant wild game and the rich soils with rivers and streams they had found. He talked about gold and silver, but then he warned about the Indians… Juan's voice got shaky as he explained they had filled the packs of thirty mules and had just started to leave the canyon when they were attacked.

There was a brutal fight and Juan's father sent him to hide. He climbed a large pine tree and did just what his father had said… he hid. Through the thick branches he watched as all of the men, including his father, were killed and all of their pack animals were led away. The Indians came looking for him but they never looked up. At nightfall, he climbed down and went back up the canyon. He crossed some rugged terrain but ended up in the valley to the east where they had descended from the canyon to meet the Rio Severo. Juan traced his way back to Santa Fe then back to El Compo, deeper in Mexico.

Juan worked in the mines of Mexico until his body was worn out, but none of the gold ore they ever found in Mexico compared to what his father had found in that mine in Utah. Now that he was old. He wanted to explore and see some of the grand things his father and the other miners had described. But his quest ended with an Apache arrow in his back. He couldn't ride or stand, for that matter, without intense pain. Having Ranger Goodnight find him gave him new direction and hope. Ranger Goodnight had become a buen amigo.

Winn Colter thought the story was interesting about the gold, but he was only looking for a place to live in peace. Gold was the last thing he was thinking about at this time, but he paid close attention to Juan's directions of how to get to Utah. After listening to his descriptions of the Rio Severo , he hoped to find the valley with the wild river flowing north. From his descriptions, the area would be well suited to settle. Winn knew the Mormons were settling on every water source in the territory and he hoped the Mormons there would be friendly. Colter hoped he could make a future with Courtney and Chase. Right now, he just wanted to make sure he could get them there safe. Winn thought about it... Within a week, they would mount their horses and be off towards Santa Fe looking for the old Spanish trail.

-Part III-

CHAPTER 20

"Look here brother, they upped the reward on us!" Jon Kennedy held the wanted bills he had pulled from the dead Ranger's breast pocket. He looked at his hand and saw there was fresh blood on his fingers from the hole in the Ranger's chest. He left bloody fingerprints on the papers he had just pulled from the man's pocket. Jon reached down and wiped his hands on a clean spot on the front of the Ranger's shirt. "Yup! Looks like they upped the reward on us!" Jon Kennedy repeated to his brothers Westlee and Preston.

Preston Kennedy turned his head to the left and asked, "What you say Jon? You say they upped the reward on us?" Preston's right ear was disfigured and his hearing was completely gone on the right side since that damn gunsmith shot his ear off six years ago.

"Yea brother," Jon spoke louder, "They upped the reward on us!" Jon looked at his oldest brother and handed him the papers. "I told you Westlee! Killin' that Lubbock Sheriff, and harmin' his wife last year would come back to haunt us!"

Westlee was in a bad mood. He looked at each of the bills then said, "How was I to know that whore was his woman! "

"She wasn't a whore brother!" Jon shouted, "You were leavin' the cantina drunk when you saw her sittin' on her porch. You broke her damn door in ,Westlee!"

"She wouldn't let me in!"

"We both know what you did brother! Texas men don't stand for anyone harmin' a woman like that, specially a Sheriff's wife!" Jon was still disgusted with his brother..

Westlee countered, "That Sheriff shouldn't of had him such a handsome woman."

"Well brother, ever since then, the Rangers have really been after us. This is the fourth one I've killed in three months. They catch us now and we'll hang!"

Westlee spoke up to Jon, " You's lucky I got the drop on this one tonight brother, or you might be dead."

"You may of nicked him Westlee, but I put two bullets through his heart." Jon thought for a minute. He was disgusted with both of his brothers. Too much tequila and poor judgment was slowly adding up to more trouble. Things were getting out of control with these Rangers sneaking up on them. Hell, they killed two other Rangers the day before. Jon knew what they had to do. "I think we need to get out of Texas for a while, Brother."

"Because of you little brother, we can't go to Mexico now. I don't think that Mexicalli General's forgave ya yet," Westlee grumbled. " The Federales almost had us before we jumped the Rio Grande the night you stole the General's stallion." Westlee took a swig of Tequila then smiled at his brother Jon, "Remember, he chased us clear into Texas 'till we peppered his men with lead."

Jon was quick to remind his brother, "That horse is the best any of us ever owned... Ain't he? Besides, I took a bullet that night from one of those Federales for that horse. I paid in blood! My leg's barely getting healed up." Jon thought again for a moment then had an idea.. "Maybe we should get the rest of the boys and go into Arizona for a while. Or how about we go up to the Utah territory? We can rustle some cows and kill us some Mormons. Nobody 'll care! I hear lots of those Mormon's don't even have guns, Brother."

"No guns?" Westlee asked.

Jon said, "And I hear there's more women than men there too. Some Mormons have more than ten wives!"

Preston shook his head, "Well I'll be dammed!"

Jon had them thinking. "We can get away from the Rangers for a while. We may even get rich."

"I'd like that brother," Preston grinned, "and who knows, I may even get me some Mormon women too."

"Keep your breeches on brother! You may have some Mormon run you through with his pitch fork!" They all got a good laugh at that.

"I'll just kill 'em!" Westlee hissed. "They've never seen a bunch of Texans like us! We'll show 'em; Kill 'em all if we have to. Who knows," he started to smile, "maybe the government will even pay us to do it!" They all laughed again.

Jon looked down at the dead ranger and gave him a vicious kick. "These Some-bitches think they's gonna kill us? They can look all they want here in Texas. We won't even be here!" Jon could see his brothers were both thinking about the possibilities in Utah. "Who knows, Brother, we may even like it up there. Chase them damn Mormon's to the desert. Take their stock and their land. Have us a big ranch."

Preston Kennedy spoke up quickly, "And keep their women?

Jon laughed, "Only the pretty ones little brother...Only the pretty ones!"

The Kennedy brothers looked at each other and nodded. They had convinced themselves it was time to get away for a while. The Rangers were more persistent and taking more effort to come after them. Jon knew it was only a matter of time before one or all of the brothers would meet a bullet or find themselves at the end of a rope.

Mexico was the other option, but his brother was right. The Mexicali General was so mad that he ran a horse to death chasing after them. He told the boarder Mexicali's to threaten and kill anyone they thought bought or sold to the Kennedy gang. Jon could have stolen the General's mistress or his wife and the General wouldn't have cared as much as he did for that black stallion.

Westlee told the others to get the word out for the men to gather at the saloon in Abilene at dusk .

"Brothers," Westlee suggested, "Y'all get a good supply of ammo and say goodbye to your whores tonight. We may not see Texas for a long time. We ride out at daylight." With that, the brothers broke. Jon looked at the wanted bills in his hand. The first bill was for his brother Preston. It read: *$300 Dead, $500 Alive for one Preston Kennedy, wanted for the crimes of Murder, Bank and train robberies. The next page was Westlee's. $1,000 dead or alive for Westlee Kennedy (Alias Wess Kennedy.) Wanted for the crimes of murder, bank robbery, horse rustling and rape.*

Then he came to his bill. It looked like Texas really wanted to stretch his neck. The bill reads: *$2,500 Dead, $3,000 alive for Jon Kennedy Wanted for the crimes of Murder of two Texas Rangers, Bank, Train and Stagecoach robberies, Cattle rustling and horse theft. - $2,500 Dead or Alive!* Jon remembered that during the war, he wanted nothing more than a bad reputation. Now that he had it, it wasn't such a good thing after all. His reputation had nearly got him killed on three occasions, two of those being Rangers. If it hadn't been for his brother Westlee and that rifle of his, the number could have been twice more.

This was a good idea he had to go to Utah where nobody was after them. He thought about the women too. He smiled to himself thinking it would be nice to have ten women. He could train them and build a female gang that worshipped him. Who would ever suspect a bunch of women robbing a stage coach or maybe a mine payroll? How would his nights be sleeping with ten women? … Tired, he decided! Jon smiled to himself again. Utah could turn out to be a good move!

CHAPTER 21

At the saloon in Abilene, Westlee and Preston Kennedy stood amongst eleven known outlaws and several other men. Jon Kennedy addressed the group. "Okay boys, we're feeling the pressure of the Rangers coming down on us. There are rewards out on six or seven of us that I know of. They all think they can track us down, that they can kill us!" The room lit up in laughter.

"Me and my brothers came up with a plan. Now since the pressures up on all of us in Texas, we thought, why not ride up to the Utah Territory and kill us some Mormons." Several of the outlaws started to hooted and hollered their agreement.

Jon sold them on the idea, "I say we go up there and either chase those Mormons out, or just kill 'em! Then we take their stock, their land and any Mormon women we have a mind to! It gets us out of Texas away from the Rangers and we may all end up rich!" With that he garnered more hoots and hollers.

One of the outlaws asked, "What do you know 'bout them Mormons? I hear tell Salt Lake City is a big town. Bigger'n Dallas"

Jon replied "We'll stay away from Salt Lake City. We'll go south, 'long the Old Spanish Trail and find us a place to hole up." Preston spoke up and chimed in, "I hear the Indians chased the Mormons out afore. Most don't even have a gun, only a pitch fork!"

Jon looked at the men and knew almost every one. He wanted

assurance that all were going so none of the men were left behind to talk. He continued, "What guns they do have is mostly old muskets. Out a this bunch, I know we have at least six Henrys, four Spencer's, a Volcanic and I'm sure there's lots more."

Preston bragged, "Me and Westlee have our .32-70's. There's not another gun in the bunch that can shoot with them." Jon agreed, "Preston and Westlee have their rifles and that's not to mention all our revolvers." Jon and Westlee studied the group and liked what they saw. These were a tough group of men. Some were real gunslingers including Thomas and Sheldon Ashby who were both noted gunmen. Then there was the hotheaded Bo Ringo. There were some tough men in this group and Jon was impressed.

Jon spoke up to the group, "We're a small army with all of us together… No bunch of Mormons can stop us!" The entire group was hooting and hollering now firing a couple of shots fired into the ceiling of the cantina. Westlee exclaimed, "The South rises again boys. Let's do it!"

All of the men were fired up and there were lots of hoots and hollars! Many of them were wanted in Texas and five others were wanted in Arizona. More than half a dozen were wanted in Mexico too. Jon Kennedy topped that list being the most hated Gringo of the Mexican Federales. This was a chance for all of them to get away and not have anybody hunting them. In the last month, two of the boys had been captured and were in jail at Fort Concho.

Donny Driscol, another one of the gang had been killed by a Texas Ranger only days before. Two more men had been killed down in Mexico by the Federales the week before. Besides the law, Jack Perry had been hung by a rancher last week when he got drunk and was caught rustling a few cows. Jon and Westlee Kennedy both knew that with the killing of another four Rangers, the pressure to locate them would be more intense and they would lose more men.

Some of the outlaws were thinking of the kind of horses and cattle they might find in Utah and some were thinking of the possibilities of land for a ranch. A few of the men, including Preston Kennedy, were thinking more about all those Mormon women.

An outlaw by the name Perry Jones chimed in. "I'll bet those women never seen a real man like one of us from Texas. They'll all come a running begging us to bed 'em!" The men all laughed again. Jon warned, "Don't get your hopes up. Them women may all be ugly!" But the men were almost crazed, thinking of what they might find in Utah. Tomorrow they would be on the trail North through New Mexico on their way to Santa Fe. Then they would go on to Utah by way of the Spanish Trail that led from Santa Fe to California. Women and riches were waiting!

The outlaws had a wild night of women, whiskey and tequila. As the sun rose over the saguaro and Mesquite, a total of twenty-two men mounted up ready to ride north. Most every man had stocked themselves with supplies and most had at least one spare horse. There wasn't a spare box of ammunition, bottle of tequila or pound of coffee left in all of Abilene as every man packed all they could.

As the men rode out, the whores could now breathe a sigh of relief and get their rest. The saloon owner closed the batwings and polished the bar. It had been a long night and he had made a lot of money. From what he overheard, it may be a long time before he or the whores saw any of these outlaws again. Some had been good regular customers, decent fellows. But there were a few of the outlaws that scared him and his ladies.

Those Kennedy brothers were bad apples! If you saw one brother, you better be looking behind you for the others. They were coyotes! It had been said the brother you didn't see was the one most likely to stab you in the back… or even kill ya with a bullet from one of those rifles they always packed. Any disagreement with one of the Kennedy brothers resulted in a corpse or two. That's what the gambler "Smiling Rob Reynolds" found out after a poker game a few months before.

Reynolds had the luck… too good of luck, and Westlee lost nearly $100. At the end of the night, Reynolds disappeared when he walked out to the privy. All that was found the next day was a left boot and two ace cards down the alley. Of course, nobody saw anything…There was no doubt, the Kennedy brothers were flat out mean enough to eat off the same plate as a rattle snake. Nobody saw Smiling Rob Reynolds again.

The saloon owner looked over the batwings at the dust of the riders in the distance. Those boys had spent a lot of money for years in his saloon on whisky and women. They had even kept him supplied with painted women on occasion. It was something they always held over his head. It scared him…What if he disappeared going out to the privy like

Smiling Rob? The bartender thought to himself, "If those Kennedy brothers didn't ever come back, that would be too soon!"

CHAPTER 22

Rangers Goodnight and Paxton had been riding hard trying to catch up to the four Rangers sent out to investigate a recent rash of cattle rustling. Rumors had it that the Kennedy brothers had been seen in the area between Big Springs and Abilene, but there never was any proof they were involved in the rustling. They were still wanted men with a price on their head, but had somehow continually eluded the Rangers for the last three years. Now the Rangers were making an effort and were moving in, hoping the cattle rustling would help them find the Kennedys and the no-good outlaws who rode with them.

Every lead the Rangers tried to track down always ended with nothing. The Kennedys were very smart and rode fast horses. Sometimes they would disappear for months at a time without a single lead. The Rangers had all heard about the Kennedy's slipping into Mexico and stealing a Mexican Federale General's horse. All the Rangers had a good laugh, but it showed what the brothers were capable of. It wasn't a crime in Texas to steal from Mexico, but it wasn't helping border relations.

Goodnight and Paxton searched but hadn't been able to locate the four Rangers, so they rode into Abilene and headed for the Saloon. It had been a long dusty trail and the two were ready for a little relief. They needed to decide where to go next, to either find their fellow Rangers or the Kennedy brothers.

Goodnight and Paxton stepped through the batwings and waited a second for their eyes to adjust to the light. The place was dead, hardly a person inside other than a couple down on their luck, ranch hands, two soiled doves and the bartender. Goodnight called out, "Couple of Beers bartender, and give those cowboys and ladies a drink on me; and one for yourself if you want one!"

"Thank you Ranger!"one of the cowboys said appreciatively. Goodnight wondered how he was spotted for a Ranger so quickly until he looked at Paxton and saw his badge displayed prominently on his chest. He would have to talk to Paxton about that. Goodnight turned back to the cowboys and said, "I've rode the range many times myself. I can recognize good men when I see 'em."

Goodnight heard a commotion to the side of the bar and turned around. Whether it was the sound of a new voice in the saloon or his generous offer for drinks, there were now four painted ladies instead of two. His generosity for drinks was going to cost him more that he expected. Goodnight needed someone to do some talking and many times found a drink could buy a lot of information. All four of the women moved towards the Rangers hoping they could score some additional business.

"What's your name, Ranger?" one of the cowboys asked.

"I'm Goodnight and this is Paxton." Paxton's focus was on the four women, three of which surrounded him and had him backed up to the bar. Paxton took a sip of his beer and carefully watched the ladies. He was a new Ranger and was planning to just listen to Goodnight who seemed to be an expert at getting information.

"Thanks for the drink, Ranger," the first young gal standing by Goodnight cooed seductively. He knew what this was leading up to so he just played along. This young woman must have been new. The other doves were willing to let it all hang out, enticeing a cowboy into a back room. This young gal was well covered and unsure of what she should really do.

The bartender had been wiping sweat off his forehead from the moment he realized the pair were Rangers. He had backed away to the corner of the bar and was busily cleaning glasses. Goodnight caught a glimpse of the bartender trying to motion the ladies away from them, but the free drink was an open invitation and possibly an opening for some additional money. Income was harder to come by now since most of the area's men had mounted their horses and ridden out of town the week before.

"Goodnight? Any connection to the Goodnight Ranch up around

Mesquiteville?"

"Not many still call it Mesquiteville, but Yeah, that's my ranch." Goodnight's attention was focused on the cowboys much to the disappointment of the ladies. "It's Jacksboro now. Only a few of us first settlers still call it Mesquiteville."

One of the cowboys took a sip of his free beer then offered "We've heard good things about your ranch Ranger Goodnight. We've heard you have plans to drive cattle north to market soon. Do y'all need more riders, because we'd be lookin'. We've been riding the range for so long I believe we know every lizard by it's first name."

Goodnight looked close at the two men again, "What's your name, Cowboy?"

"Sorry, Mr. Goodnight. I'm Sean Pickard and this is Horus Johansson."

Goodnight tipped his hat, "Nice to meet you gents."

"Nice to meet you too, Sir." Pickard declared. "There's not many men about these parts if you're looking for riders since that big group that rode out last week. I only knew a few of those men but I don't know if'n I'd trusted those men anyways."

"Who rode out?" Ranger Paxton asked.

The young woman trying to get the attention back on her spoke quickly. "It was the Kennedys that rode out!" The bartender dropped the glass he was washing. It shattered at his feet.

"Kennedys?" Goodnight looked at the bartender who turned away and went to cleaning up broken glass. Not only was the man sweating but his head reddened as if the oxygen had been cut off at his neck. Goodnight could see his hands were shaking. Goodnight turned back to face the young lady who was happy to get the attention.

Goodnight kindly asked, "Kennedy... Which Kennedy?" The bartender whirled back around and glared over the bar at the young woman. She caught his look and instantly backed away, knowing she would be beat after the Rangers left if she said anything more. The other women had quietly backed away and disappeared into the other room. The Rangers only caught quick glimpses of the women when they tried to see what was happening in the cantina without themselves being seen.

The young girl had tears running down her face, knowing now she had said something that she shouldn't have.

"You can tell us… It's ok." Goodnight tried to comfort and reassure her. She still hesitated and started to shake her head back and forth "No…" Her eyes were pleading for help and her voice was shaky. "I don't know anything."

"You can tell us," Goodnight said, "I won't let anything happen to you." Goodnight thought he could now detect some bruises on the girl's face and arms. He hadn't noticed them before. She looked like she was about to speak when the bartender slammed his hands down on the bar, glaring at her again. At the same time, Goodnight pulled his pistol from its holster and leveled it between the eyes of the bartender who jumped back, now that he was looking down the barrel of a gun. The bartender raised his arms in the air still holding his bar rag in his right hand. The man stood about five foot six, had muscular forearms and a crooked nose. He may have been a boxer earlier in his life. He wasn't fat, but wasn't skinny either. The Ranger could see the man was past his better days.

Goodnight turned back to the crying girl. This young girl couldn't have been more than fifteen. She looked older before because of the way she dressed and the way her hair had been done. She acted older by the way she had presented herself, but the child in her was lo longer hidden.

Goodnight lowered his gun and the bartender lowered his hands until he heard Paxton's Colt click, as it was cocked. The bartender's hands went higher than before. Beads of sweat covered his chubby face and balding head. His white shirt was saturated with sweat. Paxton was only about five foot six, but his big Stetson hat and broad shoulders made him look closer to six foot. The pair of Colt Walkers strapped to his hips made him look taller too.

Goodnight's complete focus was on the young girl. Her huge blue eye filled with tears was enough to poke a man in the heart. "What's your name Hun?" The toughness was gone from the Ranger and all she could see was kindness flowing from this man's face.

"It's Rose… Rose Marie."

"How did you end up in this place? I can see you don't belong here."

She started to cry again. "My Mother and Father were killed not far from here."

"How'd it happen?"

The girl said "Shots from nowhere killed 'em; we seen nobody! Then I heard two more shots and the Kennedy brothers rode up to our wagon. Said they just killed the Indian that killed my parents. Said there might be more and they would help me... I don't think there were any Indians. They brought me here and..." She was shaking and held on to Ranger Goodnight's hand then she started to weep again. She glanced at the bartender, then to the floor, "He beat me and told me I worked for him now." Paxton walked around behind the bar still pointing his pistol at the bartender's head.

Goodnight looked hard at the bartender and asked the question he dreaded, "Did he..." He couldn't even ask, but the girl looked up and nodded yes. Paxton lowered his gun barrel slightly and stuck it up the bartender's nostril making him stand on his tip toes. The Ranger was seething with disgust. "You Son of a bitch!" Paxton then lifted a knee quick and accurately hitting the bartender hard in the groin, lifting him clear off the ground then letting him fall to the floor. There was blood flowing from the torn skin of his left nostril. From the back room Goodnight heard a woman's quiet voice "I wish I had done that!"

Paxton looked down at a wet spot on his knee. "I think he just pissed on my leg." Paxton was thoroughly disgusted. "You low life Bastard!"

"Rose Marie, I'll help you if you help us. What were the Kennedy brother's names?"

"They didn't say but I think it is Winn. Winn was engraved on his gun." The name about floored Ranger Goodnight. He had been searching for this lead for over six years and the bomb just hit him. "Are you sure it said Winn?"

A woman's voice from the back room corrected, "His name isn't

Winn, it's Westlee, but that gun does say Winn." A scantily clad red haired woman moved out of hiding. What she was wearing barely left any room for the imagination for what was underneath. "He brings that gun to my room when he comes to visit."

"Shut up, Woman!" the bartender yelled angrily from the floor. Paxton's boot caught the man in the gut hard enough to lift him off the floor again. The bartender let out a horrific wheeze as all his wind escaped. Then he started to puke.

"They always keep those guns close," the redhead added. "His brother Preston has one just like it that has Weston engraved on it. Preston keeps the name covered with leather but I saw it." She could see the curious looks from the Rangers and the cowboys. "He was too drunk to do anything and passed out, so I played with his gun." There was still curious looks from the Rangers. She said, "I like guns. Is that a problem?" There was no comment from anyone. The woman thought for a moment then continued, "Jon has several guns but usually packs a Spencer." She thought again for a moment. "There was another brother but he got himself killed some years ago, about five, six years ago I believe. Same time Preston got his ear shot off."

Ranger goodnight mused for a moment. The pieces were starting to come together. He couldn't leave Rose Marie here because he was fearful what the bartender might do in retaliation. Goodnight turned to the two cowboys "Do you want a job?"

"Yes Sir!" Any prospect of a job sounded good .

"Take Rose Marie to my ranch and tell Mrs. Goodnight I sent her. Tell her this girl's parents were killed and Mrs. Goodnight will take it from there. Then talk to my ranch foreman and tell him I offered you a job. It never hurts to have a few extra men that are worth their salt."

Horus Johanson hadn't said a word but now spoke up, "We'd like to stay just long enough to strip that bartender naked and let a wild horse drag him through cactus. He's not a Texan! No Texan would ever treat a woman like he has… the yellar, carpet baggin' snake!"

The group of women looked at the bartender and the redhead chimed in, "He's pushed too far. Us girls can handle him. I've got a pepperbox and a Smith and Wesson, and Milly," another woman stepped out of the back holding a Winchester, "Milly has a double barrel coach gun." Milly stood there with a mischievous smile on her face, then tauntingly said, "And I have a Baby Bowie too." A look of shock was on the face of more men than just the bartender. Her smile as Milly talked, made every man pay attention to every word.

"Tie me to the horse!" the bartender pleaded in a panic but the Ranger just sat him in a chair facing the armed women. He looked frantically from one to the next then to the Rangers. "Arrest me! Take me with you! Look at them!" There was no doubt these girls could handle themselves.

Goodnight reminded him, "A man who beats a woman or girl in Texas eventually gets his. Let's go see the Governor, Paxton." Ranger Paxton looked at the petrified man and the look in those women's eyes. He shook his head and just said "I don't want to know."

The cowboys smiled to themselves as they helped Rose Marie mount a horse and ride away with them, headed toward the Goodnight ranch. Whatever she had endured for the past few days, she was now going to be all right.

CHAPTER 23

"Governor, we have evidence!" Goodnight looked across the desk at Governor Edmund J. Davis. "It's out of our jurisdiction!" Davis replied, "You know as well as I that we can't get permission for you to cross over into New Mexico same as we keep the New Mexico Rangers out of Texas."

"I know Governor, but this is personal!" Goodnight pleaded, "These men are smart and we may never get a chance if they figure we know."

"Can't help that. If they come back to Texas, then the Rangers can get them. But until they do, they're out of Texas jurisdiction!" Goodnight knew what the Governor said was true, but should he let the New Mexico Rangers know what they were dealing with or wait 'til they came back and show them some Texas justice! For a moment, Goodnight thought of the fate of the bartender at the hand of those ladies, but quickly put it out of his mind before he smiled.

"Besides Goodnight," the Governor continued, "When you think about it, what evidence do you really have? Some guns that you can't prove were stolen. Cattle and horse theft that we we're investigating, but haven't proved. Two dead settlers that three Kennedy's claimed were killed by Indians. Then there's a six year old murder that we can't tie them to. You can't even prove they did anything to that young girl other than help her." The Governor wiped his sweaty forehead. "Any good lawyer worth his salt would get 'em off!"

Goodnight was disgusted, because the Governor wouldn't back

him on anything. "We're missing four Rangers Governor! Over the past several years we've had other killings that never got solved. "

Governor Davis continued, "I'm not sure we can even prove the murders we've got the reward out on them for. Can we prove any of these other Rangers are missing because of the Kennedys?"

"No Governor. Guilty as sin and no "real" proof!" Goodnight couldn't think what to do.

The Governor offered, "We can charge the Barkeep you told me about. Why didn't you arrest him?" Goodnight fumbled with an answer... "We needed to come here to talk to you to go after the Kennedys! Besides, we're sure he'll get his for what he done." Goodnight was smiling and nodding as Paxton fought to hold off a laugh.

The Governor looked at the two Rangers and asked, "What you smiling for... No, don't tell me!"

The Governor was quiet for a moment. "I'll send a wire to the New Mexico and Colorado Governors to inform them of what they're dealing with the Kennedy brothers. Hell, we're not even sure if that's where they are!"

"If you won't let me go after 'em then that's all I can ask Governor Davis." As angry as Goodnight was for not trying to get him clearance to follow the Kennedys into New Mexico, he still treated the man with respect.

"You do good work, Ranger! Find a way to get evidence on 'em."

"Thank you, Governor."

****

Westlee, Preston, and Jon Kennedy led an assortment of Texas outlaws north into New Mexico and up through Santa Fe. Jon Kennedy was right, the Rangers were moving in and it was only a matter of time before they would have to face it off with them. If the reward was tempting enough, a fellow outlaw or a bounty hunter might try to collect reward money with a bullet in the back. Even as careful as the Kennedy's had been, years of killings and rustling created trails that were all be leading back to the same location, Grayson County. When the question came to who, the Kennedy name was one that kept coming up quite regularly. Four Rangers had been sent out to specifically question the Kennedys and they hadn't been heard from since. Everyone in Texas knew if someone gunned down one of their fellow officers, the Rangers would never forget! Now that they'd killed four more, it was something the Kennedys needed to remember!

Preston Kennedy was missing the security and comforts of home. He missed his visit to see Sherrie, the red haired beauty that he rode in to Abilene to see every month. A little fun right now with Sherrie, or the feisty brunette Molly was all Preston could think about. If it wasn't for those Damn Rangers! He spoke out loud to nobody in particular, "We should of just stayed in Texas and keeled 'em… Keeled any Ranger came our way."

"But how many of us would get killed doin' it Brother?" Jon had to ask the question to make his brother Preston think. Of the three brothers, Jon was the youngest but there was no doubt he had the brains. He was always the one to think through plans. It was because of him, the Kennedy brothers had stayed undetected by the law in Texas for so long.

Jon cautioned, "Think smart Brother! We just keep some of the new guys out front. If there's trouble, it'll be them that gets shot instead of us. Didn't y'all learn nothing from the war?"

Westlee was close enough to hear what Jon had said to Preston "I learned something from the war, little Brother. Even Majors and Generals got themselves killed!"

Jon added, "I'm not ready to get myself shot or hung Brother. And I don't plan on spendin' time in no prison cell! We have twenty-two good men ridin' with us, Brother, and we're better equipped than an army regiment! Ain't no group of Rangers stand a chance, or no Mormons neither!"

Jon reminded them they were doin' this to get the Rangers off their backs and to have a little fun. "Who knows, we could come out rich!"

Preston wanted to make it very clear to Jon the reason he was along. "I want those Mormon Women! That's what I'm coming for, Brother!"

"Keep your breeches on, Big Brother! Y'all have plenty of time for those Mormon Women. We just need to be smart. Do thingS right and anything that we want will be ours! Us Kennedys have done well so far and we can keep doin' it as long as we're smart!"

Preston's mind was racing. He knew Jon had kept them away from a hangman's noose and avoided the Rangers most of the time because he thought things out. Jon was right, but he wouldn't wait long to get him a woman…. No, he thought again, lots of women!

-Part III-

CHAPTER 24

It was late in the fall, 1871, in the Utah territory. Winn Colter sat on the mountain top overlooking the small valley he had called home for six years. Winn pulled the coffee pot off the small fire and poured himself a cup. He loved the aroma and the taste of coffee, but it had been a long time since he had had any. As he replaced the pot to the coals, a cool breeze went down his neck and sent shivers down his spine. The flutter of leaves in the wind made him look to his left where he saw a doe and fawn feeding along the meadow unconcerned with his presence.

The grove of aspen trees behind him were a mixture of colors in yellow, red and green and behind them was an upshot of one hundred fifty feet of granite with a small cave at the base. Winn could see the blacked roof of the cave and knew it had been used by some weary traveler not long before.

Slightly to the south, on the other side of the meadow in another grove of aspens, sat the scattered remnants of an old cabin, probably built more than a hundred years back by the Spanish as they searched for Gold in this area. It looked like it had been knocked down many years before and hidden. If Winn hadn't seen the signs of the developed spring, he probably would have missed the old cabin. Now that he looked, he could see a Maltese Cross carved in one of the old trees. There was no doubt, the Spanish had spent some time here. The way the cabin had been destroyed showed something bad had happened here.

Stories of Eldorado, the City of Gold, still lingered and occasionally strings of mules with Mexican miners were still traveling along the Spanish

Trail. Story was that a priest named Father Escalante lead a group exploring through this area in 1776. Now even a hundred years later, Winn had seen Mexican miners on two occasions. At first, hi figured, both groups continued along the Trail to California, but not long after the second group of miners passed, a lame mule came wandering out of a canyon above his homestead.

The pack had some miner's tools and an ancient Spanish map with markings indicating what Winn believed to be mines and old missions. Winn studied the map which was very detailed, but also very old. Someone had put many hours into creating this map which must have been important to the men who lost it. Winn recognized parts of the trail. The map called the valley the De Santa Isabella, and listed the river as Rio Severo. It also marked several mine locations including two to the east, several to the south and two Northwest, where the mule wandered from. The real surprise was that the pack also concealed six small bars of gold! It all started to fit together with the story he heard from Juan, the old man in Texas at the Goodnight Ranch.

From several vantage points, Winn had looked at the terrain and had seen most of the major drainages that flowed both east and west. He figured from this little meadow, which was nearly on top, he must be some five to ten miles south of the old Spanish gold mine that Juan had told him about, so the Spaniards that built this cabin had been here for another reason. Either the Spaniards had built a small Mission here, had another mine or something else close by that wasn't listed on the old map. Someday soon, he thought, he would explore this area more closely and maybe work his way over to the next major drainage that he believed held the old Spanish mine.

While riding, Winn had found Indian sign in this small flat and around the hill by another spring; he had also located the remnants of a recent Indian village. There was no doubt from the sign that the Indians liked this place too. His exploring of the area would have to wait until next spring because time was running out. Cooler weather would soon grasp the high country. Fall had left her mark and Winn needed to push on to find his missing cows.

The sun was fading quickly to the west and the shadows were already crossing the small grassy meadow behind him. Winn looked to the east across the valley at the majestic granite cliff that towered thousands of feet over the valley below. He then looked to the south at the two towering bald peaks in the Tushar Mountains which had already been dusted with the first snow of the year. It wouldn't be long before this whole area would feel the bite of winter. He was thankful, it hadn't happened yet. Looking at the sky and feeling the nip in the air, he knew winter could come any day.

Winn now took a long look at the large granite cliff face that overshadowed the valley below and felt a tightening in his chest when he thought of what had caused him to be sitting here looking at this beautiful sight. Winn thought about his incredible journey that had all started in a small hidden valley in Tennessee.

Was it fate delivered him here? Winn couldn't answer that, but it had been a turning point in his life. It was the start of a journey to a place where he hoped to live out his life away from violence. He had seen his share of death and mayhem during the war and later in Texas. He hoped for a place away from all that. Looking again at the valley, he knew this was the place. He was thankful "Fate" had delivered him here.

He knew living in the west, they would likely have to deal with some problems. It was unavoidable, but Winn hoped living amongst the Mormons would allow him and Courtney to live in relative peace; in a place that not many white men had traveled, let alone wanted to settle.

Winn found the Utah Territory and the Mormons were a welcoming people after they decided he wasn't a threat to them. He and Courtney had followed the California leg of the Spanish Trail that led north from Santa Fe, then turned west into a mountainous desert. They followed the trail into the badlands of Utah crossing the Colorado, then on to a crossing of the Green River at a stop on the Overland Mail Rout called Blake's Station. After forging the Green, they followed the trail through the San Rafael Swell, across Castle Valley, then down a steep and rugged canyon. The ride down the canyon was an un-nerving gauntlet to anyone traveling through. Winn could feel eyes upon them as they descended the canyon; but there was no other way. The canyon's narrow walls made Winn sick because of his shooting experience as he was sure he could see Indian or Yankee sharpshooters hiding behind the rocks and trees. He knew It had been his imagination…at least he hoped.

After descending the steep mountain gorge, they entered the first Mormon town at the mouth of the canyon which was named Salina. There, the settlers sent them north to a town called Manti in the Sanpete Valley to meet with church leaders; but they, in turn, sent them back south asking Winn if he would help settle in the south end of the Sevier Valley. The area they were asked to settle was a newly re-settled town, Joseph, which was named after a Mormon Stake President Joseph A. Young. Indians had driven out settlers earlier and it was just being resettled by a few families. Some who had settled there in the past had been called to settle farther south in Washington County and wouldn't be coming back.

After Winn thought about it, he remembered how the church leaders in Manti were eyeing his guns. His guns either scared those men and they wanted to get him some distance away because of the threats to leaders. It could also have been because of the recent hostilities with Indians, they wanted his guns to help protect the small groups of settlers in Joseph and over to Fort Alma at South Bend. Six towns had been established so far in the long, narrow valley including Gunnison, Salina, Big Spring, Glen Cove, Alma and now Joseph. Church leaders where now pushing to settle and establish other communities in the valley as well. Winn found the majority of the new settlers in the area were poor Danish immigrants who couldn't afford a gun, didn't know how to use one and wouldn't be able to protect themselves.

Winn found these peace-loving people had a history of being persecuted ruthlessly before they came to the Utah territory. They told him about the first leaders of the church being kicked out of New York, then being driven from Illinois as their church founder was murdered by a mob while in a jail. One of Winn's neighbors told him a story how he barely survived an attack on his family when the Missouri Governor issued an extermination order to kill all Mormons. He told Winn that many of the Mormons came west to Mexico to escape persecution. The territory was later purchased from Mexico in the Treaty of Guadalupe and was first was called Deseret, but soon changed to Utah. Even here, violence and persecution still existed and still haunted these people. No matter where these Mormons went, they were magnets for evil men that would take advantage of anyone they perceived as weak.

Winn still held the warm cup in his hands and took a sip. He found himself lost in thought remembering some of the terrible things he had seen six years ago. He still remembered how the war was nothing like he had ever imagined when he was so eager to leave home and join the fight.

He was now thankful his father held him back as long as he did. Of the three boys he was ready to join with when he was 13, two never made it home, and one came back all shot up, missing an arm and an eye.

Winn often wondered how his father could have known how bad the war would be. He knew his Pa had fought in the Mexican American War, but Weston never talked about it. Whatever he had done or experienced during that war had changed his Pa's life. It was the reason Pa had become a gunsmith. Whatever he saw had made him weary of war but fascinated with weaponry. Winn wished Pa had told him more about his fighting; but then again, knowing how determined he was at the time, such stories would probably have made him want to go fight even more. He was sure that is why his Pa never told him.

During Winn's short time in the war, he had known plenty of evil men; and, in most cases, he loathed them. He put a bullet into some. Others he despised were fighting for the Confederacy… on the same side. Both sides had their share of evil men. Soldiers followed orders. They did their duty and many thousands died. Winn knew that as the sad truth of war.

Winn assumed that the battles he saw and experienced were nothing like the Revolutionary War or the War of 1812 that he'd read about in school. He felt guilty for how he'd treated his Pa when he thought he was going to miss the war and miss his chance fighting for the Confederacy, helping win victory for the South! Now he knew his Pa was right about war. Too many senseless deaths! Too many men who never got to see home or family again. Too many went home with scars or even missing arms or legs. Winn thought of Mr. Duncan missing his arm and his sons. Life would never be the same. The war had changed everything…

Hostilities brought out the worst in some men. Winn figured many more soldiers and civilians died by the hands of men because some took pleasure in killing, creating all the destruction and pain they could, smiling while they did it. Winn recalled some terrible atrocities that still haunted him.

Besides the countless number of dead soldiers, innocent townspeople had been killed and their livelihoods destroyed by the likes of Bloody Bill Anderson and General William Sherman as he ran his "scorched earth campaign." Winn saw plantations and cities burned… and experienced the stench of death on the battlefields everywhere! He wished those memories would go away because he knew that is what had changed him.

Those memories ate at his insides and woke him up at nights. To this day, he could still see the faces of men he couldn't help. He could hear their cries or sometimes their wives' or mother's cries. The nightmarish thoughts made him thankful the war was over and now even more thankful that he had the chance to get away from his past. Thank God that war was over now!

Winn shook himself out of his thoughts and glanced back over the valley as he sipped again from his tin cup. Sometimes, old memories popped up to haunt him like this one. There were no winners in war, only losers that had to pay with their blood. His Pa was right!

Many western men who spent a lot of time in the saddle or riding alone, found their minds in constant motion. In the west, a man had better stay focused, because there were dangers out there that could kill him. After spending a significant amount of time without any sign of trouble, even the most focused mind tended to wander. When things were quiet, a cowboy could be inventing a better way to do things, thinking of women or sometimes trying to solving past mysteries. After five days riding the hills, Winn's mind was bouncing from one thing to another and he knew that could be dangerous. Winn had thought how long it had been since he heard anything from Mr. Goodnight. Winn had ridden to Gunnison some forty miles to the north two years ago to send a telegram to the Texas Rangers. It was addressed to Ranger Goodnight, and read:

Goodnight. Doing good. Rio Severo, Joseph, Utah Territory. Catch killers? He signed it only with Winn.

Mr. Goodnight had replied with a telegram two weeks later and it read:

Kid dead in Mexico. Mexican banditos and rustlers more brazen. Ranger's hands full. Have not forgotten your Ma and Pa. He signed it Texas Ranger George Goodnight.

It had been nearly six years and the Rangers still had not found the men who killed his Ma and Pa. Whoever had done the killing had kept quiet which meant they were either smarter than the average outlaw or somebody that left the area and never looked back.

Lots of soldiers returned to Texas after the war to find they had lost land and possessions to carpetbaggers. Many of those same soldiers tried to rebuild their lives in Texas, but others left and went to California or to Mexico. Some turned to stealing and taking advantage of honest Texans.

Winn heard every gunslinger with nowhere to go after the war, headed to Texas to become a bounty hunter, outlaw or both. Winn knew if "Kid Colter" had stayed in Texas, there was no doubt that unexplained killings or rustling would have been blamed on him because of the reputation that dogged him. He knew he could have been challenged to a shootout or worse yet, some gunslinger would have put a bullet in his back to collect the Union reward, prove how tough he was or to build his own reputation. The best thing… the only chance Winn had to have any normalcy in life was to do just what he had done, load up Courtney and Chase on the horses and leave Texas.

Winn had occasionally thought about the possibility of returning to Jacksboro to see Mr. Goodnight and possibly drive home some longhorns to strengthen his herd. Now looking over the Sevier Valley… the "wild river" below him, he knew he had more important things in his life now. His family and future were here! He would have liked to see his Ma and Pa's murderers brought to justice, but it wasn't important any more. Courtney and his two boys were all that mattered now.

*****.

CHAPTER 25

As they entered the Utah territory, the Kennedy Gang crossed the Colorado River at the Crossing of the Fathers, then rode north to cross the Green River at Blake's Station, a new little town just getting its start. Blake's Station served as a stop on the Overland Mail Route. Jon and Westlee talked to Thomas Farerer, the station operator, and he told them the news of what was going on in the valleys to the west. There had been some farming development in Castle Country, but Farerer was most excited about the discovery of gold in the Tushar Mountains at the South end of the Sevier River Valley. He didn't know how much gold had been found but he heard it was good find. Farerer mentioned how new gold camps were born with every rumor of gold. Two new camps had started up recently and were booming!

All of the men were amazed at the rough terrain as they rode across the San Rafael Swell into Castle Valley. They then followed the Old Spanish Trail down a rugged canyon that eventually ran into a narrow valley with a northerly flowing river. The first thing the riders saw as they came out of the canyon was the small Mormon settlement called Salina. Not too long ago Salina had been abandoned because of Indian troubles, but the town was active again.

The Texans could see these people had laid out the town in square blocks and were building a number of homes. This was the first real signs of settlement they had seen since Santa Fe. These Mormons had built a church, a school and a small fort built on the east side of town. The Kennedys saw a formation of a dozen riders holding rifles emerge from the fort heading north, so Jon and Westlee decided to avoid trouble right away before they knew what they would be up against. They decided to bypass the town of Salina and continue riding to the south. There may have been a dozen riding out to the north but there was no way of telling how many more remained. They kept riding south to get closer to where Thomas Farerer said the gold camps were supposedly located.

About fifteen miles farther south, the group decided they would go into the next town to get some information and supplies; but as they came closer to that settlement, everyone was shocked at what they saw. A Texans named Sean Applegate questioned," Is the Army here Jon? I didn't come here expectin' to fight the Army." His brother Willard Applegate looked at the rock structure, "Would y'all look at that…That ain't no Army fort. Look at it… It's huge!" Seeing the sight before them didn't offer any comfort to the Texans as they all remembered the siege at the Alamo, but that was an adobe structure and wasn't built anything like this. All the men were looking at a red rock fort the size of a city block built with solid red rock walls some twelve feet tall. They could see the top the walls were over two feet thick and the base over 4 feet. The Army didn't build forts like this out here in the west.

"I thought these were supposed to be defenseless Mormons," one of the outlaws said with concern in his voice. "Yea," another Texan spoke up. "Y'all said lots of women." There actually were a lot of women; but everyone they saw, men and women, was busy working. "Look," Jon whispered, "I don't see a gun amongst 'em."

"But they-all have a fort!" Willard Applegate replied. Sean Applegate was acting nervous and it was catching among the younger Texans. Of the twenty-two total riders, four had never been in trouble or had the law even look at them. Willard and Sean Applegate were brought along as camp cooks but their cousins, Thomas and Sheldon Ashby, had ridden with Jon Kennedy before and had reputations for their shooting skills. With the exception of Jon Kennedy, or Bo Ringo, Thomas and Sheldon Ashby were the two most noted gunmen in the group of outlaws, more noted gunmen than Westlee or Preston Kennedy. The Ashbys had been fierce fighters for the Confederacy and had ridden with the infamous John Mosby, the Gray Ghost of the South, during some of the most bitter fighting of the war. The Ashbys fast, accurate guns had been a big part of Mosby's success. They had only ridden with the Kennedys for six months and now look at them… wanted by the law in three states and old Mexico. Now they were hiding out in the Utah territory.

The large group of Texans standing around at the edge of the fort was gaining some attention. Jon told the men to scatter out a bit and wait. He looked at the group and warned, "Don't do notin' to start trouble!" The men quietly moved out trying to blend in; but in a town of 150 people, that was almost impossible. There was a school, a livery, a general store. A new hotel was being built just down the street. These Damn Mormons, they didn't even have a saloon! How were they going to fit in? Preston Kennedy was drooling seeing the women of the town. He would have grabbed one if Jon hadn't told him he had to wait. He wasn't going to wait long!

Westlee looked around the busy little town, "This is different than I expected, Jon." Jon looked around and replied, "Different than I expected too Brother, We just change plans some if we need to. Let's mosey in to the general store and ask some questions." Jon glanced around; there were a lot of women now that he really noticed.

As they stepped inside, a bell rang above their head. The store was so small Jon couldn't understand why the shopkeeper needed a bell when it was only ten steps from front to back. The first thing Jon saw was an old muzzleloader rifle leaned up against the back of the store. Jon smiled for just a second when the shopkeeper turned and said, "Welcome, Brothers!" Jon and Westlee looked at each other quickly. "How you know we's brothers?"

The shopkeeper looked embarrassed. "Sorry, it's just habit." Just then a young man walked in the front door and smiled, "Brother Jensen!"

"Good day Brother Hansen, I'll be with you in a moment." The man turned back to the Kennedys, "New to the area? Welcome to both of you! Can I help you today?" The young man had answered their question as to why the man called them brothers. "We need a side of bacon, ten pounds of beans and five pounds of coffee."

"Bacon's in the smoke house out back, take just a minute." The shopkeep turned to the other fellow that had come in the store to ask for a favor. "Brother Hansen, would you help me with that bacon?"

"Of course!" The man ran out the door and headed for the smokehouse. Westlee thought that these Mormons talked funny. "Have your beans and coffee in just a moment." The shopkeeper started to weigh the coffee on a scale.

Westlee asked, "Why y'all have a fort here?"

"Ah, you're not from around here. We've had Indian troubles…real bad! Chief Blackhawk signed a peace treaty a few years ago but he died and there's been a struggle in the tribes. We don't know if they're still honoring the treaty. Oh, there are lots of friendly Indians out there, but there's still some that would just as soon try to kill us." Mr. Jensen turned to look at the men behind him, "Those Indians are always watching out there, so be careful! We still have to keep guard and travel in groups for safety."

Mr. Jensen delivered the beans and was now working on the coffee. "We're all just getting back in the area. At least those that dared came back. There are several families moving on to St. George or a new settlement called Las Vegas. But things are feeling somewhat better now in this valley. If you want to keep your hair, you better keep an eye out for Indians."

Jon asked "What about to the south? We heard they found gold."

"Oh yea, isn't that something? They're pulling a lot of gold out of those hills to the south." The shopkeeper stopped what he was doing and looked straight at the Kennedys. "I mean lots of gold!" He turned back around to weigh coffee. The Kennedy brothers looked at each other "How much is lots… five pounds; ten pounds a week?"

The shopkeeper stopped again. "They send seventy pound bars down every couple weeks."

Westlee was astonished and thought he heard wrong. He asked again. "Did you say a seventy pound bar?"

The store keeper turned around with the beans and coffee in his hands. "No Sir, I said bar with an "S"! Nobody knows how many. That's kept secret by the mine bosses." Jon Kennedy was thinking they had hit the jackpot! The shopkeeper was a wealth of knowledge, but they would have to find out a lot more about when and how much gold was shipped from the gold camps. Jon thought if they worked this right, they could be leaving here very rich men!

The Kennedys paid for their goods and hurried out of the shop to get the men out of town. Jon excitedly looked at Westlee, "Did you hear that Brother? Seventy pound bars! We need to think this out and do this right. We need to find out all we can about that gold."

Westlee agreed, "I about fell over when he said seventy pound bars. Oh Brother, I never would have imagined!"

Jon expressed, "We need to keep the boys in close, Brother. This is big! We don't want to screw this one up!"

" No, Brother, we surly don't!"

Jon thought for a second," Let's go south and find a place to hole-up, and then, Brother, we start planning this right." Back with the Texans, Jon Kennedy told the group about the gold and the Indians. "We can't be reckless! If we do this right, boys, we'll all go home rich!"

Preston Kennedy rode up to his brothers, "What about the women, Jon? I came to get women Brother."

"Oh you'll get some women, but we're talkin' about lots of gold first! More gold than we ever dreamed of. I think we can get it! I got an idea to get some good money… good money, Brothers! I'll think about it and we can talk to the men later."

Preston was making sure Jon wouldn't forget. "Think about those women too, Brother!" Jon shook his head and laughed. "Preston, I know what you're thinking… Just keep your breeches on!"

****

The shopkeeper had told the Kennedys that Chief Black Hawk had signed a peace treaty only a few years back. Things had been mostly calm between the Mormons and the Utes, but there were still some wild Indians that didn't want peace and would still attack given any opportunity. Some of these Indians were enraged that Black Hawk had given up to the whites. They had not given up!

Occasionally a settler or a miner would haphazardly wander off into the woods or up a canyon without paying attention. Men that were careless about their surroundings and forgot about the ever present dangers that lurked in the wilds of the territory sometimes just disappeared or were found full of arrows and bullet holes. There was also a lot of danger for women who were left home alone. Those that couldn't shoot and sometimes even those that could were found dead or were just outright missing.

Nobody in these parts wanted to see the trouble between the Indians and settlers start up again. Leaders of the church had counseled members that it was better to feed the Indians rather than fight them. Though they tried, the hostilities had been bad for the Mormon settlers early on during the Blackhawk War. Threats of attack had been so severe that settlers in the valley had to abandon their homes for fear of attack.

This area remained completely abandoned for nearly three years with everyone sent back to the Sanpete Valley because of tensions with the Indians. Chief Blackhawk had gathered fighting men from the Utes, Goshutes, Piutes, Navajos and other tribes to attack the Mormons and steal cattle. Blackhawk had been a effective leader and had built an active fighting force putting terror into many of the poor immigrant's minds. Some of the Danish immigrants that settled in the area were so poor they had only rakes and shovels for protection.

When the Mormons returned to resettle the Sevier Valley, they built three forts. Fort Salina was built near Salina Creek in Salina; Fort Alma was built at South Bend which later changed its name to Monroe, and Fort Omni , the largest of the three was built in the town of Big Spring. The name of the town was changed to Omni, but soon changed to Richfield because of its rich fertile soil. It was said the soil was so rich you could put a thumb tack in the ground at night and it would have grown into a ten-penny nail by morning. That was the rumor.

******

Another day of riding and Winn was nearly spent. As he often did, Winn would find himself deep in thought about all he had gone through the past few years and how thankful he was that he and Courtney had chosen this place to build their home together. Winn was on the mountain, looking down at the valley below. This was where he had hoped would be his chance to live out his life away from the violence he would have inevitably faced had he stayed in Texas. Even though it was Utah, Winn knew living in the west would always have some problems, but he hoped living amongst the Mormons would allow him and Courtney to live in peace. After all, this small valley was a place not many white men had ever traveled let alone wanted to settle.

Given the recent troubles with the Indians, this was still considered the Wild West and a dangerous place to be living away from the forts. This area needed resilient men and women who could hold their own in settling, tough men and women like Winn and Courtney Colter.

The three forts in this valley were non-military, all built by the Mormon settlers for protection from Indians. In fact, the nearest Army Fort was Fort Douglas nearly 150 miles to the north where they were more concerned about the Mormons than the Indians. In fact, the Indians were almost encouraged to attack Mormons because the Indians knew there would be no reprisal from the United States Army. The Mormons didn't ask for help from the Army because indications were that after they handled Indian troubles, they would move on the Mormons next. The whole triangle between the Indians, the Army and the Mormons was an ugly mess!

Winn glanced to the south of the valley and spotted the willows and the line of cottonwood trees that grew along the river bottom below his home. He couldn't quite see the house itself which was hidden in a small cove a little farther to the south. The main trail by the river was actually part of the Spanish Trail which split into two legs. That was where the Sevier River and Clear Creek joined a half mile beyond Winn's homestead. One of the legs of the trail followed the river south through the canyon to Piute County. The other trail crossed the mountain to the west and dropped into Millard County where a Mormon by the name of Ira Hinkley had built a lava rock and limestone fort. Cove Fort was used as a way station along the Mormon Corridor for travelers half way between the towns of Fillmore and Beaver, as protection against Indians. Winn was aware that a sulfur deposit had just been found a mile south of the fort. Some men were talking and there were rumors a new mining town would be built there soon.

Winn and Courtney had been in the Territory for six years and the Mormons had always treated them well. The Mormons accepted them into their growing community with very few questions. Winn knew he looked young and most neighbors thought he looked too young to have fought in the war, so few questions were ever asked. All Winn knew was that no one came looking for him and that meant a lot.

There was a rumor that someone calling himself "Kid Colter" had been shot and buried down in old Mexico after a run-in with Mexican Federales. The rumor didn't bother Winn because he never wanted a reputation in the first place. If some dumb outlaw took his reputation and was buried in a grave marked for him, then the outlaw deserved it! Winn was actually very thankful that the dead outlaw took his name because it relieved the worry of anything interfering with his life. Winn and Ranger Goodnight knew the truth. That's all that mattered.

Everything seemed to be going right for him now. Indian troubles were few and far between. His cattle herd was starting to grow and he was feeling at peace. Winn thought about it and he knew for sure leaving Texas and coming to this valley was the best thing that could have happened to him and probably saved his life. He was building his future here with his family and had no doubt that he was the luckiest man in the west here in Utah with Courtney and his two boys.

Courtney was the most handsome woman in the Territory and still took his breath away with her smile or even just the sparkle in her eyes. Chase was now eight and had grown into a young man. His little tow-head brother Weston, who was named after his Grandpa, was now three and growing faster than a rag weed after a rain.

Winn was thinking about Courtney and how long he had been away from home. Feeling the cool nip in the air, he now knew how a man could get soft after getting used to having a warm body in the bed next to him. Sleeping on the ground never used to bother him, but it did now. He had been sleeping on the ground and in the saddle for a nearly a week and he was ready to turn for home. His muscles were sore and needed a good rub of liniment. Winn knew he was now only five rough miles west of his homestead and the cool breeze made him think about being home. He ached for Courtney's touch and knew he could be there in a matter of hours if he turned his horse downhill.

Winn had been searching for half a dozen lost cows that should have been in the mountain pastures west of Joseph but they were gone. While he was searching, he found new areas to expand his cattle's summer range. Because of his missing cows, Winn wondered if there was a mountain lion working over his herd, but he had only cut a couple of sets of tracks and they were old.

He hoped this cool weather had already started the cows off the mountain and he had just missed their trail. He decided on one final look for the missing cattle by searching in some of the high mountain clearings before he was ready to turn down the canyon for home. His fear was one big snowstorm could hit and trap the cattle up high, then there would be no getting them out and he could lose them all. At least these Hereford cows were easier to work than those longhorns back in Texas. If his cows had been longhorns, one man didn't stand a chance at tending the herd. A longhorn calf seemed able to outrun a jackrabbit the second it hit the ground. Herefords, on the other hand, were hearty, easier to manage and weren't near as mean.

Winn had ridden carefully on his search through the trees and upper meadows knowing the mountains were still a wild place. He occasionally cut horse tracks so seeing a group of Indians or running into some outlaws remained a possibility. For a man to be safe, he always needed to pay close attention to his surroundings. Winn realized he needed to stay focused because his family was waiting at home for him. Daydreaming could be a deadly mistake and he knew he had to make sure his thoughts remained clear as he explored and searched for his missing cattle. There would be plenty of time to focus on Courtney and the boys as soon as he got home.

Now that gold had been discovered in the Tushar Mountains, scattered gold camps were popping up around the mountain to the south. Winn knew he should be closer to home in case any trouble broke out. He had taught Courtney how to defend herself, but it was a husband's job to make sure she was okay. As the first homestead out of the Severe River Canyon, his was the first place anyone encountered as they came from the gold camps and farming towns of Piute County.

Two towns had been established in the past three years close to the best producing mines. Weber and Bullion City were both about twelve miles south of the Colter homestead above another recently established mining town called Marysvale.

Winn found many of the Mormons in the Territory had lost family getting to Utah, dying on ships, crossing the plains or killed by Indians. That was in addition to what happened in Missouri with the extermination order that legalized the murder of Mormons. These people packed up their wagons and carts with everything they could carry and came west to escape. Even here, troubles still followed.

The majority of miners in the area weren't Mormon and many would just as soon see the Mormons driven out of this area now that gold and silver had been found. It seemed no matter where the Mormons went, men wanted to take advantage of anyone they perceived as weak. The Mormons had been pushed out before. They were anything but weak and many had been pushed to their limit. Gold had a way of drawing all kinds of people, the very people the Mormons had tried so desperately to distance themselves from.

The longer Winn lived here, the more he respected the Mormons. They had welcomed him and Courtney from the day they arrived, but Winn had watched as several of the Mormon men looked at Courtney like they were sizing her up to be another wife. She shocked them by introducing this younger man, Winn Colter, as her husband.

Winn knew Courtney's figure demanded a second look by most men but he didn't mind so long as they were respectful and minded their business. Winn didn't have to worry because he knew Courtney loved him. However, there was this one incident where Winn and Courtney traveled to Glenwood to purchase a load of supplies at the ZCMI Co-Operative Store. One of the young Mormon ladies in town had been eyeing Winn up and down trying to catch his attention by smiling at him. Though Courtney could understand the young lady's interest in Winn, she informed him that if he thought about taking a second wife, she would shoot something off…A thought that he kept clearly in mind. He was married to the most beautiful woman in the Territory. Why would he ever want another? He didn't want another! If nothing else, that was safe thinking on his part!

Winn rode his horse out to a point and found a large stack of rocks some twelve feet high. Winn had seen this from the valley, but thought it was a lone pine tree out on the point. Now that he could see it was manmade, it gave him an eerie feeling wondering who and when someone had gone to such effort to build. The old Spanish cabin wasn't too far so Winn wondered if it was a Spanish marker or something much older and more significant? Winn could see some of the larger stones at the base probably weighed close to a ton while some at the top probably still weighed over a hundred pounds. Curious things such as this made Winn wonder about Anasazi … or as the Indians would say, those who were here before us.

A gust of wind brought him back, looking over the Valley. From his vantage point he could see three big towns, big compared to Jacksboro.

There was twenty homes scattered across the south end of the valley but this was nothing like some of the larger towns to the North. The small town directly east across the valley had just changed its name from Alma to Monroe in honor of the fifth President of the United States, James Monroe. The town had a fine water source coming from a large canyon to the south. In just a couple of years since the end of the Blackhawk War, the town had turned into a successful farming community.

Winn looked far to the north but couldn't see Fort Omni because the town of Richfield was close to the base of the red hills. It too had become more successful as a farming community with the end of the Blackhawk War after the townsmen dug a ten mile long canal that brought water to their crops.

Winn then looked down towards his homestead by the small town of Joseph. There were only six families scattered through this part of the valley but they were good hard working men and women, and good neighbors. There was one small homestead farther south from his own, but it had been abandoned since attacks during Indian troubles.

From his vantage point nearly five miles away, Winn could see smoke curling from the chimney of his house, but what really made the house stand out down below was its blue color. With the money Winn brought from Texas, he was able to build one of the finest homes in the entire valley. Courtney then had looked at him with those big green eyes and asked if Winn would paint the house blue. He couldn't refuse that look so… painted the house blue! Winn had also bought seed and fifty head of Hereford cattle. Things were looking good. Winn could sell all the cattle he had to the Mines and probably make more than most of the miners.

Winn thought about Goodnight's ranch and decided by now the Ranger must have thousands of head of longhorns or had already driven them to market. There was great feed in the south end of the valley and in the mountains around them. Goodnight would have been proud. There was money to be made with the cattle as long as the lions or the Indians didn't take too many.

****

Courtney could see a bit of dust coming from the far edge of their homestead but that wasn't uncommon as people passed through regularly to and from the mines. Her experiences with Winn had always taught her to look around because trouble usually came from what you didn't see.

Courtney could make out a large group of riders wearing sombreros and cowboy hats similar to what Winn chose to wear. There were more than twenty riders in the group. As she watched, they rode past and continued heading south. Courtney thought they could easily be heading for the new mining towns or might cross over to Cove Fort. She watched until they went out of sight then she continued to work digging potatoes from her garden.

CHAPTER 26

At last, Winn found a pair of cows. Now only four cows were missing. Another gust of wind whirled through his slicker and went down his neck. He decided he had searched the Mountain long enough. "Hell, the Indians or lions must have eaten them." Winn looked at his old horse who was looking back at him as he tightened the cinch on the saddle. "Let's go home!" The horse perked its ears and looked to the valley. Winn lifted his collar and glanced at the thunderheads blowing in from the distance. He was ready to head for home to see his boys… and his lovely wife. He had been gone too long and the thought of Courtney made him move faster as he was ready to mount up and put a spur to the old horse. "I'm coming home," when something stopped him. Winn heard the echo of a bear roar in the distance… then again. There were some tall pines just up over a small rise and the sound came from that direction. From the roar, it had to be a big bear. Maybe the missing cows had been eaten by something besides a mountain lion.

Winn whirled the horse and rode quietly towards the sound of the bear which his horse didn't like. He moved to better position himself downwind as he got closer. A mountain man had warned him how quickly a grizzly could move. He said a grizzly had swatted a mustang at full run out from under him and claimed a black bear was nearly as fast. If they really could move that fast, Winn didn't want to chance a run with his old horse, but he needed to see what was making the commotion over the hill.

As Winn got closer, he could hear the sound of a boy yelling and screaming at the bear, It was an Indian voice. Winn tied his horse to a tree and slipped his rifle from the scabbard and moved toward the growls and yells. Winn could see it now, a young Indian boy was thirty feet up in the top of a pine tree and a huge cinnamon colored black bear was only a few branches below moving closer, swatting and gnashing at the boy. Winn could see the boy was covered with blood on the front of his buckskins and had now climbed as high as he could. A grizzly bear would stay on the ground and try to push the tree over but a black bear, if he wanted to, would climb up and get it's prey. That's what was happening. The bear was huge and its weight was too great for the top of the tree. Winn could see the bear had started to bend the top over but in its fury, hadn't noticed the top tipping and swaying back and forth and was fully intent on getting this boy, no matter what!

Winn was only two hundred yards from the tree and wasn't about to let the boy fall prey to the big bear. Winn moved quickly, but just as he was about to squeeze the trigger, the boy tried to kick the bear in the snout and got caught. The bear sunk his teeth into the boy's foot and clamped down for the kill. If Winn shot the bear now, it would likely pull the boy out of the tree with him. His strong jaws clamped down and penetrated the buckskin moccasin giving the bear a taste of blood.

Winn's thoughts raced as the boy was screaming in pain and grasping the thin trunk of the tree so the bear couldn't yank him out. The bear was positioning himself to start pulling so he could make the kill! A second or two more and Winn was sure the boy would be done as the bear would twist until the leg would snap or the boy would fall. Winn aimed at the bear's rump at the base of the tail and pulled the trigger.

The bear reacted as he had hoped, opening its mouth for a split second, releasing the boy as it tried to bite whatever just bit him. Winn placed a quick second shot into the bears neck severing it's spine but the jolt caused the bear to jerk hard breaking off the top of the tree. Both he and his prey began to fall! The boy bounced through the branches as he fell grabbing at anything to stop his descent, but gravity had hold of him and it pulled him down.

The boys' efforts had slowed his fall enough so when he hit the ground he was battered, broken and bruised, but alive. His buckskins were a bloody mess. The skin of his hands were severely torn and bleeding to match his chest and foot. Winn had felt sick watching the boy falling and bouncing through the branches and it made him think of Chase.

Winn moved in cautiously as the boy hadn't moved since he hit the ground. The massive bear lay dead not six feet away, eyes still open and blood dripping from his huge teeth. Its paws were so big he looked like he could of taken a man's head off with one swing. Winn got to the boy who laid motionless on his belly in the pine needles and carefully rolled him over. Even with his bloody and torn up hands, the boy lifted a knife towards Winn, but he looked exhausted and could hardly hold up his hand.

The boy looked to be about the same age as Chase, fully clothed with buckskin and moccasins. His left foot was dripping blood from large holes where the bear's teeth had clamped down. Winn motioned calmly for the boy to put down the knife. He looked about ready to pass out but he was frightened and held steady pointing the knife towards Winn. Obviously the boy thought this white man was about to kill him and was still frightened, maybe as much of a white man as the bear he had just fought.

Winn looked at the bear and now saw that there were two arrows sticking out of the body, one in the front shoulder and the second in the hump on its back. Winn then saw one of his missing cows down the hill another 100 feet. It too had an arrow stuck in it and Winn could see the boy had started to butcher the animal when the bear must have caught wind of blood and came in to claim the prize.

The boy's broken bow lay at the base of the tree where he had fallen and Winn could easily put the rest of the pieces of the story together. He walked over to the bear and cut off a claw with his Bowie and then walked to the boy and offered it to him. Only then did the boy put the knife down.

Winn reached out slowly and carefully pulled pine needles out of the boy's face and cheeks. He then took off his own shirt and ripped off the sleeve to use as a bandage. Winn first wrapped the boys foot tight to stem the bleeding and then wrapped a head wound that he must have sustained in the fall. The deep cut was now bleeding more severely.

It looked like the bear had taken a swat at the boy and hooked him with one claw across his chest. The boy was lucky that's all he caught. Winn ripped off the other sleeve of his shirt and tied it tightly around the boy's forehead and used the rest of his shirt to wrap the chest wound. The thick buckskin clothing had minimized the injuries; otherwise this boy would be dead.

Winn could see the wounds needed attention and the boy should be back with his people. Wherever his pony had been, it was gone now. Probably scared off by the bear. Winn ran up the hill to his horse and came riding back to the boy; but the horse started to balk away because of the bear and the smell of blood. Winn couldn't just ride away because he was sure with the extent of the boy's injuries he would probably die. Winn had to move quickly.

He thought for a moment then went over and cut a hind quarter off the beef and tied it to the saddle then came back and gently lifted the boy up and sat him on the saddle. Winn knew what he was about to do was dangerous and could cost him his life but that didn't matter. The boy reminded him too much of Chase and he needed help.

Winn turned to the boy with a questioning look and pointed at him, then in a circle then looked back at the boy. He sat there for a moment then the boy pointed with a wobbly finger down the canyon toward the Millard Valley. It was a rugged trail but that's where the boy had indicated so Winn took hold of the reins and led on.

After leading his horse down the canyon to the west for what seemed like an hour the boy turned them on to a different trail heading south pulling them out of the main drainage. They rode for an additional half hour until they started to emerge into a small hidden meadow with two streams flowing nearby. The meadow was at the base of one of the tallest peaks of the mountain range and it was surrounded by beautiful aspen groves on three sides. A beaver was working the stream below and had built a dam creating a 300 foot wide reservoir where the cutthroat trout were growing to several pounds. This hidden valley was beautiful. Winn could sense a light smell of smoke. He asked himself quietly, "What kind of trouble am I getting myself into?"

Another 10 yards around the trail he finally could see a teepee, then many teepees and a herd of nearly fifty horses that were being tended by three young boys. Winn could hear women and children running then whooping letting others know danger was coming into their camp. To this band of Indians, the war with the whites wasn't over and a white man was walking into their camp, in this hidden valley, below their sacred peak.

Winn stayed close to his horse and the boy as he walked into the center of the camp where a number of women and children stood and watched. More braves started coming slowly out of the trees, some with bows but the majority held Winchester or Henry rifles.

Immediately Winn noticed a proud looking man that stepped forward and walked to the side of Winn's horse and just stared at him. This was Ouray, Chief of a band of Northern Utes that continued to fight with the Mormons. He looked at Winn like he couldn't decide what to do with this man who was brave enough to walk right into his camp. Winn turned to look at the boy whose blood was seeping through the bandages. The boy held his head down low like he was ashamed to be brought in by a white man.

Winn turned back to the chief, "I don't know if you understand English, but if you do, you should be proud of this young man. When I first saw him, he put two arrows into a bear then chased him up a tree! This boy climbed the tree with no fear to attack the bear with only his knife. He is a brave man, but now needs time to heal. All of the Indians stared at Colter and he couldn't tell if they understood or not.

"That bear bit him on the foot and his bones may be crushed!" The chief looked at Colter then to the boy, his demeanor never changed. The Chief talked quietly to the boy and he began to nod as the boy answered in response.

The Chief looked back at Winn and then said in broken English "You are brave man that shows no fear to come to this camp, but you showed compassion to the boy." Winn didn't want to show any fear, but standing in the middle of the Indian camp had him scared out of his wits! He was wise enough not to let it show.

"The boy is a fighter and did not give up!" Winn said, "He needed his wounds attended to. I could not leave such a brave man in trouble to die." Chief Ouray studied this brave man in front of him. Winn looked at Ouray and said "Your brave should have a great tale to tell about his scars. I was honored to watch his battle and honored to return him to his people where he can heal from his wounds." The chief nodded and waved to two women who came quickly and took the boy to clean him up and dress his injuries. The Chief never moved his eyes from Winn. "My name is Ouray and the boy is Tamhook, my son. He said you lie! The bear chase Tamhook up tree."

Winn never flinched and talked back to Chief Ouray, "No matter," he said. "He fought the bear well. My name is Winn Colter. Tamhook killed a beef and the bear came to take it. Tamhook fought bravely." Coltr motioned to his horse, " I brought the beef for your people."

The Chief looked at Colter very closely. Colter bent down and drew a C with a line over the top in the dirt then looked back at the Chief. "This is my brand. The Bar-C. If your people are hungry, take one. You are welcome." The Chief looked at Colter still trying to figure him out. Colter thought for a moment then said, "This is land of the Ute. I ask permission to fatten beeves on this land that I may share with the Ute." Chief Ouray was impressed. Most white men took and did not ask. And this white man had saved Tamhook from disgrace or from death. Ouray was thankful.

"What you say is good. Fatten your beeves on Ute land and we will only take Bar C beef when we are hungry. Utes will not attack the sky house."

"Sky house?" Winn didn't understand. The chief pointed to a blue spot in the sky and Winn knew what he meant. Winn had been told the Indians were always watching. Now he knew it was true. Winn nodded. He felt safer now than he had since the first sound of the bear.

Winn looked at Chief Ouray respectfully, "Tamhook has a bear down and the rest of a beef that I could not bring. There's meat that the Utes should have." The chief nodded. He spoke quietly to three braves who immediately mounted their horses and were ready to ride. Winn nodded to the Chief, then mounted his horse and rode out with the three Utes. This had turned into an interesting day.

Winn talked to the Utes as if they spoke English but none said a word. As they neared the bear, Colter described how Tamhook fought the bear and pointed to the broken top of the tree. "Tamhook," he motioned in a falling motion and the braves motioned in approval. The four worked on the carcass of the bear and got it balanced on two horses and the remainder of the beef on the third horse. Winn nodded at the braves and they all nodded back and started to the west. Winn felt much safer now after his meeting with Chief Ouray and the band of Utes. Little did he know the greatest danger to his life had just ridden past his homestead, all the way from Texas.

CHAPTER 27

The Kennedy Gang rode south through the valley moving closer to the Tushar Mountains and the gold camps. These majestic mountains that surrounded this valley amazed the Texans. The sheer granite cliff face that overshadowed this valley was an incredible sight. Not to mention the two bald peaks of the Tushars to the south and another bald peak far to the north known as Molly's Nipple. There had been a bit of a storm and the group looked up at the Tushars to see a light dust of snow. That was where the gold camps were supposed to be.

The Texans stopped to water horses along the Sevier River at the mouth of the canyon. Looking back to the east, Jon Kennedy could see two pine poles hanging across what looked like an improved trail that the trees had now started to reclaim. "Look there, Brother, That may be a place to camp for the night." Jon looked at the group resting by the river. "Strickland, Ringo, Y'all go check over there to see what it's like. It looks like there's another pocket over there."

The two cowboys mounted their horses and rode through the overgrowth. It had been some time since the trail had seen any significant use. As Ringo and Strickland rode into the hidden clearing, they could see there had been a pole fence where someone had spent a lot of time and effort clearing trees to establish a homestead. In the back of the hidden pocket, they saw a little broken down ranch house that looked abandoned. It was situated close to the river but the pocket offered protection preventing anyone from riding in on two sides. The remaining two sides would be easy enough to watch.

Ringo and Strickland rode back to tell the Kennedys what they had found and thought this looked to be a good place to hole up. As the Texans rode over, they all saw the arrows sticking out of the clay covered roof. Apparently there had been a battle here that had killed the homesteaders.

The Kennedys posted two guards and pulled the rest in to talk. "Okay y'all, this is where we're going to stay for now!" Jon said "We're not far from the gold camps, but not far from farms and ranches either." We need to be smart like back in Texas! We avoided questions for a long time." Jon studied the group of men before him and said, "Until we fully know what we're up against around here, we need to be safe and lay low."

"That includes killin' Mormons?" one of the men asked in from the back. Another man asked "When do we get us some Women?"

Westlee growled a response, "You're going to get some women, I promise you, but we need to do it right… Listen to Jon!" Jon had walked around the group. "There's too much gold involved to screw this up boys… I think we can get it!" Jon looked at the Texans and liked what he saw. Minus the two on guard, there were twenty of them in camp including himself. Most all of these men were tough and proven fighters with only a few young and inexperienced. Fourteen of these men were wanted in Arizona and Texas, and over half were wanted by the Mexican Federales.

Jon Kennedy studied the group of men for a moment. There was quite an assortment, ranging from rustlers and horse thieves to bank robbers. Some of the men had been involved in the Mason County War. Six were wanted for murder. Jon liked what he saw.

The Kennedy Brothers had always been smart and kept unnoticed by the Rangers even though they were the worst of the lot. It was only recently the Rangers had suspected them of being involved in any of the rustling or Murders until the Waco incident with Westlee. That had been the reason the Rangers started to question.

Mexico really wasn't an option for this bunch after the rustled horse incident. Jon Kennedy was probably the most hated man in Mexico after he stole that Mexicali General's prize stallion. The General vowed to make the Kennedy's pay and there was a $5,000 American dollar reward for Jon Kennedy's head in Mexico.

The six other Texans not wanted by the Rangers, came along because of the stories of women and riches. Three of them wanted the "bad man" reputation. Bo Ringo was young, but wanted the same kind of reputation as his famous brother, Johnny Ringo. He could shoot as fast as a striking rattler with his pistols and proved it! Scott Strickland and Tadd Wilson were just wanna-be tough men along for the ride, but they were ready to prove it. The two most noted gunmen in the entire group were Willard and Shawn Ashby. The brothers were the most noted gun hands who rode with Bloody Bill Anderson during the war. Jon looked at the Texans and knew what had to be done before winter. "Let's sure this place up and build a bunkhouse so we can get out of the cold. Y'all see that snow on that Mountain? It gets cold here in Utah!"

Preston Kennedy was feeling he needed a woman bad, "Let's get us some women to keep us warm Brother! I came for women!" There was a cheer from the men! "Let 'em know we're all from Texas and jump in their beds!" The men cheered again.

Jon and Westlee looked at the men seriously for a moment, "There's gold being shipped from these mines worth $2,400 a bar and they send bunches at a time!" Every man was quiet and listened. "How much?"

"Don't know yet." Jon commented. "But we're going to find out and we're going to take it!" Preston was fixated on one idea, "What about the women Brother? Jon thought if Preston wasn't his brother, he would have put a bullet in him. Westlee was fed up and nearly did anyway. "We'll get you some women Brother!" but Jon sternly cautioned Preston and all the men, "Don't screw this up for us… anyone!"

Westlee carefully looked at each man, "Tomorrow I'll take eight men to the gold camps. The rest stay here."

"Brother," Preston asked, "how about I just get that woman back at that blue house… It ain't far! I could see a woman lookin' our way when we rode by. They may be three of four there."

Jon snapped back at Preston, "Not yet! You'll get yours soon enough, Brother!"

CHAPTER 28

Winn made it home late after traveling back over the mountain. He gave his horse a good rubdown then went in to see his anxious wife and waiting boys. After supper he told the story about the bear, the Indian boy and his father the Ute Chief Ouray. The story scared Courtney and brought the boys in close. Courtney knew when Blackhawk had died it was Ouray who had taken up the fight. Brigham Young frowned on conflicts with Indians so many of the killings were kept secret. She knew the Mormons settlers didn't want to get excommunicated for disobeying guidance from the leaders. Brigham really didn't want the army in the territory for fear they would turn on the Mormons at any time.

Winn knew Courtney was still nervous because of the Indians. It was tough to identify bad Indians because there were a lot of friendly Indians in the area with different tribes and multiple bands. Besides the Utes there were Piutes, Goshute, Navajo. Some of the fighting bands were a mixture of tribes. Guns were always kept close with everyone knowing how to shoot. Settlers knew it wasn't just Indians that could bring trouble. It could be rowdy miners or other gentiles passing through that might be looking for trouble. There was also the possibility trouble could be wolves, bears or even mountain lions.

Winn could hear the team of mules long before he saw the heavy wagon rolling closer to his home. Winn recognized the four big Morgan mules before he even saw the driver. "Good Day, Brother Colter!" It was one of his neighbors, Newell Anderson, who had been one of the first settlers in the south end of the valley. Winn sensed Mr. Anderson was a good man and was thankful to have him as a neighbor.

Newell Anderson was a War veteran, a sharpshooter for the Union, and had packed his rifle across the plains much like Winn had. The two had developed a close friendship and were always looking out for each other's families. Anderson ran a coach and freight service between the mining camps in Piute County to the town of Gunnison. Courtney walked out on the porch to welcome their neighbor, "How are you today, Mr. Anderson?"

"Good," he said, "except I need a shotgun for a run to Webster and Bullion City today. Brother Parker was supposed to ride with me, but he's marrying another wife today." He looked at Winn and pleaded, "Would you be willing, Colter?"

Winn knew exactly what he meant but couldn't help but joke with Mr. Anderson at his wife's expense. "Courtney told me she's shoot somethin' off if I took another wife. Unless Courtney's changed her mind, Mr. Parker better marry her... I can't help you there."

Anderson laughed and slapped his knee, "I know, you've told me that before!" Courtney ducked her head. She was embarrassed that Winn would even joke about that, or had told Mr. Anderson. "You know what I meant Colter", Anderson said, "I need you to ride shotgun if you're willing. We'll leave the marryin' to Parker!" Winn had helped out several times when Mr. Anderson's employees were away on other business or there were big loads. He had only been home since late last night and wanted to spend time with his family.

Courtney looked at Mr. Anderson and she could see he was in desperate need. She knew his business was booming because of the mining towns. She looked up at Winn and said "Go!... Go help Mr. Anderson and we'll see you tomorrow!" Courtney gave Winn one of those looks, "It'll wait till tomorrow." He knew what that meant and his mouth fell open. She sure knew how to stir those feelings inside but he was sure it was always harder on her than him when she teased like this. When he did come home, he would need all his strength!

Winn looked up to see beautiful blue skies, quite a change from the day before. The storm of the previous day had blown right through and only left a dusting of snow on the highest peaks. "OK. Mr. Anderson... I'll grab my Colts."

"I got a coach gun for ya, you know that!" Anderson nodded towards the scabbard on the wagon.

"And you know I never ride without my Colts. Besides, even my wife has a Coach Gun!"

Courtney spoke up promptly and said, "And I know how to use it, Winn, if you don't get out of here!" Winn smiled. He knew Courtney loved that gun and always kept it right by the door. Being married to Winn had made her gain an appreciation for all type of guns. It had forced her to become a proficient shooter. Winn had made sure of that because there were a lot of dangers out there in the wilds of the Utah Territory.

Winn strapped on his Colts, grabbed a canteen then saw the boys standing there looking at him. Winn walked over and gave the boys a hug. "See you two tomorrow night." He gave Courtney a kiss and he was away!

There was nothing pleasant about the trail between Joseph and the mines to the south. Winn had to get into the right frame of mind for a journey like this over the rough and rocky trail that would bounce him all over a buckboard's seat. Mr. Anderson had a load of supplies today that needed to be split between Bullion City and Webster. After supplies were delivered, he and Winn would pick up the gold from the mine and be headed back down the trail to deliver the gold to the bank in Richfield. By morning, they would be back home and he could hold Courtney close to help him ease his pains.

"You're good company Colter," Anderson said, "I'm always glad to have you along." Just then, the wagon wheel hit a rock and jolted Winn over into Anderson's side. Anderson looked over at Winn and smiled, "That gun of yours keeps pokin' me in the side."

"If you'd ever learn how to drive a team of mules!" Anderson looked back after the insult then smiled again. "My Grammy taught me how to drive mules. You sayin' something about Grammy's teaching?"

"No I'm not!... I'm saying something about your learning!" They both turned to the front and both smiled again.

"I'm serious, I am glad to have you along." Anderson said, " Ol' Parker tends to fall asleep every time I have him along. I'm afraid I'm going to run him over when he falls off the Studebaker."

"He's got too many wives!" Winn said, "Courtney 'bout does me in as it is! What would I ever do with more than her?"

"You'd get your thing shot off is what would happen!" Jokingly, Anderson showed a look of concern.

"You get that from Courtney?"

"You've told me Colter! Anderson chuckled, "Besides, next to my wife, she's the handsomest woman I ever saw!" Anderson just smiled. He really did enjoy being around this man beside him. Winn Colter was a good man and both of them enjoyed taking little jabs and insults at each other. They both knew it was all in fun. It was a way to burn up time and miles on such a rough road.

Anderson all of a sudden said, "It's a good thing Parker lives close to us."

Winn couldn't figure where Anderson was going with this.. "Why you say that?"

"If he keeps marrying all those sisters, then neither your wife or mine will have any grounds for a shootin' on our homesteads!"

"Amen to that!" Both of them thought about Parker marrying his fifth wife and were so glad not to have to deal with his troubles.

After they rode for a few minutes Anderson thought about Chase. "Went by your homestead and saw that revolving rifle you cut down for Chase. You did a fine job with that gun."

"My Pa taught me a thing or two about smithin'," Winn said. "I wish I had his shop and some of his tools!"

Anderson was truly impressed with the gun work. "Chase is eight? Looked like you had that gun fitin' him fine!"

Winn was pleased Anderson had noticed. "Yea, he's only eight and can shoot like someone twice his age!" They bounced over more rocks. Winn said, "You know that church bell you and I found in the river? It's up in a cedar tree behind the homestead two hundred yards out and I've had Chase shooting at it for practice."

" Is that the ringing I keep hearing?" Anderson asked smiling, "I thought it was the ghost of the schoolmarm who lost the bell ringing it because you moved it!"

Well, I don't know about a ghost, but Chase's bullets ding that bell about every shot! He has to protect the homestead when you drag me away to help!"

"And all you do is complain about my driving! Anderson said, "Sometimes 'ol Parker sleeping ain't so bad . At least he ain't complainin' about my Studebaker."

"I told you, it ain't the Studebaker!" Both Winn and Mr. Anderson couldn't help but smile as they continued to banter each other.

As the wagon rolled on, Bullion City came into view. Fifteen minutes later as the wagon rolled into town, eight horsemen who had already been to the saloons and looked the town over were now just riding west heading up the canyon to see Webster. Jon Kennedy had a funny feeling, but shrugged it off and kept riding. They had given Bullion a good look-over and visited all three saloons. They found the saloons were an excellent place to find out what was happening in town and how much gold was coming out of the mines. Jon wanted to see the other gold camp up Bullion Canyon so they decided to ride out.

Anderson pulled the wagon up to the mining office, threw the cover off and started unloading boxes.

"Dynamite?" Winn read the box in surprise, "Y'all didn't tell me we were hauling dynamite. You could have killed us bouncing over those rocks down the canyon!"

Anderson just smiled, "Grammy taught me better than that. Besides you didn't ask what we were hauling!"

"The way you drive mules," Winn said, "you could have blown up your team and us too!" Winn paused for just a moment. "That wouldn't be fair to Parker." Anderson stopped to look at Winn now wondering what he meant. "Two more wives for Parker," Winn explained, "He couldn't handle our two wives." Anderson nearly dropped the box of Dynamite as he laughed. "Get to work so we can get home, Colter!"

****

172

Jon Kennedy rode into Webster City and went straight to the Bella Star Saloon. Besides needing another drink, Jon hoped there would be several miners willing to talk. Jon got his best information in Webster as he talked to a drunk miner who had just come from the Bully Boy Mine.

Kennedy found one thing for sure--these miners were a fickle lot. No matter which gold camp they were in, the stories of gold at the next mine or at a new discovery always sounded better. Many of the miners jumped from one mine to the next. Webster was slowly dying and Kennedy could see that. He was feeling pretty good about what he was hearing and new ideas were jumping into his head. As he sat there enjoying his bottle of whiskey, it was clear from the miner's talk, they needed to be in Bullion. One of the better producing mines, close to Bullion, the Bully Boy, was producing high grade ore. Jon choked on his whiskey when he heard one of the miners say the ore pulled out last week assayed thirteen ounces of gold and two hundred ounces of silver to the ton! Miners were also talking of two new discoveries, one north and one south, so Bullion definitely was the place to be.

There were about fifty buildings in Bullion including two hotels, three saloons, a boarding house, a newspaper and a house of ill-repute. There was lots of money flowing through those towns. Jon knew he better get his brother and some of the men here to visit those ladies before anyone did something stupid and messed up this golden Goose!

Jon Kennedy had an idea that offered great cover for a bigger plan; one of the saloon owners in Bullion would have an accident (with a little help if needed) and need to sell immediately. That could be a perfect cover to get the Texans into the town and find out when the biggest shipments of gold and silver were being transferred out. Then they could be smart and take several shipments rather than just one. Playing this smart would be the key! His plan would work and every one of the Texans would ride out of here rich!

****

Anderson and Colter rode in to Webster and went straight to the Mine office to deliver the boxes of dynamite, but before they left, Winn talked to one of the bosses to ask a favor. Winn needed a stick of dynamite to blast out that big rock in the canyon that they bounced over every time they brought supplies to the mines. The boss knew the exact rock Winn was talking about because he had hit the same one as he traveled through the canyon breaking a wheel. He turned around and pulled three sticks out of a box and inserted a blasting cap and fuse into each one. "I gave you three sticks with two-minute fuses. You can cut 'em off if you want to blast the hell out of that rock and a couple more if you want to!"

Winn looked at the sticks with the words "Nobel's Blasting Powder" on the side. He smiled looking back at the mine boss, "I'll get it done! He tucked the dynamite into his pocket and rushed out to jump on the Studebaker.

Anderson climbed back on the wagon with Colter and started back down the street. "You want to get a drink before we head out?"

"No, let's get to the mill and head out. I can wait."

A special feature was built into every one of Anderson's Studebakers. Every wagon had a false floor in the back with a hidden compartment. That was added security to help protect their valuable cargo. Anderson rode into the back of the mill and after passing security, he moved the wagon over to a specified spot and waited. The boxes were opened and two ten inch by ten inch by seven inch bars of solid gold were lowered into the hidden boxes. Both Anderson and Colter had to sign. They then lowered three more bars of silver into the back of the wagon on top. Only Anderson had to sign on this one. Mill bosses always had a look outside to make sure nothing was out of the ordinary before the doors opened and the wagon headed down the hill and out of Bullion.

****

Back in camp, the remaining fourteen Texans were milling around trying to find something to do. Six sat around a table playing poker. Of the remaining eight outside, the two youngest went wandering out behind the house in the edge of the trees. "Look what I found!" Willard Applegate held two gold pans in his hands to show his older brother. "Listening to Jon talk about that gold last night got me excited! What if we take these pans and slip up the creek coming from the west. Sounds like that hill is loaded with gold and maybe we can find the lode!"

Sean looked at the pans and was hesitant. "Jon told us to start on the bunkhouse."

"He ain't our Pa!" Willard snapped. "Besides if we find gold, Jon would forgive us."

"I'm not so sure." Sean knew about the Kennedy's reputation and wasn't sure he wanted to push it.

Willard suggested, "How about we go for three hours up the creek and if we can't find any gold, we come back and get busy on logs." Willard looked around to see no one was paying them any attention. "Let's just slip away. Nobody will notice." The two brothers just meandered to the edge of the clearing then dove into the thick to get away from the group of Texans. Nobody was watching. They walked about a mile upstream before they found a spot they both agreed upon and started panning. Neither knew what they were doing but they dove in head first and tried their best. They didn't find a speck of gold.

As they went further up the canyon, they both had an eerie feeling come over them as they walked by rocks covered by Indian writing. Every few feet there was more writings and designs painted on the rocks. There in the creek looked like a likely spot for gold so Sean took a scoop of mud from under a rock and started to swirl it in the pan. As the mud began to wash away, Willard saw the first speck of gold in his brother's pan. When he was done, there were five little specks of gold in his pan. He didn't have his thousand yet but it was a start. The two walked up the trail farther and this time Willard took a scoop and started to swirl the pan. Through the muddy water he was it... color... Gold!. Both men were hooked!

The two kept following the creek up and running a sample wherever it looked promising. They also saw more and more Indian sign to the point it was scary but the two pushed on. Sean looked up at the sun and was concerned. "I think we been gone for six, seven hours."

"But look at the gold we're getting!" Sean looked down and his pistol was gone from its holster. He had been so excited about the gold that he hadn't noticed it falling out. Willard looked ahead and there seemed to be a wonderful spot that he wanted to sample. Sean was now so extremely nervous because he didn't have his gun. Willard pleaded, "Just that one more spot. Then we go!" Reluctantly Sean followed.

As the two tried to sample the mud, Willard lifted a nugget out the size of his little finger nail. Both Sean and Willard looked at it in awe then jumped up and stated to hoot and holler doing a celebration dance around their find. They were so excited they hardly noticed when an arrow whizzed through the air and stuck Willard's back. It hadn't occurred to him what the sudden stab of pain was until he looked down to see the shaft of an arrow protruding six inches out of his chest. The black obsidian tip had a smear of red...his blood. The shock finally took hold and he fell to his knees in the creek with blood gushing from the wound and now from his mouth. The arrow had gone just above his heart and through a lung. The pan fell from Willard's hand and then he fell face first into the water. Nearly half an ounce of gold that he had recovered was now back in the water.

Sean had watched the whole thing. He was looking at his brother from the side when the arrow hit. He could see the shaft sticking out front and back. Willard looked at him, then looked down at the arrow and didn't say a word, just fell forward. In horror Sean watched his brother die.

Suddenly all the gold in the world wasn't important any more. He dropped his pan and grabbed for his gun, but came up with an empty holster. Willard's gun was useless too as his old revolver had fallen into the creek. The wet powder in the 1861 Remington Army was useless. Sean tried to see where the arrow had come from, but couldn't see an Indian or any movement at all. He was sick to think he would have to leave his brother where he lay or join him.

Sean ducked down and started to move fast when an arrow buried itself in his buttocks. He felt it hit bone and he screamed in pain. "Oh God, why did I come here?" He stated to run but after about ten steps the pain stopped him. He turned around and looked at his brother's dead body as an arrow hit him in the chest. He looked down at the shaft and feathers and tried to take a breath but couldn't. He could see the blood pumping out of his chest and now could taste it. How he wished he was back in Texas. Darkness was closing in all around him. He was tired. He closed his eyes and was gone.

CHAPTER 29

Preston Kennedy looked around. Nobody was paying him any attention and he wanted a woman bad! We're Texans! These women were supposed to want us to bed 'em. Kennedy looked around the camp. He could just slip out and ride back to that blue house. He may have to kill a Mormon but there may be three or four women waiting for him. He was a Texan and he was sure that woman he saw the day before was dreaming about him and the boys...No... dreaming of him... Wanting him! That was the plan Jon had come up with anyways. Kill some Mormons and take their women!

Kennedy walked out to the horses and caught his bay gilding then saddled him up. "That's my woman back there." he said to himself. That woman was waiting! He was going to tell Westlee and Jon that he went to take what was promised him back in Texas. He assured himself and said aloud, "Those women in that blue house are mine!" Preston Kennedy rode out without saying a word. That house was only back about a mile and a half. He was going to get a woman!

Tad Wilson, Scott Strickland, Bo Ringo and two others sat outside the house quietly talking. "How come the hell Jon Kennedy rides into town and leaves us here?' Wilson asked. "Maybe I wanted to go see Bullion City!"

"I bet there's saloons," Strickland said, "and I'll bet they're getting drunk or spendin' time with a painted lady!" Just then the five saw Preston Kennedy riding out of the hidden camp. Wilson called out, "Where ye goin'?" but Kennedy only mumbled a few word as he went by and kept riding. Bo Ringo looked at the others and asked, "Where the hell is he going? I say if he can go out for a ride, we all can go for a ride.

Strickland was concerned "What about Jon and Westlee?"

Wilson said, "For all we know the Kennedys robbed a gold shipment and ran off to California with all our money!" Ringo was stirred up, "I say the five of us go for a ride and if we come across that gold shipment, we take it for ourselves!"

Scott Strickland and Tad Wilson had listened to the stories and both wanted the bad man reputation. Bo Ringo was already making a name for himself by killing three men who accused him of cheating in a poker game. He had been cheating, but that didn't matter. Right now it felt like Jon and Westlee Kennedy were holding all three of them back. The other two, Sanchez and Deaton, had ridden with the Kennedys off and on for four years. They had the Rangers after them and knew these three were pushing for trouble.

When it came to a fight, the Kennedys would give these boys their chance by sticking them right up front. Sanchez and Deaton knew the Kennedy's well enough to know that's why they probably brought them. Let them take the lead and the Kennedys would take the prize. That's also why they tried to never let the brothers ride up close behind them. They both knew the Kennedy's back-shooting reputation and trusted them about as much as a den of rattlesnakes.

Sanchez and Deaton were both former soldiers and both proficient rustlers and thieves with no qualms about killing. After hearing this conversation of the three younger Texans, they didn't mind the option of taking more for themselves.

The five looked around the camp and then at each other. Sanchez had been nursing a cup of coffee as they talked but now threw the rest in the fire. The decision was made; they all walked to the horses and saddled up. Ringo was anxious, "Lets ride up the canyon. That's where the gold is supposed to come from." After a few minutes they were all mounted and checked their guns. They rode south up the canyon towards Bullion City.

Ringo looked at the group and said "If we want to keep riding to Bullion for a drink… or women, I say we do it! And if we run into Jon, he won't dare stop us if we stick together!" The five rode up the canyon trail towards the gold camps. They rode like Texans! Nobody was going to stop them!

****

Preston Kennedy could see the blue house in the distance. Its style reminded him of a house back in Texas that he watched burn many years ago. He also remembered he had been shot in the ear at that house and his brother had been killed. Kennedy had been waiting to have a woman since they left New Mexico and was ready to kill any Mormon who tried to stop him from taking his wives. This is what he came for and he couldn't wait any longer to start taking!

Courtney was working in the yard pulling weeds from her garden. The harvest moon was only a few days away and it would be time to put up their fall harvest. They had cattle, hogs, and chickens and were growing wheat, potatoes, maize, beets and carrots. Add some venison and it should be a comfortable winter if they worked hard the next few weeks.

The boys had been working and playing hard that morning and now, during the hottest time of the day, were in the house taking a nap. It seemed this was one of the few times in the day she could actually get work done uninterrupted; but she could see a lone rider coming her way from the south. It wasn't uncommon for travelers to stop at their homestead so she wasn't concerned. As the man got closer, there was a certain manner about his actions that reminded her of something.

Courtney dusted off her clothes and fixed her hair. She could see the man rode with a rifle across his saddle and he wore two pistols tied down. Winn had explained to her many times the kind of rider she needed to watch out for and this man fit everything Winn had ever warned her about. Of course so did Mr. Anderson the first time she saw him and that man Winn had introduced as Porter Rockwell , but both had proven to be harmless and this man probably would too.

As the man approached, his hand never left his rifle and she could see his eyes were searching everything looking for something. When his eyes first met hers, a burst of panic ran through her body. The last time she had seen eyes looking at her in that manner was the day when Winn had killed those Yankee soldiers that were attacking her over six years ago.

Kennedy looked around, "Where's your man?"

"He'll be home soon, Can I help you? Courtney could see a smile come on his face and there was no mistaken the lust in his eyes. Courtney knew what he was planned to do by his looks and manner. She prayed the boys would stay asleep.

"I'm from Texas!" he said it as if that made a difference. Courtney just looked back. The man staring at her had haunting eyes... pure evil! He repeated, "I said I'm from Texas!" He gripped his rifle tight and had a crazed look about him that made Courtney want to cry. She was a tough woman, but his eyes brought back all the nightmares she ever had. Where's Winn to rescue her? She knew Winn was still hours out. Winn had taught her…. It needed to come back.

The man looked like he was getting impatient His eyes terrified her! She saw the gun start to lift then she remembered, "Make him think he's going to get what he wants."

She said "I've been waiting for a man from Texas to come along!" She hadn't even lied to the man, Winn was from Texas. The man eased up on the grip of his gun.

"I've been waiting for so long!" Keep him thinking… she said, "What do you want?"

"I came here for you! I'm going to have you!" He had a hungry look in his eyes… terrifying!

She had to bluff, "I've been waiting!" The thought of this man was incomprehensible but she had to play the part. "Come to my bed. I've been waiting." She stated undoing buttons on her dress slowly. She smiled at him, it was a horrible thing but she had to play the part so she could get to the house.

"Come here!" He motioned for her to walk closer where he sat on his horse. She couldn't let that happen.

"No." She had to play him but keep control, ""I've dreamt of having a Texan share my bed. Come with me." She was undoing more buttons on her dress but moving towards the front door.

Jon was right! He wasn't sure at first but these Mormon women couldn't wait to get a Texan to their beds. Kennedy dismounted and started to follow Courtney to the house. He was glad he had come back to this house now. What a beautiful woman and he was going to have her in moments!

As he walked forward he still packed the rifle in his left hand. Courtney reached the house a dozen steps ahead of the man and as she calmly reached the doorway she reached inside and grabbed her double barrel coach gun and whirled, leveling the barrels dead center on his chest. The thought of the arrogance! The thought he could walk in here and take her from the man she loved... The Texan was surprised by the turn of events and went for his pistol, but flames flew from both barrels of the coach gun. It knocked Courtney back four steps into the house but the 00 buckshot picked the man up off his feet and threw him several feet as he did one complete roll on the ground that ended with him sitting on his knees. He sat there with 18 blackened holes in his chest, staring at her. In his last thoughts he was thinking to himself, "How could she do this to me... to a Texan?"

There was no breath in his lungs and he sat there with an open mouth staring at her. There were spots of blood on the man's front and ugly, bloody holes in his back where the shot left his body. His eyes stayed open but he was gone, his outlaw days were at an end. Courtney walked out and looked down at the gun on the ground and with shaking hands, picked up the rifle the man had dropped. It was built exactly like the one her husband prized and protected except didn't have the fancy gold in-lay on the receiver and it had a smooth piece of leather covering the stock. Courtney carefully rolled back the leather and she saw four fancily engraved letters on the gun stock... "Winn". She looked close at the top of the gun which had a drop of blood covering where she wanted to see. She pulled her finger across the spot of blood and looked carefully at the top. It read Colter Arms, Mesquiteville Texas. She started to shake and dropped the gun.

The boys came peeking around the corner of the door to see their mother, but they saw her standing over a dead man. "Ma?" She quickly wiped the blood off her finger and tears from her eyes then turned to hug them. What could this mean? She was afraid something bad was about to happen. With her boys in her arms, she cried!

CHAPTER 30

Anderson looked ahead down the trail. "Colter, you see those men?"

"Yea, I see five of 'em." The wagon rolled forward over the rocky trail. Five riders were slowly moving toward them about two hundred yards out. The way they rode across the trail was meant to look natural but from keen eyes, both Anderson and Colter could see the men were setting them up for a stop. If you're rolling with fourteen pounds of gold and more than double that in silver, you have to read a man's manner. These five men looked like a pack of wolves moving in for a kill.

Winn casually loosened his Colts and studied the actions and movement of the five men who rode their horses towards them. "Recognize any of them?"

"No" Anderson said, "but I think I've seen that gray horse. It was with a big bunch of riders in Richfield yesterday. Didn't hear if they were coming or going."

The distance was disappearing fast. Perry Deaton and Abe Sanchez rode on the left and were older than the rest in their mid-30's, but the two rode half a horse length back. Anderson and Colter could both see they rode like calm and experienced Cavalry soldiers. These two were definitely dangerous.

The other three riders were younger, all in their teens or early 20's. They must have been too young to have fought in the war. The two in the middle, Strickland and Wilson, kept glancing at the riders on both sides, obviously scared, inexperienced and not knowing what to do. Colter saw the length of gun scabbard Strickland wore. He was shooting a Colt Walker or something else big and heavy. He wouldn't be a danger unless he got the gun out. The young one on the right was Bo Ringo. He was a small framed man with a Van Dyke mustache and a fancy hat. Ringo wore two 1869 .45 caliber Schofield pistols and a bandelero full of bullets. Everything about him read trouble. His eyes were steady and he rode forward with a confidence. There was no doubt this was the natural leader of the group. He thought he was fast with a gun which made him the most reckless and aggressive of the five.

Winn quietly told Anderson to stop the wagon and lock the brake which he did. Anderson carried three guns for these runs, a .56-56 Spencer and two ten Gauge double barrel Coach Guns of which one was in his hands both barrels cocked and loaded. Winn just sat still in his seat. He cocked the coach Gun and sat in front of Anderson so he had a second gun with a quick grab. Winn said "Let's see how they play their cards."

Deaton and Sanchez saw the Spencer roll out being held by the driver and remembered facing them in the war. A Spencer could fire seven shots in fifteen seconds and at this distance the Spencer had the advantage and neither of them liked. The Mormons weren't supposed to have guns but this one had a deadly one and looked like he knew how to use it! They were just ready to back out when the second man in the wagon stood up.

"What you doing, Colter?"

Winn whispered, "Stay focused!" And he did, keeping his gun on Deaton, riding on the far left.

When Winn stood up, Ringo looked at this as a challenge. They had five men against two and this man standing there in the wagon didn't look like much. Who was he to think he had a chance against Bo Ringo!

Ringo rode forward cutting the distance from 100 to 70 then 40 and he stopped at 20 yards. He watched for Colter to act scared but he showed no emotion. He wore two old short barreled Navy Colts butt forward, but they didn't impress Ringo. His pair of Smith and Wesson Sheffield's were far superior weapons to old Navy Colts. Ringo smiled and started the play, "What's in your wagon Mr.?"

"Something you don't want." Colter was quick with his response but short.

"And what might that be that I don't want?" Ringo was having fun thinking he was scaring these Mormons until Colter's came back with his response. Colter's stare turned ice cold…. "Lead!"

Ringo was getting angry. These men should both be scared! "I'm Bo Ringo! You hear of Jonny Ringo from Texas? I'm his brother and I can shoot faster and more accurate. Do you think you can take me?" The kid was arrogant and the Texans were all laughing except Perry Deaton with the Spencer trained on him. He had seen that gun drop on him at a hundred yards and not even a flinch since then. Those four Morgan-Mules pulling the large wagon weren't giving him any help either as they stood docile and the wagon sat solid. Even the mention of Johnny Ringo didn't cause that Spencer to waver a speck from his chest. Either they didn't know who Ringo was or these men didn't care.

Anderson spoke up now for the first time and said, "It's been nice visiting with you gents now I think it's time you rode away."

Wilson laughed out loud at Anderson's suggestion. "You Mormon's really don't know when y'all should be scared." Ringo's eyes were steady on Colter's as Ringo said, "Yea, they should be damned scared!"

Anderson casually said "I ain't scared. You scared, Colter?"

"Colter… Kid Colter?" there had been a slight pause before Abe Sanchez looked closer at the man standing on the wagon and he now felt panic and sickness sweep his body. He was about the right age, wore two old style short barreled Navy Colts and he stood there facing Ringo with no indication of fear.

Winn casually said, "I've been called that before and I didn't like it!" Colter was talking to the older riders but his eyes stayed locked with Ringo. The name "Kid Colter" was recognized by every one of them including Anderson, but being on the wrong side of his gun was nothing any of them had ever expected. Now robbing these Mormons didn't seem like such a good idea after all. They should have waited for the whole gang!

"This is your last chance to ride out of here," Colter offered. "Ride and don't look back!" Wilson's hand started to slowly reach towards his gun. Colter warned, "You touch that gun and I'll put my first bullet between your eyes." Wilson's hand froze then moved away from the butt of his gun. Deaton, with the Spencer held on his chest was the first to speak, "I don't want trouble with you. I'll ride and you'll never see me again." Sanchez spoke up quickly too with panic in his voice, "I'm not here to face Kid Colter, I'll ride too!" Wilson and Strickland didn't know what to do and just sat there quietly looking back and forth.

Bo Ringo was a natural shooter and had practiced his draw to the point he was as fast as his brother Johnny or possibly even faster with his Schofields! Back in Texas, Bo had killed three men that accused him of cheating at cards and two of those men had reputations for being fast. Ringo had heard of Kid Colter but thought he was a made-up story. To find him living here with the Mormons… It couldn't be true! If it really was true, he could claim to be the one who gunned down the famous "Kid Colter." Then, Bo Ringo would be more famous than his brother back in Texas!

Adrenalin filled Ringo's veins. He was confident that he could outgun this man but he wanted all of these men to see him do it. Perry Deaton would probably get killed but Ringo thought he could kill the Mormon before he could get his second shot off. That is if the others hadn't already shot him first. Then he would deal with that Yellar Sanchez for backing out of a fight. Deaton was unnerved being under sight of that Spencer. Now that was understandable, but not Sanchez!

Ringo was thinking it was now or never! Colter saw it in his eyes and as Ringo's hands streaked for his guns, Colter's hands were a flash faster. As Ringo's guns started to clear leather he saw the flash of Colter's guns. He couldn't believe it! His eyes must be deceiving him! In almost the same instance, there were four more flashes. Colter should have been on the ground by now. His guns should have fired but…

Ringo was running on adrenalin. He felt a sudden jolt and his breath was gone. He could see his horse and three others running away. One of his Schofields lay right in front of him. For some reason, he couldn't lift his hand to reach it. Colter had put two shots into Ringo's chest then turned his Colts on Wilson and Strickland, both receiving a single bullet to the head. When the smoke cleared, four horses were running. Colter saw Deaton still sitting his mount with a scared look on his face, his hands lifted high. He had stayed out of the fight. The body of Sanchez laid in a crumpled mess with his Navy Colt still clenched in his hand. Apparently he had decided to get back in the fight and Anderson had put him down.

Deaton gave up his guns and then helped Colter load the bodies of the four Texans into the wagon. Anderson thought to himself that as long as he had known Colter, he had never even thought Winn Colter could be "The Kid." They had talked a little about sharpshooting but nothing had ever been said about his Dragoons.

Anderson thought no matter what happened during the war, Colter had always been a fine neighbor. This wouldn't change that. In fact, it made their trust in each other stronger! Anderson was thankful he had Winn Colter instead of Parker today or he may be the one lying on the ground.

Winn quietly said, "Anderson, let's keep this quiet as far as the killin'. I don't want people searching me out to hunt me down or shoot me in the back. I came here to get away from all that."

"You have my word , Colter… Thanks for saving my life!"

"I think you're mistaken."

"You saved my life, Colter. I never fired a shot. You took all four of them outlaws! Anderson pointed at the last outlaw who stood out in front of them looking like a defeated soldier. "I was bore down on that one when Hell's fury unloaded on the other four. Only that Cavalry soldier got off a shot that whizzed by our heads. He grabbed for his gun at first movement but he went down with the others." Winn then could only remember seeing his gun and pulling the trigger.

Winn looked at the defeated Texan standing there shaking. He had only avoided his own death by keeping his hands stretched high. Winn looked at Anderson. "We can take him to the Sheriff in Richfield or send him packin'. He said he was out of the fight and kept his hands high."

Anderson thought, "They'll probably let him off 'cause he said that."

Colter turned back to the man in front of him. "What's your name Cowboy?"

"Deaton... Perry Deaton. I'm from Cowtown, Texas."

Winn said, "Get on your horse and ride Mr. Deaton. I'll be holding a double barrel coach gun on you the whole time. You know I'm steady! We're going to see the Sheriff, Mr. Deaton." Four hours later they reached Richfield.

Anderson said, "You have two choices, Mr. Deaton. We turn you in to the sheriff and you risk hanging or you point your horse out of here and never look back!"

Deaton looked up dumbfounded at Anderson and Colter. "You'll let me go after what they did?"

Anderson studied Deaton's face... "You said you were out and didn't make a move otherwise."

Colter coldly stared the man down, "But if one person shows up here from Texas claiming some crazy story of some Mormon, killing Bo Ringo, I'll come looking for you... And I know my way around Texas!" Colter tossed Deaton his empty pistol.

Deaton was very careful with the gun and sat silent. "I'll ride and never look back... and I ain't going to say a word to Johnny Ringo or no one! I faced lots of guns in the war, but I never saw anything like yours." Deaton was shaking his head, "I won't give you any reason to come looking for me... Never!" Deaton tipped his hat and turned north spurring his horse on the run. He had just had a brush with death so he was getting away from here as fast as he could, thankful to be alive and not in jail. The Kennedys ... They're on their own!

CHAPTER 31

"Anderson, Colter!" It was Sheriff Franks, "We were rounding up a posse... Your wife, Colter!" Winn was instantly sick. The Sheriff saw his look then said "No, No, No, She's ok. There was trouble at your homestead... She killed a man."

"What?" Just then he saw Courtney come out of the Sheriff's Office. When she saw Winn, she ran across the street and nearly knocked him off his feet. He was so relieved that she was ok. Tears were flowing down her cheeks as she clung to Winn. His arms and kisses were the comfort she needed. Winn led her back to the Sheriff's office and sat her down in a chair but she wouldn't let him go. "I'm not going anywhere." He sat there and held her while Anderson took care of business outside.

"We have something for you, Sheriff." Anderson went to the wagon and pulled back the cover revealing four bodies. "These boys tried to rob us."

"Nice shooting, Anderson!" Anderson started to correct the sheriff then remembered his promise. All he could do was to answer sheepishly "Yea!"

Franks asked, "Couldn't you have left one alive so I could question him?"

"Wasn't thinking about that at the time, Sherriff. They're from Texas! That one there" pointing at Ringo, "is Bo Ringo. He's Johnny Ringo's brother and made it a point to tell us who he was."

"I don't know who Johnny Ringo is." Sherriff Franks didn't have a clue.

"Me neither, Sheriff." Anderson said, "Can we get 'em out of the wagon so I can finish my delivery?"

"Okay but don't shoot anybody else." There was a short pause then the Sheriff said "Anderson, that man Mrs. Colter killed was from Texas too."

Winn drove his own wagon home with Courtney sitting on the seat close. Anderson followed right behind. Courtney had left the boys with Mrs. Anderson as she took the wagon with the dead Texan to the Sheriff. She clenched her coach gun all the way to Richfield and the Sheriff had to pry it out of her hand to get her to put it down.

Anderson told them to leave the boys for the night and to get some sleep. If there was any trouble, Winn could shoot that bell and he would come on the run. It took them nearly three hours from Richfield, but they finally made it home. Normally Winn would have sat down and cleaned his guns but Courtney led him to their bed. She needed a Texan in her bed...needed him bad! The long day turned into a long night... an incredible night. Courtney knew she would have to show Winn something in the morning. She dreaded it. Something she knew was sure to bring back memories... and the hurt. It was the stolen rifle his father had made for him.

****

"Where the Hell is everybody!" Both Jon and Westlee were furious! "Nobody was supposed to leave! Where the hell is Preston?" The seven outlaws who stayed in camp had been so focused on their poker game they hadn't seen anyone leave. Jon and Westlee were beside themselves! They had come here to get away from the Rangers but the first day these guys were riding out recklessly. Jon had told them to stay in camp! They were looking at some big money... more than they ever imagined, but it all came down to planning and not messing up!

Jon was storming around the cabin when he remembered his brother talking about the woman in the blue house. "By hell, Preston better not have gone after that woman at the blue house," Jon turned to Westlee,

"If Preston wasn't our brother, I'd probably put a bullet in him if he's messed up our chance at the gold... And where the hell are the others!"

The cabin door creaked and everyone in the room grabbed for guns. It was Albert Fredricks. He and the Ashby brothers had stayed behind in Bullion to visit the whores. While they were there, news of the dead Texans made its way to Bullion from Richfield.

Fredricks looked like he had been kicked in the gut. His hat was off, he was sweating and he had a look of panic in his eyes. Jon's stare drilled right through Fredricks, "What's with you?" Fredricks dropped his head. He cautiously said, "They're dead... at least five of them"...there was a look of unbelief on every face in the room.

Westlee asked "Dead... Who?"

Fredricks talked really slow, "From the description, it's Ringo, Strickland, Wilson, and either Sanchez or Deaton." Fredricks looked at the Kennedys and ducked his head, "And your brother Preston." How could this have happened? Jon had left very little to plan. This was supposed to be easy against these Mormons and nothing should have happened!

Fredricks explained what he heard at Bullion City, "Bo Ringo tried to rob the gold shipment and got him and three others killed.....by a freight driver named Anderson." Fredricks paused again then continued, "Your brother Preston was killed by a woman...The one in the blue house!"

Jon Kennedy finally settled down sitting at the table. Someone had brought out their private stash of Tequila and sat it in front of Jon. "Tomorrow we ride!" Westlee took a swig of the Tequila, "First I'm gonna kill them Mormons! Every one 'em in that blue house. Burn it to the ground... Kill every man, woman and child! Then we'll hunt down that freighter and kill him too! Nobody does this to a Kennedy!"

Jon took a long hard drink of tequila and just sat there holding the bottle with hatred burning him up. He had a look on his face that kept every man from saying a word.

Jon looked around the room at the group of outlaws. There were some really bad men in the room with him and a few that wanted to be. Counting the two on guard, there were fourteen here. Maybe a few more would come riding in.

Westlee walked over and pried the bottle from Jon's hand and took a couple of big swallows. Jon took the bottle back and drank hard again. "Well get even, Brother."

Westlee said, "Who are these Mormons who think they can shoot up us Texans…"

Fury was burning him up. Jon slammed the bottle on the table and yelled "They can't! I'm going to skin that woman and hang her hide on her gate post! These Mormons think Indians are bad… they never messed with Texas outlaws before!"

"Keel 'em all, Brother," Westlee said with a deep seething growl, "We'll keel 'em all… Every last stinking one of 'em!"

The outlaws scattered, checking and cleaning guns. Jon sat at the table gripping the bottle and staring blankly into the room with an ugly, mean look warping his face. Two of the outlaws sitting across the room were assessing the situation and talking quietly. Fredricks said "Look at him" (meaning Jon,) "If I didn't know better I'd say the Devil himself is sittin' right there… I don't like this." Fredricks was checking and cleaning his old Volcanic rifle that he won from Westlee in a poker game. "No, I don't like this!" he said, "Ringo was fast, probably faster than his brother and I would bet faster than Jon." Ashby looked around the room to make sure Westlee couldn't hear, then whispered "Sanchez and Deaton were steady gun hands as well. If one of 'em's dead, where's the other one? And where's those damn Applegate brothers? No, I don't like this at all!"

Jon whirled his pistol and cocked it directly it at Ashby and Fredricks talking in the corner, "What y'all talking about… You turn yeller?"

"No, we ain't yeller!" Fredricks said, "I's just saying we better be ready cause Ringo wasn't no slouch! Neither was Sanchez or Deaton! And where's the Applegate brothers?"

Jon was furious! He had been asking himself the same questions and couldn't come up with an answer. "Them Applegate brothers come through that door right now, I'm gonna kill 'em!" The tequila was having its effect on Jon but it didn't calm him, he only got madder. "Damn Mormons!"

****

Perry Deaton had headed north until he was out of sight of Richfield. He waited until just about dark then turned back to the east and skirted around the small settlements. He needed to tell the Texans that Kid Colter was there and had killed the rest of the men. Deaton's horse was spent from too many fast miles but Deaton put the spurs and whip to him and he kept moving fast. Four miles from the hideout, his horse went down splattering Deaton in the mud. The horse was exhausted and dying and might even have a broken leg but Deaton couldn't chance that someone would hear his gunshot. Deaton pulled out his Bowie and cut the horse's throat spewing blood over him and the mud. Deaton gathered himself up and started on a fast walk. In the dark he had ridden into a swampy area and now had to backtrack, adding miles to his walk.

It was nearly midnight when he finally made it back to the hideout. The guards were asleep but a light was still on inside. He walked up to the door and gave it a shove looking in at a drunk Jon Kennedy. Kennedy looked up and saw a dark, blood covered creature coming through the door at him. Deaton saw the gun raise and tried to stop him but it was too late. Deaton took a shot in the throat.

The other men that were awake were horrified watching Jon shoot one of their own. Westlee grabbed Jon who was so drunk he was having a hard time sitting in the chair. "He's out of control!" One of the men shouted, but just as swiftly as Jon, Westlee had his gun pointing between the eyes of the talker. "Y'all have something to say?"

"Deaton could have told us what happened." Ashby said, "Then we'd know what we're riding against." Westlee looked at Deaton on the floor with a pool of blood forming around his body. "Don't matter; we're killing Mormons in the morning!"

The killing of Deaton was too much for a couple of the new men, Jenkins and Webb. An hour later, they quietly slipped out into the darkness to their horses and saddled up. Jon Kennedy was going to get them all killed! The two men mounted their horses and rode away. By morning they would be twenty miles away..

CHAPTER 32

Courtney woke with Winn already out of bed and could smell the aroma of fresh brewed coffee coming from the kitchen. She needed to show him what she had taken from the man the day before and didn't know how he would react. Courtney came around the corner wrapped only in a blanket and looked in to see Winn sitting in the low light of an oil lamp. He was sitting there shirtless with suspenders holding up his breaches while he cleaned and loaded his Dragoons.

Winn took a sip of coffee and saw Courtney's reflection in the glass on the window pane. "Hello, beautiful!" He turned to look and smile at his lovely wife standing there with bare shoulders looking at him. Her green eyes sparkled in the light and her smile… well it could melt a man's heart. Winn knew he was the luckiest man in the west. He was ready to put the Dragoons down and crawl back in bed with her when she said, "I have something I need to show you." Courtney walked to a corner in the room and brought something wrapped in a blanket over to him and sat it down on the table. She paused for just a moment before she let Winn start to unwrap the gun. "I took this off the man I shot yesterday." When the blanket came off, he could only stare at the gun sitting before him. He hadn't seen this gun for more than nine years when it had been stolen from his Pa's gunsmith shop.

Winn quickly glanced at Courtney then back to the gun. He very carefully slid his fingers across the engraving in the stock… His Pa had made this gun for him. He looked to Courtney but was choked up and couldn't say a word. How could this gun show up here over a thousand miles away from where it was lost back in Texas? Winn kept rubbing his fingers across the engravings… He couldn't believe it. What's the answer? He finally said, "I'm afraid there may be more trouble out there. I need to see Mr. Anderson first light! "

Win looked outside at the darkness then at his wife still standing there wrapped in her blanket with a scared look on her face. He sat the guns down and walked to her and leaned in to kiss her on the cheek. She looked back with those eyes and the blanket fell to the floor. More than anything, she needed to feel safe in the comfort of his arms.

****

As the morning hours started to break, the outlaw camp slowly came alive. Most of the men had slept outside and a coffee pot was on the fire. The night had been cool and the men all knew a bunkhouse should be built soon. Snow was already on the mountain above them, but it would be down to the valley soon. "Why's coffee cooking outside?" Turner, one of the youngest and newest riders to the group, asked Brooks Jones who was nursing a headache and tending the fire. "Look through that window."

The young Texan slowly peeked through the opening. The oil lamp still burned from the night before and Jon Kennedy still sat in the same chair staring at the wall with an empty bottle of tequila in his left hand and his pistol in his right. The look on his face was a man burning up with hatred who probably hadn't slept at all last night. Even though Turner was new, he knew enough not to grab a rattler by the tail. He turned back around, "I'm not going in there."

Jones sized up the other outlaws. Most of these men were bad and could hold their own. What the Rangers had failed to do in the past five years, these Mormons were doing in a matter of days… and one by a woman none the less! Had they rode together, their twenty two riders were a large enough force that they could have stayed in control! But now only fourteen remained… Jones glanced at the horses tied to the picket line and counted saddles… Ten?… He glanced around the camp and saw two more. He counted again, "Look, there's only twelve saddles!"

Jones spoke a little louder, "Who's missing?" All of the outlaws were up looking at each other then back at the horses. Jones looked over at the saddles. "Jenkins and Webb's is gone! "Why those yella Sons-A-Bitches!" The door swung open and there stood Jon Kennedy still wobbly, holding his pistol in his right hand. His bloodshot eyes and blind stare made them wonder if he was still drunk. He looked at the group of sorry outlaws scattered out around him with those scared looks on their faces. Jon's voice was almost like a snarl of a puma. "What the hell is going on out here?" Nobody wanted to be the bearer of bad news, but Jones finally confessed, "We looked at the hosses . Jenkins and Webb's hosses are all gone… and their gear is gone too!"

A look of death came across Kennedy's face. What was going on? All his plans were falling apart. Jon always planned and always had success. He glared at the remaining men. These were all tough fighters and Jon knew he couldn't afford to see any others turn away. He'd learned a valuable and costly lesson. He must keep every last one of the gang together. It was time to put some fear in the hearts of the Mormon settlers starting with the woman that killed his brother.

CHAPTER 33

Winn got back out of bed. He had fallen asleep with Courtney snuggled in close under their blanket and now it was light outside. He had wanted to be at Mr. Anderson's door before now but Courtney's persuasion had kept him in bed. Now that he was up he again looked at the rifle with his name engraved on the stock. Other than being a little dirty, the gun had been kept in perfect condition. Winn gave it a careful cleaning then sat it aside.

Courtney hadn't seen her husband like this since they left Texas six years ago and now she was feeling scared. Winn had said they were probably in for more trouble and now two horses were saddled and tied to the hitching rail. She could see he was stocking his saddle with guns like a Cavalry soldier... like he had during the war. He wore his pair of short barreled .44 Colt Dragoons but then he had a pair of .36 caliber Colts in saddle holsters and the Smith and Wesson Schofield revolver taken from Bo Ringo.

Courtney looked at her husband and knew he was a force to be reckoned with, but she was scared he would be riding to his death. Winn looked at her and saw the concern in her eyes. Winn walked over, took her by the hand and pulled her in for a hug. "I'll be all right." She held him tight until he pushed her back. "I'm taking you to stay with Mrs. Anderson for the day then Newell and I need to discuss a few things." Courtney was relieved. Winn wasn't going on his own. She turned back to the house and went to the door, reaching inside for her coach gun. It wasn't there. When she turned around, Winn was smiling and pointed to her horse. There it was in the holster he had made special for her. The butt of his long lost rifle stuck out of the scabbard as well.

They mounted and rode north towards the Anderson Homestead. As they reached the crest of the small hill, he glanced back to see a man on big black horse coming from the river canyon trail. He and several other riders were headed towards their homestead.

Winn turned to Courtney and commanded, "Get to the Anderson's quick and tell him I need backup as fast as he can ride. If his horse isn't saddled, put him on yours and send him to the bell. There are bullets for that gun in the saddlebags. Tell him to trust the sights! I need a distraction!"

Courtney was in a panic and wanted to ride with her husband but knew Mr. Anderson would be better. She whirled to the north and started the mare on the run. The Anderson homestead was only a mile away from the point of the hill. On the run she could be there in just a few minutes!

Where Winn sat he could see the group of riders filing off the trail and riding towards his homestead. He counted twelve riders in all riding cautiously towards the home he built for his family and now it was time to defend it. He thought quick... The dynamite was in his saddle bag. He quickly took the sticks out and cut three inches off one of the fuses and six inches off a second. He looked over the rise at the men scattering out and moving in on his home. It was time to meet these men head on!

****

A hunting party of Utes had ridden south from their camp for several miles through some grassy valleys known as three creeks. They swung to the east riding down the canyon of the ancient ones. The Utes and Paiutes had claimed this territory as their own for many years, but even when they came to the area, there were signs of ancient dwellings and writings on the canyon walls. It was treated as sacred ground. Yesterday the hunting party had killed two prospectors that had come to search for the yellow metal in the streams. They killed them like they killed the Spanish when they came to this canyon many years before.

Chief Ouray wanted to see Winn Colter who lived in the sky house not far from this sacred canyon. Colter had shown bravery riding into the Ute camp with his son and had honored the Utes with beef. He had also worked with his braves to take care of the bear his son had battled. Colter had shown compassion to his hurt son and treated him with great respect.

As they came to the mouth of the canyon, the Indians saw a large group of riders moving north with their leader riding a magnificent black stallion. Ouray thought, "That would be a horse for a Chief!" Those men below looked like the prospectors they had killed the day before up the sacred canyon.

The chief ordered his braves to stay wide and see where the white men traveled. Surprisingly, they turned off the main trail rode toward the sky house which sat back in a little cove.

There were eight Utes in the hunting party including the two who had ridden with Winn Colter a few days earlier to get beef and bear. The Chief motioned for them to stop in a gully and leave their horses, then they moved in closer on foot to see what was happening by the sky house. From the actions of the men, the Chief could see they were moving in to attack.

Over the hill to the north, a lone rider came galloping toward the group of men and the Indians could see it was the horse Colter rode into the Indian village three days before. Chief Ouray looked at what was happening and thought this would be the day that Colter would die.

With a match, Winn lit all three fuses on the Dynamite and held the three sticks off to the side of the horse. As he kicked him into a light gallop, he dropped the dynamite with the shorted fuse on the hillside. None of the riders had seen him yet. Another twenty yards he dropped the second. Winn held the third stick of Dynamite until he was one hundred yards from his house. The riders had spotted him and Colter only had one juniper tree to ride behind where he dropped the last lit stick. If all went right, the dynamite would start blowing in sixty to seventy seconds, hopefully giving him the distraction he needed.

The twelve riders saw this man riding down the hill that now made a sharp left turn and came straight at them on a trot. All, but Jon Kennedy, held a gun on the man riding towards them. "Who the hell are you?" Weston Kennedy demanded.

"You're on my homestead." Colter said, "If you don't want trouble, y'all need to leave now!" The group of men didn't know what to think of this man riding in here thinking he could demand anything of the Texans. They all laughed at the suggestion and knew either Jon or Westlee would gun him down at any moment.

It took a few seconds for Jon to remember, but the voice was a clear giveaway. Jon Kennedy's mouth fell open as he took a second look at this young man on horse challenging them to leave. In a suddenly scared voice, Jon gasped, "Brother, that's Kid Colter!" Jon looked at the house again and now he could see it. It looked just like Weston Colter's home that they burned back in Texas many years ago.

Jon had dreamed of facing down Kid Colter but now that he actually looked at him eye to eye, he didn't like the idea. The men behind the Kennedys couldn't believe what they heard and took great satisfaction having Kid Colter at gunpoint. They were thinking about the stories they all had heard about the famous "Kid Colter." Now every one of them could tell how they had him under the gun and watched him die!

Westlee looked at the forward facing Colts Winn wore, "Toss those guns of yours slow and careful!" Winn looked around at the eleven guns pointed at him and could see the smug satisfaction in the looks on these rough outlaws faces. Winn knew he still had another fifteen seconds before the first blast. He moved slowly pulling his two colts and tossed them to the ground in front of his horse. The tension on Jon's body eased slightly when the Colts hit the ground.

Westlee Kennedy was pleased that he was the one that held the life of "Kid Colter" in his hands. He was going to kill him, and then the woman that killed his brother. "Where's your wives, Colter?" The outlaws were enjoying this and started moving in closer so they all could see. Jon Kennedy had always claimed to be faster than Colter but every man there knew Westlee and Jon would never give him the chance at a fair fight.

Westlee looked at a disarmed Colter sitting on his horse looking death strait in the face. One thing he had to give the man, he sat with no fear in his eyes. Colter's rifle stock was sticking up but they all knew if Colter touched that gun he would be shot before he cleared leather.

Westlee was prodding to get Colter to jump for the rifle. "I see you have my brother's rifle." Colter knew what was coming. He had already figured all this out and was ready for what was ahead. Jon Kennedy watched Colter's eyes closely and said, "You know, this looks like a house I saw burn back in Texas." He was looking for a sign that he had shocked Colter but his gaze remained cold as ice.

Westlee blurted, "I burned your house after I killed your Pa!" Colter still didn't show any sign that what Kennedy said affected him.

Chief Ouray watched this brave man who had saved his son's life. He bravely stares death in the face with twelve riders moving in to kill him. Ouray's braves had three Henry rifles while the rest shot bows and arrows. Ouray and two Indians moved in to within fifty yards. He kept the rifles and two others back to protect their escape if necessary. This was Colter's fight, but the Chief could offer a distraction. The rider closest to the Indians was Thomas Ashby.

Ashby didn't want to miss any of this so his full attention was on what was happening before him. The three Indians drew their bows letting arrows fly long and Ashby didn't see it coming. One of the arrows hit Ashby in the chest from the side and a second hit him on the hip bone makeing a sickening and painful thud. The third arrow missed but flew only inches from his brother Preston's nose. Preston looked back at his brother Thomas who was looking down at the arrows sticking out of his hip and side. Preston yelled out in fear "Injuns!" He started to whirl but saw nothing out there.

An unexpected explosion blasted the hillside and shook the riders, then a second one closer. Something went off in Jon Kennedy's head… he had seen this before. His mind screamed but he couldn't say a word. With all the commotion and explosions none of the outlaws could understand what was happening as horses whirled shying away from the explosions.

Ashby had arrows sticking from his body and was desperately trying to hang on but before the third blast of dynamite, Winn had grabbed his saddle dragoons and started pulling the trigger sending lead into the outlaws, causing more confusion! Adrenaline filled Colter's veins and now the guns in his hands were true and deadly.

Westlee Kennedy didn't have a chance as he took the first bullet between the eyes. He rolled off the back of his horse. Jon remembered the shootout with the Yankee Soldiers many years ago so he knew what was coming. Jon ducked behind his horse before the second blast, but still took a bullet in his upper thigh as his stallion whirled to get away from the oncoming explosions.

Colter's guns had already turned on the group of outlaws and without thinking, systematically started firing into the men with deadly accuracy. Bullets whizzed by Colter's head and around his body like a swarm of angry bees until his horse took two hits in the neck then one to the head and fell out from under him. He never stopped firing. Colter rolled off his mount and had lead kicking up dirt all around him, then something bit at his side. When the smoke and dust cleared, Jon Kennedy, Brooks Jones and Preston Ashby were the only three riders alive out of twelve that rode in. The three were all on the run heading east toward the river bottoms.

Ashby and Jones came out unscathed, but Jon Kennedy was hit in the thigh and riding a little behind with his hurt leg out of the stirrup. All three riders knew they needed to get to cover and disappear.

****

Courtney came on the run into the Anderson homestead as Mr. Anderson stepped from the barn. "Winn's in trouble and needs you now, Mr. Anderson!" He turned to saddle his horse and Courtney stopped him, "Take mine, please!" Winn's rifle in the scabbard and he said to tell you to trust the sights. "He said to get you to the bell!"

Mr. Anderson knew what Winn meant and took Courtney's horse back out of the yard on the run heading to the point of the hill. Before he got there, he could tell all hell had broken loose at the Colter homestead as rapid shots were being fired. As Anderson reached the edge of the hill, three horses were headed on a dead run towards the lower river bottom. Mr. Anderson could see smoke in the air and bodies lying all over the homestead but they were too far away to know for sure what had happened.

Anderson pulled the rifle from the scabbard and he saw President Davis's gun for the very first time. It was an incredible gun but there was no time to look now. He saw the riders on the run to the east. It was nearly 400 yards to the riders and they were riding fast heading for the trees along the river. They would be gone in half a minute. Anderson found a place to set down for a rest. Time was nearly gone. He checked the telescopic sight first but couldn't tell how to make adjustments. He had seen one of these German telescopic sights during the war, but it was mounted on an English made gun called a Whitworth.

Anderson had never shot anything like this gun. Courtney had said "hold true to the sight" so he did. The riders were going south by southeast on a slight angle. Anderson took sights on the lead man and held four feet to the left of the man to compensate angle and speed.

Anderson took a breath and did a quick fire but actually led the man too far given the speed of the bullet. It caught the horse behind the ear as it missed the rider. The dead horse went tumbling, throwing Ashby hard to the ground flipping and rolling with the rider. When everything stopped, neither horse nor the rider moved. Anderson then realized this was a falling block rifle design. He only had the one shot... Courtney had neglected to tell him bullets were in the saddlebag and now with the commotion, the horse was gone, trotting toward home. How he wished he had grabbed his Spencer, but if he had, he would have been too late. The last two riders were going to get away and there was nothing he could do about it!

Anderson watched through the telescope as a shot rang off to his right from the Colter homestead. A burst of red mist filled the air around Ashby who grasped onto his horse for almost three seconds before he toppled forward and fell. Anderson looked back towards the Colter homestead and saw Winn leaning over a post with his rifle. That shot was an easy 800 yards, but Colter's bullet had held true.

Jon Kennedy watched the two men in front of him fall. How could this happen to them? They were Texans! They had come here to get away from the Rangers. They were here for the gold and to rape and plunder these Mormons. Now both his brothers were dead along with every other man that rode with them. This couldn't happen, but it did. His plans were all shot to hell by a Texan turned Mormon...

Jon pulled his horse to a stop and turned around. If he was going to die it wouldn't be from a shot in the back.

The big black stallion pranced after being pulled up from a run and still wanted to go as one horse continued to run away. Jon looked down at Preston Ashby who was the first to fall with his dead horse not ten feet away. Ashby was alive but it looked as if he had a broken back because of the angle he laid. He didn't make a sound. Ashby looked back at Kennedy with pleading eyes but Kennedy just rode away leaving the man to die slowly.

Jon Kennedy was about to face his Devil... The dreams... His nightmare was standing down the hill waiting for him. Winn looked down and saw his short barreled Navy Colts in his hands and couldn't remember how he got them from the ground. He looked around at the men lying before him, nine men and three of their horses were dead or dying.

Colter reached in his pocket, pulled out his spare cylinders and reloaded his Colts. He looked to his right at his old horse lying dead with three bullet holes that he could see. The horse was like an old friend that had traveled many miles and taken care of him in some tough situations.

Jon Kennedy was riding back towards the battle site sitting up proud on his magnificent Mexican black stallion. Kennedy pulled out his nickel plated Scofield and popped it open, empting the spent casings then thumbing in new .45 caliber bullets. He always packed two Scofields but in the commotion, he had dropped his left gun when the horse was spinning and about threw him. Kennedy closed the gun and slipped it back into his right holster reminding him that his leg hurt like hell from the bullet wound. He couldn't think about that right now.

Colter walked forward to meet Kennedy beyond the dead men. On his left, Winn could see Mr. Anderson had watched from the rise on the hill and couldn't do anything without bullets. On the right, three Indians stood watching the man returning to the battle site and Colter moving forward.

Kennedy looked at Colter with a burning hatred. He rode up to face Colter still not believing it was him. "Of all the places we had to choose to hide out, you had to be here!"

"I've been here for a long time." Winn said, "I came to get away from the shooting." Kennedy carefully pulled his injured leg up and slid it over the horse to dismount. There was a lot of pain but he wanted to face Colter for this. If there was any chance, he had to have all factors in his favor… none of it was.

Jon stood facing Colter. The adrenalin was still flowing because of his fear and anger. "You killed my brothers!"

Winn just looked at this sad excuse of a Texan trying to steady himself. "I didn't come looking for trouble. It was you who brought this whole thing down on yourself."

Jon was quiet for a moment and Winn sensed a sudden change. Jon paused then said, "I thought you should know, I didn't know it was your Ma and Pa until after they was dead. Westlee went back for bullets for that gun he stole and your Pa drew down on us...My brother William shot your Pa and your Ma killed Will. She was lifting the gun on me and I had to shoot her." Jon paused for a moment then said, "I may be a bad man, but I had no intention of shooting a woman." Jon could feel his anger and hatred start to burst again. "But your woman here," he said, "I wanted to kill her, and would have!"

The confession of the killings of his Ma and Pa hurt, but Winn didn't waiver. The comments about killing Courtney brought the fire back into his veins and he was ready.

Jon was almost yelling, "You and your kin brought nothing but trouble for my family and I've dreamt of killing you since I watched you gun down them Yankees during the war!" He spat on the ground, "You had what I wanted and you didn't want to take credit for any of it!" Jon took a step closer and yelled "Damn you Colter! Damn you to hell!"

Kennedy grabbed for his gun and for a split second, thought he would beat Colter's draw but he was mistaken. The short barreled Dragoon slid from its holster and fired three shots to the center of Jon Kennedy's chest. He was beat! Darkness filled his vision as he fell. His body tried one last time for a breath that wasn't there and he died at Colter's feet.

Three Indians walked forward to the edge of the battle site and looked around at the dead men and horses. The Chief looked back to Colter and said in his broken English "It was an honor to watch you fight." Colter knew from Chief Ouray that was a great compliment and he could see it in the eyes of the other two as well. The Indians turned and disappeared into the brush. A minute later, horses could be heard galloping away back to the south.

Now that it was over, Mr. Anderson had to sit down. First the outlaws then the Indians. Sitting with an empty gun... it was too much. From the north, Mr. Anderson could hear running horses and the panic came back to him. As the riders crossed the rise on the hill, he saw it was Sheriff Franks and a ten man posse coming south to find where these outlaws had come from.

Winn recognized the horse Westlee Kennedy had been riding and saw the familiar shape of his rifle butt sticking up in the air. Winn walked over to the horse that shied away just a little with the smell of blood in the air. Winn caught the animal then slowly pulled the gun from the scabbard to reveal what he was expecting. He gently ran his fingers over the engravings on the stock… "Weston." All he could think was "Welcome home!"

The Sherriff looked around at the number of bodies, amazed. He finished, "Good work Anderson. Looks like you saved Colter's life!" Andersons jaw fell open as he looked back at Colter who was looking at him and slightly shaking his head side to side. Anderson wouldn't take credit, but just quietly said, "These boys came looking for trouble at the wrong place!"

Franks looked at Colter. "You're a lucky man, Colter, to have a good neighbor who can shoot like Anderson!" Another horse came racing over the rise with a buckboard following close behind. Courtney was on the horse and raced down the hill to find Winn standing there with a spot of blood on his shirt.

Winn saw that she had tear-stained cheeks. As she got closer to him, she came off the horse running into her husband's arms. As she kissed him, the tears started to flow again. She quickly checked his wound to find it was only a slight graze where a bullet had burned his side and left a small furrow. The buckboard pulled up with Mrs. Anderson driving, Chase and little Weston holding on. They too jumped off as soon as they could and ran to their Pa and wrapped their arms around him. Sheriff Franks watched Courtney and the kids and said it again, "Colter, you are a lucky man!"

EPILOGUE

The Old Spanish Trail was a trade route approximately a 1,200 mi long which connected settlements near Santa Fe, New Mexico with Los Angeles, and southern California. It ran through areas of high mountains, arid deserts, and deep canyons and is considered one of the most difficult of all trade routes ever established in the United States. It was explored by the Spanish as early as the late 1500s and saw extensive use by pack trains from about 1830 until the mid-1850s.

From the journal of a traveler: In 1848 Lt. George Brewerton, and his guide Kit Carson, entered a gorge along the Old Spanish Trail, on the Fish Lake Cut-off and came across seven human skeletons. Six of the skeletons lay on the ground, probably scattered by hungry wolves. The remains of the seventh persons were undisturbed, being sheltered by rocks and a fallen tree. Arrows embedded in the surrounding trees of this unfortunate party suggest a one-sided battle. – Source: fs.usda.gov.

REFERENCES OF KEY LOCATIONS

Names and places in this book/ dates settled/name changes:

Jacksboro, Texas, 1858 First known as Mesquiteville, Texas, renamed, 1878.

Green River, Utah , 1876 - Blake's Station started as a river crossing for the U.S. Mail. In 1876, In 1883 the <u>Denver and Rio Grande Western Railroad</u> was built and a train station was opened. The west side of the river became known as Greenriver (later changed to Green River) and the east side of the river became known as Elgin.

Salina, Utah, 1864 – Abandoned 1866, resettled 1871 after the Blackhawk Indian War. Salina Fort built in 1871.

Richfield, Utah, 1864 -First settled as Big Spring, renamed Omni 1865. Renamed Richfield in 1871 when resettled after the Blackhawk Indian War. Fort Omni built in 1865.

Joseph, Utah, 1864 – First settled as Jericho, Utah, Abandoned 1868 due to Indian troubles. Resettled and renamed Joseph 1872.

Monroe, Utah, 1864 – First settled as South Bend, Name changed to Alma in 1866. Abandoned and resettled in 1871 Renamed Monroe in 1898. Fort Alma built in 1866.

Manti, Utah, 1849 – First settlement south of Provo, Utah.

Cove Fort, 1860 – Current stone fort built in 1867.

Elsinore, Utah, 1874 – First Known as Little Denmark, later changed to Elsinore 1874.

Glenwood, Utah, 1863, changed to Glenwood in 1865 Abandoned in 1867, resettled 1868.

Bullion City, Utah, 1868.

Webster City, Utah, 1869

Marysvale, Utah, 1863. Originally called Merryville, Merry Valley or Merry Vale, later changed to Marysvale.

More upcoming adventures of Winn Colter in:

KID COLTER...
Dead Men keep good secrets!

– After Winn Colter's shootout with the Kennedy Gang, he hopes his troubles are finally over so he can live at peace with his family in the Utah Territory, Two Texas outlaws could see what was coming and slipped away from the outlaw camp during the night, before the gangs final shootout.

Back in Texas, word about the death of Bo Ringo reaches the notorious gunfighter and big brother, Johnny Ringo, and he vows to avenge his brother's death! Jonny Ringo and his band of outlaws ride for Utah to do what the incompetent Kennedy gang apparently couldn't... kill the Mormon that killed his brother Bo Ringo.

Nobody's telling Johnny that he will be riding against the infamous Kid Colter and a former Yankee sharpshooter. When it came to answers about his brother Bo or any of the Kennedy Gang, no-one was talking. It seems... Dead Men Keep Good Secrets...

Memories of Another Man...

At 51, Chet Taylor has a beautiful wife and a family that is nearly grown. He's lived a normal life in a small town in Utah but in the past few months his mind had started to slip he was forgetting little things. It was starting to scare his wife. Later he's diagnosed with early onset Alzheimer's and something's changing.

Chet's mind is getting worse but he's been having dreams… The kind of dreams that you don't wake up and tell your wife. He's dreaming about a beautiful woman and she seems so familiar. Like she's been somewhere in his mind for many years, but he's sure he doesn't know her.

Then his life begins to change as the Alzheimer's advances and strange things begin to happen. Chet wakes up in a sweat holding his Ruger pistol but can clearly remember the feel and balance of a Colt Peacemaker. Thing is, he's never held one in his life.

Chet goes target shooting to relieve some stress, but on the range, he throws up his pistol firing three shots in a flash. He hit dead center of a target the size of a dime. He then realized he'd done that shooting with his left hand… he was right handed. What was going on?

When Chet Taylor glanced in the mirror, for a second, he thought he saw a battered and bloody young cowboy. He needed to help that beautiful woman… He then realized he was having Memories of Another Man."

210

About the Author :

SCOTT CHRISTENSEN grew up in Elsinore, Utah, loving the outdoors and the old west. He grew up in a coffee shop/service station listening to stories of hunters and ranchers. He rode horses, worked a farm and spent every spare second hunting and fishing. He now lives in Richfield still exploring and enjoying southern Utah.

Scott served in the Sheriff's Search and Rescue squad for 17 years as well as other community organizations including the Chamber of Commerce and Rotary Club.

Scott has a knack for telling stories and has lived the adventure. He's been attacked by a mountain lion, met a bear face to face with only a bow and tackled a four point buck. He's been on the radio, written for newspapers, magazines and recently written and performed cowboy poetry.

Many locations described in this book are real and based on historically accurate information. The Old Spanish trail, Spanish gold mines, old cabins, stone marker and ancient petroglyphs stand as part of the inspiration for this novel.

Made in the USA
San Bernardino, CA
10 November 2014